THE BODY IN THE COFFIN

Savannah looked at the "wound," the deep hole in the chest through which the wooden stake had been thrust. Reaching out, she touched the darkened area next to the wood, then looked at her fingertip. It was dried paint. "This is a dummy," she said.

"No! Not that one!" Bunny cried. "It's him!" She pointed to the male in the adjacent coffin.

But Savannah was already looking at the male figure, her heart in her throat. Even in this dim light, she could see the difference in this body and the female's. The features were far finer, more realistic. The hair was real, not a phony wig. The hands, the fingers, and the nails were all too beautifully detailed to be fake.

As before, she dabbed her finger into the dark area around the stake, and this time, she felt the telltale wetness.

Blood.

The real thing . . .

Books by G.A. McKevett

Just Desserts
Bitter Sweets
Killer Calories
Cooked Goose
Sugar and Spite
Sour Grapes
Peaches and Screams
Death by Chocolate
Cereal Killer
Murder à la Mode
Corpse Suzette
Fat Free and Fatal
Poisoned Tarts
A Body to Die For

Published by Kensington Publishing Corporation

G.A. McKevett

Poisoned Tarts

A SAVANNAH REID MYSTERY

KENSINGTON BOOKS
http://www.kensingtonbooks.com

KENSINGTON BOOKS are published by

Kensington Publishing Corp.
850 Third Avenue
New York, NY 10022

ISBN-13: 978-0-7582-1553-6
ISBN-10: 0-7582-1553-3

First Hardcover Printing: May 2008
First Mass Market Printing: January 2009

10 9 8 7 6 5 4 3 2 1

Printed in the United States of America

Dedicated to

Joleen and Arden

With such joyful beginnings,
How very blessed,
And how deeply loved you are.

I want to thank all the fans who write to me, sharing their thoughts and offering endless encouragement. I enjoy your letters more than you know. I can be reached at:

sonjamassie.com

Chapter 1

"**P**alm trees and jack-o'-lanterns. Yuck," Savannah Reid said as she entered the supermarket and skirted around a display of chrysanthemums, colorful gourds, and pumpkins—some of which had snaggletoothed smiles scrawled on them with black permanent marker. "I hate autumn and winter in Southern California. I mean, I love California in the spring and summer, but holidays just bite if you don't have the right weather to go with them."

Her companion Dirk Coulter answered with a disgruntled grunt, communicating his disgust at being dragged along on this little shopping foray. Dirk hated grocery shopping nearly as much as he hated watching soap operas and chick flicks or listening to "female prattle." And in his opinion, any discussion that didn't revolve around sports or things police-related, constituted "female prattle."

"How's a body supposed to get into the Halloween spirit when it's eighty degrees out?" Savannah said as she yanked a shopping cart out of the queue. "No frost on the pumpkin. Nary a fodder in the shock in sight. How depressing."

"Fodder in the shock? What the hell's fodder?" he asked as he took the cart from her and began to push it himself. Detective Sergeant Dirk Coulter might not be up on his Victorian poets, but he was a gentleman when it came to opening doors and pushing shopping carts.

"Oh, shoot, I don't know," Savannah said, her Georgia drawl even more pronounced than usual—as it tended to be when she was aggravated—"but I need some of it around to get in the mood. How am I going to give a good Halloween party without the smell of burning leaves in the air, that crisp morning cold that gets your blood flowing and—?"

"Oh, enough of your griping, woman. You'll give your Halloween party the same way you do Thanksgiving and Christmas. You'll decorate your house with way too much junk and cook way too much food and invite all of us over and make us dress up in stupid stuff and . . ."

"I told you last Christmas that you don't have to dress up anymore. I just plumb gave up on that after seeing you as a maid a-milkin'. Lord help us, I still have nightmares about that."

"*You* have nightmares! My skin still crawls when I think of how I allowed myself to be talked into wearing a dress and putting a mop on my head."

"Free food."

"What?"

"I told you that if you wanted to sink your chompers into that fine holiday feast of mine, you had to play along." She giggled, recalling the sight—Dirk with milk bucket in hand, yellow yarn mop on head, inflated boobs straining against the front of a pink floral jersey dress. He had balked at the ruby red lipstick and chandelier earrings. Dirk had a *few* standards, free food or no.

"Don't worry, buddy," she said. "I won't ever ask

you to do that again. I have to draw a line somewhere at how much humiliation I heap on a body. Even you."

"Gee, thanks." He followed her past the jack-o'-lantern display and into the produce aisle. "So, what do I have to do to earn all the good food you're going to feed us at this party you're giving?"

"Just help me shop," she said. When he grinned brightly, she decided to push her luck. ". . . and help me carve a couple of pumpkins." His face fell until she added, ". . . you know, scoop out the guts—the gross stuff that us girls don't like to do." He perked up again.

She chuckled, reminding herself that manly men like Coulter needed special handling. "Why don't you take the cart to the other side of the store and load up on some beer? And on the way back, hit the chip aisle and get whatever you think we need."

"Really? Wow. Okay. Cool."

In seconds, she was watching him retreat with far more vigor in his step as he headed across the front of the store to the refrigerated beer coolers on the opposite side. And not for the first time in the many years she had known him, it occurred to Savannah that watching Dirk walk away wasn't totally without its rewards. He might be over forty and not the hard body he'd been when they had met nearly twenty years ago, but he still filled out his Levi's quite nicely.

And among his other nice assets was the fact that after all these years, she could still feel him watch *her* walk away with the same rapt attention. And since she had gained two decades and thirty pounds since they'd met, she couldn't help being grateful.

You just really had to love a guy who sincerely liked his women well-rounded.

Once he disappeared around the corner, she focused on the task at hand. It wasn't easy putting on a successful Halloween party. The devil was, indeed, in the details . . . or the vampire, or zombie, or whatever ghoulish creature one chose to be. No fairies, butterflies, or ballerina princesses in pink tutus at *her* extravaganza! Nope, a Reid Halloween party was not for the squeamish. She had been present at enough crime scenes to know what real gore looked like . . . unfortunately.

And now, there were decisions to make. In a dimly lit room, which would feel the most like real eyeballs, olives or peeled grapes? Grapes were best, and she could probably pawn the tedious task of peeling them off on her best friend and codetective, Tammy Hart. So—

"Sit down, you stupid little shit, before I knock you in the head!"

Savannah jumped, nearly dropping the bag of grapes in her hand, and whirled around to face the angry male standing about ten feet behind her. He wasn't a particularly large man, but he towered over the tiny toddler sitting in the shopping cart. The child, a little boy no more than two, stared up at the enraged adult with terror on his innocent, baby face.

Not for the first time when witnessing something like this, Savannah longed for the old days when she could walk up to a bully like this, flash a badge, and have a serious talk with him. When she and Dirk had been on patrol, they had done it at least five times a night.

She knew better than most that domestic abuse, in all its hideous forms, kept law enforcement employed.

Beside the man's cart stood a woman with a bag of potatoes in her hand, a guarded, pained look on her face. In spite of the fact that she was well-dressed and wearing expensive jewelry, she had an air of defeat about her. The hang of her head, the slump of her shoulders betrayed a wounded, heavy spirit.

She started to put the potatoes into the cart, but the man snatched them out of her hand. "Baking potatoes?" he snapped. "I told you to get red potatoes. What's the matter with you? Can't you do anything right?"

"I'm sorry," she whispered as she took the bag of potatoes from him and replaced them in a bin. "I forgot."

She picked up a bag of red potatoes, and as she put them into the cart, the child strained in his seat, reaching for his mother. The father raised his hand as though to strike the boy, and the child cringed in a move that was obviously well-practiced.

"You try to get out of that cart one more time," the man said, "and I swear I'm gonna bash you."

"Honey, please, don't . . ." the mother whispered, casting a quick look around. She saw Savannah watching, and a look of pain and embarrassment swept over her face.

"Yeah, well," he said, "you don't discipline the little brat. Somebody's got to, so shut up already."

The man looked in Savannah's direction and realized that she was not only watching but also disapproving of his words and actions. But instead of sharing his wife's embarrassment, he actually smiled. The self-satisfied, cocky smirk that appeared on his face was one she had seen many times before. Far too many times.

Savannah could feel her pulse rate soaring, her face growing hotter by the second.

Yeah, yeah, you're the big man, she thought. *Gotta show everybody how in control you are. You keep your woman and your kid in their place—under you where they belong. Way under you.*

She gave him a sweeping, disgusted look up and down and added, *What you need is somebody to jerk you down a notch or two.*

Another voice in her head whispered a word of warning. *It's not yours, Savannah. It's not your situation. Stay out of it. Mind your own business.*

"I thought you said you were coming in here for a couple of things," he told his wife. "I've got better things to do than hang around in a damned grocery store all day. Get your lazy ass in gear, and let's get out of here."

Again, he shot Savannah that arrogant grin that set her teeth on edge. She thought of all the times she had heard the myth, "Abusers have low self-esteem. That's why they abuse."

I know your nasty little secret, she thought as their eyes locked in an unspoken challenge. *You don't have an insecure bone in your body. You truly think you're better, smarter, stronger, more valuable than your wife and kid. You think the world revolves around you.*

Savannah had seen the end results of such an attitude: broken homes, broken women, broken children. She despised the attitude. And she tried very hard not to despise the men who harbored it. She tried desperately to give them a break, remembering that a rotten attitude was often handed down generation to generation, a sickening heritage, like some sort of decomposing corpse in the family cellar.

But she seldom succeeded. Too many years of too many visions of too many victims haunted her in the wee hours of the morning when she woke up from a nightmare and couldn't get back to sleep.

Some people were good enough, highly evolved enough, to forgive and feel compassion toward abusers.

Long ago, Savannah had come to terms with the fact that she wasn't one of them.

The wife walked away from her husband and baby and began to sort through some bananas. Savannah could see her hands shaking as she reached for a bunch and tried to shove them into a plastic bag as quickly as she could. But her fear made her clumsy, and her husband glared at her as she fumbled and nearly dropped the bag.

Shaking his head with disgust, he said, "I'm gonna go up front and get in line. You better be up there in two minutes. Two minutes, you hear me?" He looked at his watch, marking the time.

"Yes. I hear you," his wife mumbled.

Savannah gave him her best You Rotten Creep, I Hate You look as he walked away, but he sent her a nasty little smirk in return. She knew the game all too well. He had just shown her that he ruled his family, that he could do anything he wanted to his wife and kid, and even though she obviously disapproved, there wasn't a thing she could do about it.

As far as he was concerned, it was a game. A game he enjoyed because he always won.

The moment he was out of sight, Savannah reached into her purse, pulled out a notepad and pen, and scribbled down a phone number: 1-800-799-7233. Glancing around to make sure he was gone, she hurried over to the woman, who was grabbing apples and dropping them into a bag. Savannah shoved the paper into the woman's hand.

"Here," she said. "That's the number for the National Domestic Violence Hotline. They can help you. Please call them."

The woman's eyes widened, and her mouth opened and closed several times. "Domestic Violence? But . . . but . . . I don't need, I mean, he doesn't . . ."

"He doesn't?" Savannah gave her a sad, knowing look. "Call the number, sweetie," she said, her voice soft and pleading. "They'll help. Really. You don't need to be alone."

Tears filled the woman's eyes, and she blinked several times. Then she shoved the paper deep into her purse.

"What the hell's going on here?" Again, Savannah heard the angry male voice behind her. She spun around. He was practically on top of her, his face red with rage. "What are you doing talking to my wife? What did you give her?"

Savannah felt her fists tighten as the warrior inside her rose to fighting stance. Oh . . . she was in it *now.*

She fixed him with a cold, defiant stare. "I beg your pardon," she said without the slightest hint of apology in her tone. "Are you speaking to me?"

"You're damned right I'm talking to you," he replied, taking a step closer, leaning far into her personal space. "What the hell did you give her? What did you say to her?"

Savannah took a step toward him and seriously breached *his* boundaries. "I will speak to anyone I choose about anything I choose," she said to him, "and it's none of your business what I say. So, back off! Now!"

He did take half a step backward, but his face was still contorted with rage when he said, "I know your type. You're one of those women's lib bull-dykes who hate men. You think men should go around henpecked, kissing women's asses and—"

"That's quite enough," she said, her words even, clipped.

"You think just because I set my old lady straight and discipline my kid that I'm some kind of abuser. I watch the TV talk shows. I know what shit they say about guys who are just trying to keep their families in line. I know what they say about us being abusers and crap like that."

Savannah felt her tether strain, strain, and then snap. Yes, she had to. She just had to . . .

She looked around for the cart with the baby in it. He was out of sight behind a salad dressing display.

"Okay then," she said with a nasty little smirk of her own, "if you're that all-fired informed, you know about the latest scientific findings."

He looked confused. "What? What findings?"

"About abusers like you. Oh, you *haven't* heard? Then let me tell you." She held her little finger up in front of his face, only a few inches from his nose. "They've done tests and discovered that abusers, guys who yell at their kids and belittle their wives in grocery stores just for the fun of it, just to prove what a big shot they are, this . . . this right here . . . is the average size of their—"

"Hey, your news story is coming on next," Tammy called from the living room. "They said they've got film and everything!"

In the kitchen, Savannah grabbed plates laden with rocky road fudge and peanut butter chip brownies and scurried into her living room.

Her guests were stretched out on the sofa and across the floor, holding their bellies and moaning in pain. They were soldiers laid low, not from battle but from Savannah's determination to make sure that every morsel of food possible had been consumed—and then some.

She wasn't content until the aftermath looked like the scene in *Gone with the Wind*, with casualties stretched as far as the eye could see. When no one could move, or even breathe, only then would her job as hostess be finished.

"A little post-dessert repast," she said.

The chorus of groans mingled with pleas of "No, no! I couldn't eat another bite!" as they snatched up the offerings.

Even the svelte and health-conscious Tammy took a piece of the fudge before passing the plate to Ryan Stone and John Gibson.

A couple of Savannah's closest friends and honorary members of her Moonlight Magnolia Detective Agency, Ryan and John had fought the urge to eat every delectable morsel that Savannah had forced on them for years—but with pathetically little conviction. If not for the hours spent at the gym and on the tennis court to counteract the effects, their ultratrim physiques would have disappeared long ago.

And that would have been a shame because lusting after the two of them—hard bodies and all—was one of Savannah's favorite pastimes, second only to watching Dirk walk away.

With Ryan's dark good looks, his six-foot-plus frame, and his impeccable sense of style, he could set any female heart pitter-patting. And although John was older than Ryan, his life partner, John's thick silver hair and his soft, aristocratic British accent was enough to make a girl melt.

For all the good it did her, Savannah had been pitter-pattering and melting into puddles in their presence for years.

"Hey, Van, bring some of those brownies over here," Dirk called from the other side of the living room. "And is that fudge? Is it rocky road?"

Snuggled into her favorite rose-print chintz easy chair, he leaned back and unbuckled his Harley–Davidson belt.

"What are you doing there in my chair?" she asked as she brought the plates of goodies to him. "I've told you time and again not to sit in it. I've got the cushion molded just right for my own hind end, and you're gonna wreck it. Get out! Now!"

"It's comfortable," he objected as he reached for the plate. "I can see now why you like sitting here, even if it is a sissy, pansy chair with stupid flowers all over it."

"Get out of it!" she said, kicking him on the shin with her fuzzy red slipper. "You insult my chair and expect me to let you sit there? Move your carcass over to the couch and take those boots off. They've got mud and heaven knows what else on 'em." She took a sniff and wrinkled her nose. "Lord have mercy, boy, what have you been wading through? Meadow muffins?"

"Meadow whats?" He lifted his boot and stared at the sole.

"Cow pies," she said. "You know . . . bovine biscuits."

"Ah. You mean bull shit," he said. "Yes, as a matter of fact, I—"

"Sh-h-h," Savannah said, seeing her grandmother descend the stairs, a cloud of Hawaiian print in her floor-length pink and red muumuu. "Watch your mouth. Gran's coming down."

"I heard that," Gran said, a twinkle in her eye as she joined them in the living room. "Who's been tippy toeing through the bullpucky?"

"Me," Dirk admitted as he quickly stood and offered Gran the chair. "I had to chase a suspect through a pasture yesterday out in Mooney Canyon. I guess I haven't gotten around to scraping off all the . . . uh . . . forensic evidence yet."

He held Gran's arm as she settled into Savannah's easy chair and gently placed the ottoman under her feet. Then he handed her his brownie and a piece of fudge.

Savannah smiled, loving him just for a moment, then she said, "Go put those boots out on the front porch and get back in here before my news story comes on."

Glancing at the television, she could see that the weather report was nearly finished. And that meant the colorful, local story would be next. She wasn't sure how she felt about her latest exploits being broadcast for God and everybody to see. With cameras everywhere these days, a body had precious little privacy.

On the other hand, the footage had convinced the cops who had appeared on the scene that the other guy was the one who had thrown the first punch . . . or at least attempted to before she'd effectively blocked it.

There were times when a bit of store security videotape could be a girl's best friend.

"I don't need to see it on the screen," Dirk said as he plodded off to the hallway. "I was there. I saw the whole bloody, gory scene in person."

"Bloody?" Tammy was all ears. "Gory?" She looked anything but appalled. In fact, she looked deliciously intrigued—embarrassingly so.

Ghoul, Savannah thought proudly.

She'd taught the kid everything she knew about crime scene gore, its significance, and how to process it.

Granny settled her generous self into the easy chair and looked perfectly at home, the golden light of the reading lamp setting her white hair aglow with a fire that matched the one burning in her bright blue eyes.

Granny Reid might be an octogenarian who had traveled a lot of long, bumpy, pothole-pitted roads, but her passion hadn't dimmed one bit over the years. And one didn't need a second glance to see where Savannah had gotten her feisty spirit.

Gran took a bite of Dirk's brownie, closed her eyes, and savored it for a moment, then she said, "Perfection, Savannah girl. Sinful, scrumptious perfection." Then she opened her eyes, the moment for savoring over. "Now, what's this business about you committing murder and mayhem at the local supermarket? I thought I taught you better than that."

"You did, Gran," Savannah said as she sat on the floor beside her grandmother and rested her head on Granny's knee. "You taught me to be a lady, but sometimes a lady has to . . . well . . ."

"Hey, it's you!" Tammy said, nearly jumping out of her chair and pointing to the television. "Oh, you look great! I'm so glad you were wearing that turquoise sweater. That's one of your best!"

"Oh please. Tammy Hart, stylist to the stars," Savannah said, giving her friend a grin.

"Actually," John said, "Tammy's right. You do look stunning in that sweater."

"I agree," Ryan added

"Oh, right." Savannah snorted. "Like either of you would even notice."

"We notice." Ryan lifted one eyebrow and gave her a quick once-over that set her pitter to patting all over again. "Notice is all we do, but we notice."

Dirk reentered the room and shuffled across the floor in his socks. He sat down on the rug next to the television, reached over, and turned up the volume.

The blond cutie at the anchor's desk began the story. "And this afternoon in a San Carmelita supermarket, an altercation sent a local accountant to the hospital. As seen here on the store security videotape, two shoppers exchanged words, and their discussion rapidly escalated into an argument. The woman you see there at the bottom of your screen is Savannah Reid, formerly a police officer with the San Carmelita Police Department."

The living room erupted in whistles and cheers. Savannah held up both hands, "Quiet! Quiet! Listen now; throw cash and gifts later."

The newscaster continued, an amused look on her face. "At this point in the argument, Reid held up one finger—no, ladies and gentlemen, not *that* finger—her pinkie—but even that appeared to enrage Timothy Barnett, who took a swing at her. As we can see, Ms. Reid has not forgotten the self-defense training she received from the S.C.P.D. and there . . . only a few seconds later . . . you see Barnett on the floor amid a pile of fallen produce, tumbled cans, and broken bottles." The reporter grinned her perfect, bleached white smile. "Yes, folks, we *do* have a major cleanup on aisle five."

"Yay-y-y-y! That's our girl!" Ryan shouted.

"Here, here!" John saluted her with his cup of Earl Grey.

"Oh, Savannah! I'm so proud of you," Tammy said, her pretty face shining, tears in her eyes. "You blocked him with an exquisitely executed *gedan barai*. The *mae geri* kick to his chest was flawless, and that *nage waza* was the perfect choice to put him on the floor."

Savannah stared at her for several seconds, then said, "Uh, okay. Thanks, Tam." And she decided to cut back a bit on Tammy's martial arts training.

Dirk smirked. "I see you're still using that 'the average size is . . .' line to provoke suspects," he said.

Savannah winked at him. "Hey, the classics hold up."

The only less than jovial person in the room was Gran, who sat with her arms crossed over her ample chest, a scowl on her face.

From Savannah's seat on the floor beside her grandmother, she looked up into that infinitely dear face and cringed. Her grandmother had raised her and her eight brothers and sisters. Savannah knew the look all too well—she was in trouble.

"What was that business you did with your finger there?" Gran wanted to know. "Is that what I think it was?"

Savannah giggled and nudged Gran's leg. "Naw, it wasn't that at all. Like the gal there on TV said, it was my pinkie. A perfectly innocent gesture. I'd never do that other one . . . after you teaching me to be a genteel Southern lady and all."

Dirk cleared his throat, and Savannah shot him a warning look.

"Well, you must have said something pretty unladylike for him to take a swing at you like that," Gran said.

"He was being nasty to his wife and little boy, mouthing off and threatening them," Savannah told her. "And I just couldn't abide it. You know, like ol' Leon Hafner used to do. And Gran, I remember all too well what *you* did to Leon that Saturday night when he came calling uninvited."

A mischievous grin flitted across Gran's face. She shrugged. "Eh, well, Leon deserved to get a skillet upside his head," she said. "He was always thumpin' on poor Alice and her too scared and broke to leave him with three little young'uns in tow. She came over to our house that day with a bloody nose and a black eye, and when he came bustin' through my kitchen door after her, hollering and carrying on, I had to do something. So, I grabbed a twelve-inch skillet and gave him a good talkin' to."

Savannah laughed. "After their little, uh, conversation, Leon needed seven stitches to close that gash on his forehead. But he never came over to our house in a rage again. Not even when Alice finally left his ugly a——, I mean, left him flat."

"It looked like that accountant in the grocery store was needing some stitches himself," Tammy said. "There was blood everywhere!"

"Naw," Savannah laughed. "Most of it was ketchup."

"Most?" Gran asked.

"Ketchup?" Ryan added.

"She was next to the condiment section," Dirk explained. "You work with what you've got."

John nodded. "Our Savannah is resourceful, if nothing else."

"Did they arrest that fellow?" Gran wanted to know. "Are you going to have to go to court and testify and all that rigmarole?"

"Naw, I didn't press charges," Savannah told her. "He never actually got the chance to lay a finger on me, so why bother?"

Dirk reached for the plate of fudge. "I'd say he got the point when that shelf full of ketchup and mustard came crashing down on him. I swear I saw a pickle sticking out of his ear."

"Oh, you did not." Savannah chuckled. "But I wasn't trying to make a point with him. Guys like that never get the point anyway, so what's the use? My statement was for his wife. I wanted her to see that he's not God Almighty, no matter what he's told her. Seeing another woman take him down a notch or two might have done her some good. I sure hope so."

A cell phone began playing the theme song to *The Good, the Bad, and the Ugly.* Dirk reached into his shirt pocket and pulled out his phone. "The captain," he offered in explanation. He shrugged and added, "Seemed appropriate somehow."

They nodded, understanding perfectly. Dirk's rocky relationship with his captain—and everyone else in the S.C.P.D.—was common knowledge. The brass didn't like him. He hated them. And most of his fellow cops respected his work but would have run ten miles in the opposite direction to avoid working with him.

Dirk had only slightly less luck with partners than with women. And the only person who had actually enjoyed working with him, had been Savannah. Since she and the S.C.P.D. had parted ways years ago, Detective Sergeant Dirk Coulter had been the proverbial lone wolf, and nothing made him happier than to be pack free.

When he wanted companionship, howling at a full moon or whiling away the boring hours of a stake-out, he invited Savannah to come along.

She was so much better than Detectives Demitry, Averick, or Bura—way better looking, and she always brought food.

"Coulter," he barked into the phone, chatty as always. He listened for a few seconds, then began to scowl. "Why? No. I don't think so."

Savannah perked up as they all listened intently. While they wouldn't have admitted it for all the rocky road fudge in the world, they lived vicariously through Dirk and his cases. Since Savannah was no longer a cop, Ryan and John had long ago left the FBI, and Gran and Tammy were merely Nancy Drew wannabes, they had to get their true crime fix somehow.

"If it's only been nineteen hours, what's the big deal?" Dirk was asking. "Whatever happened to the twenty-four-hour rule?"

Ah, a missing person, Savannah thought. *Not as interesting as some cases, but it could turn into something.*

"Just 'cause it's a fat cat's daughter." Dirk shook his head in disgust. "Yeah, okay, that's even worse . . . a fat cat's spoiled rotten daughter's friend. She doesn't come home from partying, and I'm supposed to go club hopping to find her? I mean, it's not like she's a little kid who went missing from a local playground or—" He sighed. "Yeah, yeah. Okay. I'll get right on it. In fact, I left ten minutes ago. Happy?"

He snapped the phone shut.

"Teenager didn't make it home last night?" Savannah asked.

"Yeah, an eighteen-year-old named Daisy O'Neil. She's a friend of that Dante kid. . . ." He thought for a moment. "You know, that gal that's always in the tabloids, the skinny one."

"Tiffy Dante." Tammy turned to Gran. "She's sort of a local celebrity around here, she and her friends. Her dad is filthy rich, and she and her high society girlfriends are always getting into some sort of trouble."

Gran waved a dismissive hand. "Oh please. I know who Tiffy Dante and her girlfriends are—the Skeleton Key Three. I read the papers and watch some TV. I mean, we may live out in the toolies there in Georgia, and McGill may be nothing but a wide spot in the road. But I'll bet you that more girls at McGill High School know who Tiffy Dante is than know the name of the first lady of the United States of America. Sorry state of affairs, but true."

"Oh yeah," Dirk said. "I've heard of them, too. Read something about some sex–drug parties they were having there at her father's mansion last year when . . . oh . . . sorry, Mrs. Reid."

Gran gave him a wry look. "We know about sex and drugs there in McGill, Georgia, too." She grinned. "Not that we'd have nothin' to do with either one."

"No, of course not." Savannah turned to Dirk. "So, who did you say is missing? Tiffy? Bunny? Or the third one . . . what's her name . . . ?"

"Kiki," Tammy supplied. "The third one's name is Kiki."

"But it's Daisy O'Neil who's missing," Dirk reminded them.

"Where do they get these names?" Gran said. "Can you imagine sticking a perfectly sweet, innocent little baby with a stupid tag like Kiki for the rest of her life?"

Savannah bit her tongue and decided not to mention that Gran had named one of her sons Sebastian and one of her daughters Annameena. Gran might be over eighty, but she still had a fast hand, and Savannah was within slapping distance.

"So," Savannah said, "if the Skeleton Key Three is Tiffy Dante and her friends Bunny and Kiki, who is Daisy O'Neil?"

Tammy was fast with the answer. "Daisy is sort of a hanger-on, an appendage to the Key Three. She's not as rich and certainly not as thin as the others. I've seen her pictured many times with them. She's never quite as put together as they are. Though I must say, she's the prettiest of the group, in my opinion."

"Well," Dirk said, rising from the rug and shoving his phone back into his pocket. "Whether she's rich or thin or good-looking, I couldn't tell you. All I know is that she didn't come home last night and her mother is worried about her, and Tiffy's dad, Andrew Dante, is raising a stink about us looking for her."

"And when you've got the kind of wealth that Andrew Dante has," John said, "it's enough to make certain that your complaint is heard."

"Yeah, the chief is after the captain to get after me. So, I'll have to call it a night here." He turned to Savannah. "Thanks for the good dinner, Van."

She didn't even bother to ask; she just started to wrap up some brownies and fudge in a napkin to go.

More than anything, she was itching to tag along. But Gran had only arrived from Georgia two days before, and with her other guests there, it would just be too rude. Southern hospitality just didn't allow for such things.

She knew Dirk was thinking the same thing as he glanced around the room, then gave her a questioning look.

"Oh, go ahead and go," Gran said, standing up and offering a hand up to Savannah. "You know you want to."

"I don't want to," she lied.

"You do, too. It's as plain as the fudge on your face." Gran reached down and wiped a smear of chocolate off her granddaughter's lip. "Don't stick around on my account. I'll be trottin' off to bed in a minute anyway. Gotta read my Bible and my *True Informer*. There'll probably be something in there about this missing girl. You know how they beat everybody else to the scoop."

Gran's unwavering confidence in the *True Informer*'s journalistic integrity had always amazed Savannah. Whether something was written between the well-worn leather covers of her King James Bible or within the pulp mill pages of the national tabloid, it was gospel, according to Gran.

"Go ahead and go with him, Savannah," Ryan said as he stood and stretched his long limbs. "John and I have an early tee time at the club tomorrow morning. We'll be getting going ourselves."

Only Tammy appeared to mind. Her lower lip protruded in predictable fashion. Tammy didn't mind the fact that Savannah would be leaving as much as that she wouldn't be accompanying her.

Savannah felt for her, but not enough to invite her along. There was a limit to how many civilians Dirk could bring with him when he was on the job. And since Savannah brought along carbo-rich goodies and Tammy irritated him to distraction, Savannah was always his first choice.

"You coming?" he asked her.

She grinned, winked at him, and out of respect for her grandmother, decided not to give him her usual X-rated reply to that question. "Absolutely," she said. "Let me get my weapon and—"

"You won't need it," he said with a smirk. "I've got mine. I'll keep you safe."

"Yeah, right," she said. "I'll just bring along my own, if you don't mind. I've seen you at the target range."

Chapter 2

Savannah gazed out the window as they passed one mansion after another after another in the exclusive enclave of Spirit Hills. As they drove deeper into the valley, each estate seemed grander than the last. Here in the heart of the canyon, the trees grew thicker, and the road curved more tightly and rose in elevation with each twist and turn. And with every crook in the road, more and more of the panoramic view was revealed.

If you lived in San Carmelita and were rich enough, you could afford to live in Spirit Hills. If you were filthy, stinking rich, you could afford to live on one of the hillsides at the end of the canyon, overlooking the valley, the town, and the Pacific Ocean. And you could feel pretty darned good about it.

Or at least, Savannah figured they should feel pretty good about it. Heck, if she lived here, *she* would!

In McGill, the little rural town where she had been born, most people had looked down on her immediate family. Her barfly mom and never home trucker dad had made pretty sure of that. Their deeds and misdeeds had secured the family's reputation as white trash in the better part of three counties. Other than turning out a new baby every year and naming each one after a town in Georgia, neither of them had accomplished anything that would have garnered any respect from their neighbors.

But Granny Reid was respected and deeply loved by all who knew her—with the possible exception of Leon Hafner, who respected her but harbored precious little affection for her since the skillet incident. And when the courts had taken Savannah and her brothers and sisters away from her parents and put them in Gran's care, their lives had taken a decided turn for the better.

But not before Savannah had learned the pain of having people look down on you. Way down. And she had to think that living here on what seemed like the top of the world and literally looking down on everyone else . . . that would go a long way toward healing any inferiority complexes one might have incurred during a rocky childhood.

"Do you ever wonder what they eat in joints like this?" Dirk said as he guided his ancient Buick Skylark around another curve and shifted into low gear to climb a particularly steep hill.

"Is that all you ever think about?" she asked him. "Food?"

"No, sometimes I think about sex and baseball."

She groaned and shook her head. "What do you mean, what do they eat? They eat just like the rest of us. Well, they probably wash it down with wine instead of beer or soda pop, but—"

"I mean, do people who live in a place, like say, that one there . . ."—he pointed to a sprawling Tudor mansion on their right—". . . do they actually bring home a bucket of chicken when everybody's too tired to cook? Or do they eat pheasant under glass every night?"

"I don't want to have this conversation again. We both agreed last time that very few people actually have pheasant under glass for dinner anymore. And no, I'm not going to try to make it for you. Ever. Barbecued game hens are the closest I'll ever come."

He didn't reply, and they sat in silence for a while until she added, "And to be honest, I'm plum confused as to why you, of all people, would even give a hoot about a fancy schmancy dish like that. You're more of a hot dog and hamburger guy. What's with this obsession you have about pheasant under glass?"

He shrugged and looked mildly uncomfortable. "I don't want to tell you. You'll laugh."

"So what? I always laugh at you. Spit it out. What is it?"

"It's a James Bond thing, okay?"

"James Bond?"

"Yeah, I read somewhere or heard that he likes it, like it's his favorite dish or whatever. And you know I'm a big fan of his."

She shook her head and stared at him. "I never heard that."

"Well, believe it or not, Miss Smarty Pants, you don't know as much about some stuff as I do."

"Besides, James Bond is a fictional character. Do you mean Sean Connery likes it?"

"No, I mean *James Bond*. Never mind. I didn't think you'd understand."

"Lord help us," she mumbled under her breath. "Next thing you know, he'll want his beer shaken, not stirred."

She rolled down her window to let in some of the fresh evening air and to release some of the less refreshing aromas of the burger and taco wrappers that he had tossed onto the back floorboard. *Pheasant under glass, indeed.*

"I want to talk about this case," she said. "Like, why are we going to Dante's mansion rather than this Daisy O'Neil's house?"

"Because her mother called 9-1-1 from Dante's, said she wasn't leaving there until they told her where to find her daughter. She's convinced that the other girls had something to do with Daisy's disappearance, and she's causing a big stink about it."

"Seems like Dante would have been the one calling the cops if she's harassing him on his own property."

"Yeah, you'd think so. We may wind up having to toss her out of there if we can't settle her down."

"The thought of 'tossing' a worried mother anywhere doesn't exactly agree with me," Savannah said. "If I had kids and one went missing, I'd be beside myself. I lost one of my kid sisters—I think it was Atlanta—in a Wal-Mart one Sunday afternoon for twenty minutes, and I about went out of my mind imagining what might have happened to her."

"Yeah, that's just gotta be the worst. The absolutely worst thing that can happen to a parent . . . having a kid go missing. But this gal will turn up. I can feel it."

She sniffed. "Oh yes, the infamous, infallible Coulter intuition."

"Hey, don't knock it. My instinct has gotten you out of some nasty jams over the years."

"And gotten me into plenty of them, too."

"Be that as it may."

They rounded a curve, and on a separate hill above them and to the left was the most magnificent mansion Savannah had ever seen. Crowning the hill,

the palatial home looked like a cross between a Tus-
can country villa and the Acropolis.

Illuminated by exquisitely placed architectural
lighting, the limestone façade glowed golden against
the darkening twilit sky. Arched and shuttered windows, some two and three stories tall, reached to or-
nate eaves and a red-tiled roof.

They drove through an avenue of giant, mature
oaks that momentarily obscured the view of the
house. Something about their black, gnarled trunks
and the way their thick foliage blocked out even the
last rays of the fading sunlight gave Savannah a
creepy feeling. She felt like she was watching the pre-
lude to some sort of horror movie as they passed between them.

But the sense of foreboding left the moment they
exited the oaks and entered the circular motor court.
Giant palm trees danced in the evening breeze,
throwing lacy shadows across the front of the mansion, and in the center of the court, a four-tiered
marble fountain was lit with golden floodlights. The
water that cascaded from layer to layer sparkled like
streams of liquid topaz.

"Wow, I heard about this place when they were
building it two years ago," she said, "but I had no
idea it was so grand! Glory be, what a spread!"

"Eh," Dirk replied. "My trailer looks this good
when the neighbor's mutt runs too close to my front
door and the outdoor security light flips on. It's all
done with lighting."

"Yeah, right."

They parked in the court between a new Porsche
convertible and an older rusty and dented minivan.
On the van's bumper was a faded sticker that read
"My Kid Is On the S.C.H.S. Honor Roll."

"Something tells me that van belongs to Daisy

O'Neil's mom," Savannah said. "I can't imagine the guy who lives in this place driving it. And I'm sure they'd expect any servants who owned that to park around back and out of sight."

Dirk nodded. "And from what I've read about her, I don't think Miss Tiffy would be caught dead in any vehicle that didn't cost as much as your house and my trailer combined."

Savannah recalled the appraised value of her own house on her last tax statement and added twenty-five cents for Dirk's single-wide monstrosity that still had vestiges of dinosaur poop on its tires. "No," she said, "I doubt that she would."

They left the Buick and walked across the granite-paved courtyard, through a gracefully arched colonnade, to a wrought iron double door. The delicate iron work formed two letters—a T on the left and a D on the right.

"Andrew Dante," Savannah mumbled, mulling the initials over in her mind. "Should be an A, not a T."

They both looked at each other with raised eyebrows. "Don't tell me," she said. "He put his kid's initials on his door?"

"Maybe his wife's name is Tiffy, or something equally stupid that starts with a T."

"Or he's a doting father. An *extremely* doting father."

"That would explain some of the stories I've read in the tabloids. To hear them tell it, she's a brat who gets everything she wants and then some."

Savannah pushed the button next to the door and heard the Westminster Chimes echo inside. "Ah, don't believe everything you read. Rich people get a bad rap just because everybody's jealous of them. Some of the nicest, most humble, and most generous people I've ever known were rich."

"Naw. I hate 'em all. You can't be a decent person and be rich."

She shook her head and sighed. "Coulter . . . there isn't one single solitary group of people under the sun that you trust, respect, or like."

"That isn't true."

"Is, too."

"Is not. I like dogs."

The door opened, and a tiny woman in her early twenties stood there in a black and white maid's uniform. Her thick dark hair flowed around her shoulders in a manner that struck Savannah as impractical for the active work of a housekeeper. And the skirt on her uniform was so short that should she need to bend over, she would have to squat ever so gracefully so as not to expose her diminutive derriere.

It also struck Savannah that both the person who had designed this costume, as well as the one who had decided that this young lady should wear it, were well aware of the clothing's limitations—or benefits.

Savannah gave Dirk a sideways glance and saw his eyes flit, ever so briefly, over the outfit and then lock on the maid's face. She had to give the guy some major points for professionalism. Better than anyone, she knew his predilection for French maid and cheerleader garb.

"Hello. May I help you?" the maid asked in a breathless, half-panting voice that sounded like it was straight from an 800-Call-to-Talk-Dirty phone line. She ran her fingers through her long hair and then shifted her weight from one foot to another, sticking her hip out to one side in what she undoubtedly thought was a sexy pose.

A quick look at Dirk told Savannah that he thought so, too.

His eyes bugged out just a bit as he looked her up and down one more time. But he cleared his throat, and apparently his mind, because he managed to dig out his badge, flip it open under her nose, and say with only the slightest squeak, "I'm Detective Sergeant Dirk Coulter, San Carmelita Police Department. This is my colleague, Savannah Reid. We received a call that you have a problem here tonight. Is there a Ms. O'Neil around?"

The maid glanced uneasily over her shoulder. "Uh, yes, but . . ."

Savannah could hear a woman's angry voice deep inside the house, and a man's, too. They sounded as though they were arguing.

Dirk looked past the maid and tried to see into the massive foyer behind her. "Is that Ms. O'Neil I hear?" he asked. He didn't wait for an answer. "I need to talk to her right now."

He gave his best, most authoritative cop wave of the hand, and predictably, the young woman stood aside to allow them in. Savannah decided then and there that the maid was more legs and hair than backbone. But she cut her some slack. After all, when she'd been that age, her composition had been much the same.

Hey, she thought, *you live and you learn, and you eventually learn how to stand up on your hind legs and roar . . . like at abusive jerks in supermarkets.*

She grinned at the fresh and refreshing memory as she followed Dirk into the mansion. A vision of her would-be assailant lying on the floor, soaking in a marinade of ketchup, pickle juice, and balsamic vinegar, brought a grin to her face and a resolution to her heart.

I simply must do that more often, she thought before pulling her mind back to the business at hand.

The two-story foyer was depressingly large . . . depressing only because it occurred to Savannah that she could probably put her entire house inside its confines and still have room to park her Mustang, Dirk's Buick, and Tammy's VW bug. But even in her downhearted state, she had to admit it was impressive. From the marble floors to the turned oak staircase with its curved railings to the stained-glass rotunda ceiling, this architectural introduction to Dante's domain said it all.

Andrew Dante had it all.

Or at least, one might say more than his share of it all.

If it just hadn't been for the pink walls.

They weren't a delicate, apple blossom pink. They weren't a hint of smoky pink.

Nope, not even close to anything that could be called classy, Savannah thought. The walls were the color of the medicine that Granny Reid had dispensed by the bottleful over the years, curing everything from stomachaches to adolescent crabbiness. And while it might have been a welcome color to a person suffering from what Gran called "the green apple quick step," it didn't belong on walls. And certainly not the walls of a magnificent mansion.

They passed through the foyer and into a great room, following the ever escalating sound of the argument. Again, Savannah was struck by the sheer enormity of the room. The fireplace to her right was large enough for even a tall person to stand inside. And she could see at least three distinct seating groupings: one around the hearth, another near an ornately carved bar to the left, and another at the far end of the room, close to a nine-foot concert grand piano.

But for all its grandeur, the pink curse seemed to have infected this room as well. The walls were a slightly less vulgar shade of pink, but the furniture was upholstered in shockingly bright raspberry velvet.

Again, Savannah wondered who might be the source of this decorating nightmare. But her curiosity was satisfied when she saw a life-sized painting that hung over the fireplace.

The oil was of a pretty, if somewhat haughty-looking, young woman in a ball gown, her platinum blond hair spilling over her bare shoulders. The voluminous dress gave the impression that its wearer was floating in a cloud of organza . . . bright pink, of course. And in the painting's background was a garden of roses, again every unnatural shade of pink imaginable.

Something told Savannah that the teenager in the painting had been responsible for choosing the color scheme for this palatial home.

And definitely should not have been, she added to herself, as they hurried past islands of velvet, diamond-tucked furniture to the other end of the room where the woman and man stood arguing beside the piano.

"The cops are going to be here any minute now," the tall, blond Viking of a man was telling a tiny redhead who glared up at him with clenched fists and a look of fury on her tear-wet face. "And I'm going to have you arrested for . . . oh, I don't know . . . disturbing my peace or something like that. I told you to get out of here or—"

"I am not leaving here until I've spoken to that no-good brat of a daughter of yours. I want to know what she's done with my Daisy, and don't tell me she isn't here because I saw her look out her upstairs bedroom window when I drove up."

"It wasn't her," he said. "It was probably one of her friends or a maid or whatever. And it doesn't matter anyhow whether she's here or not because I've already talked to her, and she said she doesn't have a clue where Daisy is."

"She's a liar! A rotten, spoiled brat, dirty little liar. She's hurt Daisy. Those girls have hurt her and—"

The blond man was handsome, his features fine and chiseled, his physique muscular beneath his polo shirt and designer jeans, but his face turned ugly with anger at the insult. He took a step closer to the redhead just as Dirk and Savannah reached them. "You better watch your mouth when you're talking about my daughter! Tiffy's a good person who's done a lot for your kid! A whole lot! And you don't appreciate it! Why I ought to—"

"No! Hold it right there!" Dirk said as he took hold of the man's arm. With his other hand, he reached into his jacket pocket, pulled out his badge, and held it practically under the man's nose. "You called the police? Well, we're here. So everybody just settle down till we get this all ironed out. What's going on around here?"

"My daughter is missing," the red-haired woman said as she started to cry. She covered her eyes with her hands for a moment and let the sobs overtake her. Then, after ten seconds or so, she recovered herself and managed to say, "My Daisy is gone, and she would *never* have just disappeared on her own like this. Those girls she hangs out with . . . those pampered, rotten girls . . . they've done something bad to her. I just know it! They've always treated her like dirt, made fun of her, used her, and acted like they were way better than her because she doesn't have *their* money. And now, now I know they've hurt her. They've done something horrible to her. I can just feel it."

When she dissolved into tears again, Dirk gave Savannah a helpless look—the one he always gave her when he had a crying female on his hands.

Dirk didn't particularly mind if a male perpetrator was screaming with fury or blubbering like a kindergartner who had just been told there was no Santa. But when it came to weeping women, Dirk caved every time.

Savannah reached for the distraught mother and wrapped one arm around her shoulders. "Now, now," she said. "Why don't you and I come over here and sit down and talk for a while. You tell me all about Daisy and what's been going on with her, and we'll leave Detective Coulter with . . . uh . . . is it Mr. Andrew Dante?"

Dante nodded, his pale blue eyes sweeping over Savannah's curvaceous figure with practiced skill, missing nothing.

Savannah glanced down, saw the wedding ring on his left hand, and decided that she didn't like him much. Curves or no curves, married men had no business noticing . . . or at least, being quite so darned obvious about it.

"Yes," he said, giving her a slightly lascivious smile. "I'm Andrew Dante. And you are . . . ?"

"Savannah Reid," Dirk barked. "She's with me. And you and I need to have a little talk. Come along."

Dirk directed Dante out of the room as Savannah led Daisy O'Neil's mother to the nearest sofa and sat her down.

Fishing some tissues out of her purse, Savannah handed them to her and said, "I'm so sorry, Ms. O'Neil. I really am. I can't even imagine what you must be going through, but I'm sure it's just awful."

She nodded and sniffed. "It is. I'm just worried sick. I didn't get a wink of sleep last night, and I'm shaking like a leaf inside *and* out."

"Have you eaten anything today?"

She thought for a moment, then shook her head. "No, I don't think so."

"We'll get you something to eat as soon as we finish talking here," Savannah promised her. "You have to rest and eat at least enough to keep your strength up, or you won't be able to help Daisy."

As the woman wiped her eyes and blew her nose, Savannah gave her a quick glance over. She might be attractive if her eyes weren't red and swollen, her bright red hair was combed, and her simple cotton shirt and jeans didn't look as though she'd slept in them.

Savannah judged her to be in her early forties, but she seemed to have experienced some rather difficult years. The deep lines on her tanned face and the roughness of her hands suggested that she worked outside in the sun with little time for feminine niceties like salon manicures.

Reaching over and placing her hand on the woman's freckled forearm, Savannah said, "Ms. O'Neil, please tell me about your Daisy."

The mother ran a trembling hand through her tousled hair. "What do you want to know?"

"What sort of girl is she? Has she ever run away before? Things like that."

"No. Daisy's a very good kid. She's never given me a bit of trouble. She was on the honor role at school, and she's always hung out with nice kids. Well . . . until she went to a fancy club in Hollywood one night to celebrate a friend's birthday. That's when she got hooked up with this gang, these Skeleton Key girls."

"So, you don't consider the Skeleton Key Three good kids?"

The mother gave her a disgusted look. "Oh, come on. You read the tabloids, or at least see them on the stands and read the headlines. They're trashy, these girls." Looking around the opulent room, she added, "Having a ton of money doesn't make you classy . . . just more interesting to the media, I guess."

Savannah smiled. "Well, what's more interesting than an extremely rich person? A rich person who behaves worse than we do. A rich person we can feel superior to."

"Yeah, I guess that's a large part of the appeal."

Savannah remembered some of the tabloid headlines she'd read, about how the cops had been called to hotel rooms where the Three had been throwing wild sex and drug parties. She thought of this good kid, this honor role student who had never given her mother a moment of trouble. She cleared her throat and asked one of the most obvious and difficult questions. "Have you ever had any reason to believe that Daisy does drugs of any kind?"

"No. Well, I think maybe some of these girls smoke pot or maybe take some of those party drugs when they go to clubs. But I don't let Daisy club hop with them . . . for that very reason."

"Does Daisy attend their private parties, parties here at the mansion or . . . um . . . in hotels?"

Ms. O'Neil gave her a guarded, unhappy look. "She doesn't attend *those* parties. The ones you've read about in the paper."

"Okay." Savannah wasn't sure she believed that one, but apparently, Daisy's mom did. "Does she have a steady boyfriend? One she might have run away with? Or an ex-boyfriend she might be having problems with?"

"No one now. She had a boyfriend for a long time . . . over a year. She liked him a lot. But a couple of months ago, this Tiffy Dante made eyes at him or—more likely—flashed him some body part, and he dropped Daisy cold."

"So, would you say that Daisy was depressed?"

The mother considered her answer a while before giving it. "No, not really. She was earlier this year. But Tiffy started taking acting lessons at a studio in Hollywood, and she let Daisy tag along—to keep her company on the drive, I suppose. And even though Tiffy wasn't doing all that well, Daisy took to it like you wouldn't believe! She's great. A natural actress. The teacher recommended her to an agent, and he landed a bit part for her in a sitcom. They start filming tomorrow, and she was so excited about it. That's why I know there's just no way possible that she would run away. She was like a kid counting the hours before Christmas morning."

Savannah thought of her youngest sister, Atlanta, and her obsession with being a movie star someday. Or a country-singing Nashville hit. Or a runway model or . . .

"Yes, I'm sure she was *very* excited to have a part on a TV show," she told the mother. "Most people would be jazzed about that, but especially a teenager."

A rather ugly thought ran through Savannah's mind. "Uh, how did Tiffy and the other girls feel about Daisy's good fortune?"

"Tiffy was tiffed. Big time. But then, Tiffy's always miffed and throwing a temper tantrum about something. She couldn't understand why they would cast Daisy for a part when she's . . . well . . . she's not as slender as the other Skeleton Key Three. Daisy is . . . how do they say it? Pleasingly plump."

"A full-figured beauty. Like me." Savannah smiled.

The woman gave Savannah a quick look. "My Daisy is larger than you. And she's beautiful."

With those words, the woman started to cry again, and Savannah searched her purse for more tissues.

"When was the last time you saw Daisy, Ms. O'Neil?"

She sniffed. "You can call me Pam," she said. "And the last time I saw my daughter was when she left yesterday afternoon to come over here. She said she was going to be studying her lines with Tiffy, Kiki, and

Bunny, that they'd offered to help her. That'll be the day, when *those* girls want to actually help my Daisy."

"What time did she leave your house?"

She thought for a moment. "It must have been about four. I had only been home from work a few minutes when she told me she was leaving."

"Where do you work, Pam?"

"I have a job with the city—road repair and maintenance. I'm a flagman. So you can see why my daughter is so enthralled with all this crap." She waved her hand, indicating the house and its furnishings.

"Well, money on this kind of scale can turn anybody's head," Savannah said softly, "especially an impressionable teenager."

Reaching into her purse and pulling out her notebook and pen, Savannah asked, "Other than these girls, Tiffy, Bunny, and Kiki, does Daisy have any other friends she spends time with?"

"No. These girls just sort of absorbed her. She doesn't have time anymore for anybody or anything. Just hanging around here or tagging along behind them, when they allow her to, when they need somebody to make fun of and feel superior to."

Glancing again at the ostentatious painting over the fireplace, it occurred to Savannah that Tiffy Dante probably felt superior to almost everyone. But if what Pam O'Neil was saying was true, it certainly did sound as though Daisy was the Omega dog in a pretty ruthless pack.

"You say they make fun of her. What exactly do they say when they do that?"

Pam twisted the tissue in her hand and fought back more tears. "Oh, the usual stuff that teenagers ridicule each other about, I guess—her clothes, her hair. Of course, none of that is up to *their* standards. But mostly they harass her about her weight."

Savannah nodded. "Yes, sadly, that's an easy target

today, what with all the emphasis on being abnormally thin."

"Oh, and with these girls, it's an obsession. They're always dieting and purging to stay super thin, but my Daisy won't do that. I've raised her to love herself as she is. You know . . . a . . . a . . ."

"A well-rounded young lady," Savannah supplied.

"Yes. Well-rounded. And she's very pretty just as she is."

"I'm sure that's true. Do you have a picture of her with you?"

Pam reached into the back pocket of her jeans and pulled out what appeared to be a man's wallet. She flipped it open and took out a much handled creased and faded picture.

Savannah took the photo and looked into the face that was so much like the woman before her. Daisy was just a softer, prettier version of her mom.

"You're right. She *is* pretty. A lovely girl. And she has very intelligent eyes. Smart and strong."

Pam nodded. "She *is* smart. I mean, she's a little dumb where these girls here are concerned because she wants so much to be a part of their little club. But she's no fool. If they wanted to hurt her, they'd have to be very quick about it, plan it all out and surprise her. Otherwise she'd get the jump on *them*, not the other way around."

"May I keep this picture? I promise I'll get it back to you later."

The mother hesitated, then said, "Sure, if it'll help. I want to do anything that might help."

"Can you tell me what she was wearing yesterday the last time you saw her?"

"The uniform," she said with a sarcastic tone. "The stupid Skeleton Key Three uniform."

"And that is?"

"Designer jeans and a pink T-shirt with a skeleton

key in rhinestones on the front. Tiffy's favorite color is pink, so everything has to be pink. Daisy hated pink."

Savannah never got used to asking the hard questions, but they had to be asked. "Pam, do you really feel that those girls would seriously harm your daughter? Deep down in your gut, do you believe they would?"

Pam gave it a few moments' thought, then she looked straight into Savannah's eyes, and Savannah could see her fear, raw, potent, and painful. She nodded. "Yes. Tiffy was so upset that Daisy got that part. I mean, really furious about it! And she isn't the kind of kid who takes disappointment well. I truly do think she might have hurt my daughter . . . or talked the other girls into harming her."

Savannah put her hand on the woman's shoulder and gave it a firm squeeze, then a comforting pat. "We're going to do everything we can to find your Daisy," she told her. "Detective Coulter is excellent at what he does, and I'm pretty good, too, if I do say so myself. We'll find her."

"But when you do find her, do you think she'll be okay?"

Pam's eyes searched hers, and Savannah knew she was trying to read the future on her face. Victims' families always did that, and Savannah was miserably uncomfortable when they did it. She felt like a crystal ball that was trying to hide its dark, ugly mysteries.

Savannah fought the urge to look away. She also pushed down her thoughts: *The girl went missing yesterday afternoon. That was over twenty-four hours ago. And when we don't find them in the first twenty-four hours, it's not good. Sometimes, it's really not good.*

"I think you're a strong woman, Pam O'Neil," she said. "And from this picture, I can see that you and your daughter are very much alike. Not just your red hair, but the strength and courage I see in your eyes. As my Granny Reid would say, 'Twasn't a very windy day when that apple fell from the tree.' "

"What?"

"Never mind. Granny has a lot of sayings. Anyway, if Daisy is anything like her mom, and I suspect she is, I'd say that she'll take care of herself, do whatever she needs to do to protect herself, her life, until we can find her. Try hard not to worry yourself sick."

Pam sighed. "Easier said than done."

"Oh, I'm sure it is. But meanwhile, let's go get you something to eat."

"Where? Here?"

"A place this big has to have a kitchen somewhere—or even two or three kitchens—and plenty of food. At least a fruit bowl that we can raid."

"Andrew Dante isn't going to give me permission to eat anything of his. He's always looked down on me, and after what I just said to him, I'm sure he hates me."

"Nope. He probably wouldn't offer you even an apple or a banana. And that's exactly why we're not going to ask him. We're just going to nab you something and run."

"Grab food and run with it?"

"Sure. Hey, I was one of *nine* kids, raised in a house where there was never an overabundance of anything but love. Believe you me . . . I know how it's done!"

Chapter 3

After Savannah had raided Andrew Dante's kitchen counter fruit bowl and had refueled Pam O'Neil and sent her on her way, she decided to take an unauthorized tour of the mansion's ground floor.

Somewhere off to her left, perhaps in a library or study, she could hear Dirk still questioning Dante, and judging by both men's tones, the interview wasn't going well. Dirk sounded cranky, and Dante testy. She decided that since the conversation could come to an abrupt end at any moment, she'd better get her snooping done ASAP.

From the kitchen, she passed through an arched doorway and into a delightful breakfast area. The room was octagonal, with windows reaching from waist high to the conical ceiling. Green plants of all types hung in long, twisting vines from baskets suspended from the ceiling, and Savannah couldn't help but pause for a moment and think how lovely it would be to sip a morning cup of coffee and read the paper in a room like this.

From the windows, she could see a lush tropical garden that, like the front of the mansion, was artistically illuminated with architectural lights of gold, blue, and green.

And in the midst of that garden, she saw movement among the palmettos, banana trees, bird-of-paradise, and bougainvillea. Somebody—or several somebodies—was out there milling about.

After one quick glance over her shoulder, Savannah opened a small door that led from the breakfast room to a patio and walked outside.

The moment she did, she heard raucous laughter coming from the garden and recognized the sound instantly—it was a gaggle of female teenagers.

Having been raised in a family with two boys and seven girls, Savannah was all too familiar with the sound of adolescent females who were up to no good.

Quietly, on rubber-soled loafers, she crept toward the center of the garden, closer to the voices. In her mind, she wasn't exactly sneaking up on them; she just wasn't going to announce her presence right away.

She knew there was a fine line between being plain old nosy and possessing a healthy curiosity. And it didn't bother her one bit to skip back and forth from one side of that line to the other.

She believed that a private investigator who wasn't gifted with an inquisitive nose wasn't worth taking behind the barn and shooting.

That was one of her most cherished mottos, and she lived by it. It was right up there with, "Don't flip on a light switch with wet hands or climb out on the roof to adjust the TV antenna during a Georgia thunderstorm."

As she wound her way down a stone path through the thick, mature plant growth, she saw that there were, indeed, three young females ahead of her. They were lounging around an Oriental fish pond on chaises like any other trio of teenagers, hanging out with friends, chatting and laughing, enjoying each other's company.

Except that as she drew closer, Savannah could hear a tone in their voices that didn't sound all that friendly. Although she could only catch a word, then a phrase here and there, their conversation didn't seem to be lighthearted chitchat about boys or the latest fashion trends.

". . . she'll miss her big shoot . . . boo hoo . . ."

"Eh . . . won't embarrass herself . . ."

"I couldn't believe it was going to happen anyway."

"Tiff, you *so* should have . . . way better . . . just disgusting!"

". . . doesn't matter now . . . she . . ."

"Who did she think she was . . . ? If my dad . . . nothing. If I hadn't felt sorry for her, she never would have even . . ."

Savannah strained to hear, but bits and pieces were all she could catch, and as she took a few steps closer, she heard one of them say, "Sh-h-h, somebody's out there."

"Where?"

"Over there . . . coming this way."

Rather than waiting to be "discovered" snooping among the banana plants, Savannah stepped into the clearing around the pond.

"Good evening, ladies," she said brightly. "I was hoping I'd find you back here somewhere."

One of the girls, a thin gal with long, blond hair, jumped up from one of the chaises and rushed toward Savannah. Even with only the dim glow of the property's accent lights to see, Savannah knew it was the girl whose picture hung over the fireplace.

Savannah also recognized her face from the grocery store magazine displays. This was the tabloid queen Tiffany Dante in all of her Skeleton Key rail-thin glory.

The first thing that struck Savannah was how petite the girl was. Somehow, Savannah had imagined her to be much taller. Maybe it was the perpetual high-high heels that she wore. Even now, dressed casually in pink silk pajama bottoms and a lacy camisole with rhinestones across the chest that proclaimed her to be, "HOT! HOT! HOT!," she was wearing ankle strap sandals with four-inch heels.

Her heels clicked out a fast staccato on the stone walkway as the young woman hurried up to Savannah with an ill-tempered frown on her face. "Who are you?" she demanded. "And why were you spying on us?"

"Spying? Who was spying? I was just coming out here to talk to you. You're Tiffany Dante, right?"

The girl rolled her eyes and gave Savannah an indignant, "Well, yeah . . . duh."

Savannah chuckled.

"What are you laughing at?"

"Nothing," Savannah said evenly. "I just didn't realize that people still say, 'Duh.' That's all." She held out her hand to the girl. "My name is Savannah Reid. I came with Detective Sergeant Coulter. He's a San Carmelita police officer. We're investigating the disappearance of one of your friends, Daisy O'Neil."

Tiffany Dante did not shake Savannah's hand. Instead, she gave her a quick once-over, head to toe, then lifted her nose slightly as though she had just sniffed something unpleasant.

Savannah withdrew her hand and resisted the urge to lift her middle finger in salute to the disrespectful girl.

Granny Reid wouldn't have approved.

Tiffy glanced over her shoulder at her friends, a

pretty brunette and an almond-eyed beauty with waist-long black hair.

"Daisy . . . disappeared?" Tiffy said. "I wouldn't say she's 'disappeared.' Would you?" she asked the girls. They simply shrugged, shook their heads.

Turning back to Savannah, she said coyly, "I mean, Daisy probably just decided to take off for a week or two and not mention it to her mom. We do that kind of thing all the time. Don't we?" Again, she turned to her friends for some sort of affirmation.

"Yeah," said the brunette. She stood and walked over to Savannah and Tiffy. Savannah noticed that she was wearing the same exact pajamas as Tiffy, only in bright blue. And according to the rhinestone embellishment, she was equally, "HOT! HOT! HOT!"

The girl continued in the same cocky tone as her blond friend. "We take off all the time, like to South Beach or Cancun or Aspen, you know, to party a little when we're really stressed out about something. And Daisy's a bit weird. She does crazy stuff sometimes. I don't think anything . . , like . . . *bad* . . . has happened to her."

The brunette shot Tiffy a quick glance, as though looking for her approval, and smiled when the blonde gave her a slight nod.

"And you are . . . ?" Savannah asked, thinking that this girl couldn't be a day over sixteen.

Savannah remembered reading something about Tiffy's garish, outlandish high school graduation party last year. But this teen looked more like a sophomore at most.

And Savannah remembered that this girl had some sort of silly name, too. She just couldn't recall what it was. Kitty? Puppy? Chickie-pooh?

"I'm Bunny Greenaway," she said. "I'm a friend of Tiffy's. We're the Skeleton Key Three. The three of us, that is. You've probably heard of us. We're like . . . famous, you know."

Savannah smiled and nodded. "Of course, I've heard of you. Anybody who buys groceries knows about you three. How very exciting for you to be so well-known, and at such a young age." She mentally added, *And for having done absolutely nothing but starve yourselves to death and wear designer clothing and spend your parents' money with wild, vulgar abandon.*

Tiffy shrugged and tossed her hair back over her shoulder. "It's not that great, really. You have to put up with all the paparazzi all the time. I mean, we can't go anywhere or do anything without getting our pictures taken. Especially *me*. A lot of people probably think it's fun being me, but it's really a pain in the ass sometimes, having to look good everywhere you go. It's actually quite a lot of work and responsibility."

Savannah wondered if this young woman would ever grow up and realize how very transparent her conceit was to others and learn to at least tone it down a bit.

Something told her that Tiffy's strong sense of herself and her indispensability to the world at large was firmly in place and was going to remain so throughout her life.

Savannah also decided that someone had done Tiffany Dante a terrible injustice, teaching her that she was extraordinarily valuable while neglecting to mention that every other being on God's green earth was equally precious.

Savannah couldn't help feeling sorry for her. But she felt a lot sorrier for any husband or children this girl might have down the road.

Savannah looked beyond Tiffy and Bunny to the almond-eyed, black-haired girl who remained seated on a chaise, staring down at her own high-heeled sandals. Her silk pajamas and lace camisole were bright yellow, and her rhinestones declared her, "GORGEOUS!"

Savannah had to agree. Of the three of them, this girl was by far the prettiest. Her exotic looks made Savannah wonder if maybe she had both Asian and African ancestors. Her skin was an exquisite golden tan, her lips full and sensuous, her eyes tilted upward at the edges, giving her an almost feline beauty. She appeared to be around the same age as Tiffy—maybe eighteen or nineteen.

Savannah walked over to her. "And you are . . . ?" she asked, unable to remember what this third Key member was named. Biffy? Dippy? Sneezy or Goofy?

"Kiley Wallace," she said softly. "But everyone calls me Kiki."

The girl glanced up at Savannah but just as quickly, looked away. In spite of her reluctance to make eye contact, she didn't strike Savannah as a particularly shy girl, which made Savannah wonder if perhaps she had something to hide. Something she wasn't proud of?

Savannah decided she simply must have some serious private time with Kiki Wallace.

Experience had taught her that if she could find one person in a group who had a tender conscience, they could be the key to solving a case.

"And how about you, Kiki?" Savannah asked. "Is Daisy a friend of yours, too?"

Kiki replied, but in a voice so low that Savannah couldn't hear her.

"I'm sorry. I didn't catch that."

"I said, 'Yes, Daisy is my friend.'"

"And do *you* think that she would have just gone off, disappeared without telling anybody—her mother, any of you girls—where she'd gone?"

Kiki shot a questioning look over at Tiffy, then

shrugged her thin shoulders. "I don't know. Maybe. Yeah, I guess so," she said.

"Would you do that? Would you just take off somewhere without telling anybody?" Savannah asked her.

"I don't know. I might."

Kiki looked like she was about to start crying. *Yes,* Savannah decided. *I'm definitely going to have to get Kiki here alone. Maybe hold her upside down by her high heels and see what I can shake out of her.*

Tiffy hurried over to them and stood between Savannah and Kiki. "Do you have, like, a warrant or something? My dad doesn't usually let cops on his property unless they have a warrant or something."

"No, I don't have a warrant . . . or something. I don't need one. I'm not even a police officer."

"Then what are you doing on our property?"

"I was invited." Savannah didn't feel the need to mention it was the maid who had let them in. "I'm sure everyone, including your father, is concerned about Daisy's disappearance and would be relieved if we could find her safe and sound. I'm sure you would like that, too, right?"

Tiffy locked eyes with Savannah and gave her what, no doubt, was intended to be an intimidating glare. But since in the course of Savannah's career, she had been glared at by hardcore street thugs, members of organized crime, a serial killer, and a rabid pit bull, she didn't scare easily.

In fact, she decided to get a little rough with Tiff.

"I understand that Daisy came over here yesterday afternoon," she said with all the steadfast authority of a practiced liar. "In fact, I hear that you girls were the last people to see her alive."

"We were not! No, we weren't! I mean," Tiffy stammered, "we couldn't have been the *last* ones to see her . . . what do you mean '*alive*'? She's not dead!"

"She's not?"

"No!"

"Then where is she?"

"How would *I* know?"

"Well, if you're so sure that she isn't dead, you must know where she is."

Tiffy took one step backward and nearly lost her balance, teetering precariously on her four-inch heels. "This is all just stupid," she said. " I'll bet that it's Daisy's stupid mom who put you up to all of this, isn't it? She just doesn't like us, and she blames us any time anything goes wrong with her precious little baby Daisy."

"Like what?" Savannah wanted to know.

"Like when Daisy's boyfriend dumped her, and Daisy got all depressed and went around moping about it for months. Pam blamed that on me! Said I took him away from her daughter, lured him away with my feminine charms or something stupid like that." She chuckled, and Savannah thought that she had heard warmer laughter rippling through the city jail cells. "He dumped Daisy because she got *fat*, that's all. But no-o-o-o. Neither Daisy nor her mom wanted to face the truth. God forbid that Daisy would go on a *diet!*"

"You should say fatter," Bunny added.

"What?" Savannah turned on Bunny.

"I was correcting Tiffy. Daisy didn't get fat—she was already fat. She got fatter. And, I mean, like what guy is into *that*? It's just so gross."

Savannah flashed back on some delicious chapters in her own history book: sultry summer evenings in Tommy Stafford's old '56 Chevy, parked in moonlit Georgia orchards, the fragrance of fresh peaches scenting the night air.

Ah, yes . . . Tommy and few others since him had more than enjoyed her own ample curves.

She gave Bunny a sly grin. "Oh, you'd be surprised what guys like. What they *really, really* like. But that's neither here nor there. I want to know what happened here yesterday afternoon when Daisy dropped by."

"Daisy wasn't here," Bunny said a little too desperately. "Really! She wasn't—"

"Okay, okay, so she was here for a little while," Tiffy interjected. "She dropped by and asked me for a favor—like she always does—and when I didn't come running to her rescue as usual, she left in a huff."

"And what favor was that?"

Tiffy sighed and tossed her head in an impatient, It-Isn't-About-Me-So-I-Can't-Be-Bothered move. "She wanted me to go over her stupid lines with her. She was supposed to be on this stupid sitcom thing, and she had four friggen lines. Four! And, oh my gawd, you'd think she was going to be giving an Oscar-winning performance the way she was going on and on and on about it."

"And did you, help her with her lines, that is?" Savannah asked.

"No way. I had things to do. I'm having a big Halloween party, and the party planner is screwing it up bigtime. She hasn't even hired the fortune teller, or the belly dancers, or the makeup artist yet! I don't have time to mess with stupid Daisy and her stupid lines."

Savannah quirked one eyebrow as she contemplated the pleasure of tattooing the word STUPID across Tiffany Dante's forehead. "You wouldn't be just a wee little bit jealous now, would you?" she asked her.

"Jealous? Jealous? Are you kidding me? I wouldn't

stoop to doing some stupid sitcom! I'm a *real* actress. I've trained with Beverly Diamond *and* Malcolm Whitmore! Do you know who *they* are?"

"Not a clue."

"Well, that figures because *you* aren't in the business. They are the most prestigious acting coaches in the world. And I studied under *both* of them last July. I have an agent, and a Screen Actors Guild card, and fantastic head shots and everything! Stupid Daisy wouldn't even have this little sitcom walk-on if it weren't for me! Jealous of Daisy O'Neil, that fat, no talent cow? That'll be the day!"

Savannah listened to the tirade, watched the young woman's face contort with pure, hot rage. And Savannah asked herself the standard question she always asked when interviewing potential suspects:

Is this person capable of hurting someone . . . really, seriously harming another human being?

Tiffany Dante was only three degrees away from frothing at the mouth, from having her eyes bug out of her head like a cartoon character.

Yes, Savannah thought. *This spoiled rotten little brat could hurt another person. Badly.*

Or pay someone to.

She looked at the two girls, Bunny and Kiki. Especially Bunny, who so obviously ached to be a Tiffy clone.

Savannah thought, *Tiffany Dante is perfectly capable of doing it herself, paying someone . . . or manipulating others to do harm to a perceived enemy. No doubt about it.*

Deep in her gut, Savannah felt a stirring of very real fear. Fear for Daisy O'Neil. Fear for her worried mother. Fear that this girl in front of her, a child who had apparently been raised without boundaries or empathy, could have done something truly terrible.

She stepped closer to Tiffany, deliberately invading her space, and fixed her with a laser stare that had melted far harder-bitten characters than Tiffy Dante would ever be. This time it was Tiffany who looked away, breaking eye contact.

"I'm going to find Daisy O'Neil," Savannah said, her voice low and even, but with an ominous underlying tone. "I'm not going to rest until I find her. And when I do, she had better be alive and healthy. Or someone is going to pay a very, very dear price for hurting her."

The girls said nothing. But Savannah carefully noted all three of their facial expressions. Tiffany looked cocky, as usual. Bunny seemed a bit nervous, maybe worried.

But it was the look in Kiki's eyes that bothered Savannah most. Kiley Wallace looked sad, deeply sad . . . and guilty.

And that didn't bode well for Daisy O'Neil.

Savannah left the girls to ponder her threat and headed back to the house. Entering by the same door she had exited in the breakfast room, she could hear male voices in a nearby room. And from the tone of those voices, she surmised that Dirk's interview with Andrew Dante was going even worse than before.

But that was no great surprise. Dirk was highly skilled at leaning on street thugs and threatening the truth out of them. He was a lot less accomplished in dealing with "regular" folk.

In fact, most regular folk considered Dirk Coulter boorish, overbearing, and antagonistic, and they spent as little time as possible in his presence. And while Savannah agreed with their evaluation of him, she also knew that most of his less than gracious behavior sprang from his deep concern for crime victims and his passion to find justice for them.

And realizing that, she had decided long ago to cut the guy a lot of slack. She felt the same way he did about crime solving, and for the same reasons. She just had slightly better manners, having been raised by a Southern granny.

Except for abusive jerks in grocery stores.

And cocky, arrogant teenagers.

And the occasional street punk who rubbed her the wrong way and . . .

Okay, so maybe she wasn't all that much better behaved than Dirk. She could live with that.

As she walked from the breakfast room into the kitchen, she heard Dirk saying something about search warrants, and Dante reply with the name of a powerful, prestigious local attorney.

No, things weren't going all that well in the Coulter-Dante interview.

Any business of her own that she wanted to conclude had to be done right away. She had a feeling she and Dirk were due to be tossed out on their backsides at any moment.

Hoping she would run into the maid again, she walked through the formal dining room and back into the great room. But instead of the maid, she ran into yet another young woman.

Sitting at the grand piano, running the fingers of one hand lightly over the keys in a practiced scale, the woman appeared to be in her mid-twenties. She also looked deeply sad. With a pretty, heart-shaped face, enormous blue eyes, and extremely short, platinum blond hair, she had a fey quality about her, exuding fragility and vulnerability.

She, too, was abnormally slender, but instead of the Skeleton Key silk pajamas uniform, she was wearing an exquisite dressing gown of silver jacquard. And even though the fabric was most complimentary to her figure and coloring, the style seemed more befitting to an older woman.

She looked a little like a kid playing dress up in her mother's clothes.

Except that she appeared anything but playful. Her big blue eyes were filled with tears, and her head was bowed in a defeatist pose as she practiced her scale with first one hand and then the other.

Savannah took a few steps closer, and the woman noticed her. She ended her playing instantly and stood.

"Oh," she said. "I didn't know you were here. I . . . uh . . . you probably want to see Tiffany. I'll go get her for you."

"No, that's okay, thanks," Savannah replied, thinking that even though this woman was wearing a dressing gown, she must be a visitor, probably another friend of Tiffy's. No one would feel this ill at ease in their own home. She seemed painfully out of place.

"But she's been expecting you," she said, holding her robe tightly closed in front of her. "She was really upset that you weren't here earlier, and you know how she gets when, well, you know."

"I'm sorry. Obviously, you've mistaken me for someone else." Savannah held out her hand. "My name is Savannah Reid. And you are . . . ?"

"Savannah . . . ? Oh, I thought you were the party coordinator. You aren't here about Tiffy's Halloween party?"

"No, I'm with Detective Coulter." She nodded in the direction of the raised male voices. "We're investigating the disappearance of one of Tiffany's friends, Daisy O'Neil."

Savannah watched the woman's eyes closely to see what effect her words might have. But nothing seemed to register, beyond the sadness she had already shown.

"Daisy is *missing?* What do you mean, 'missing'? Is that why her mother was here?"

Apparently, this member of the entourage is seriously out of the loop, Savannah thought.

"Yes. She hasn't been seen since yesterday afternoon. Didn't come home last night, and hasn't contacted her mother in over twenty-four hours. Pam O'Neil is terribly worried."

"I'm sure she is. That isn't like Daisy at all. Daisy's a sweet girl, very responsible. And she and her mom are really close."

The genuine concern and compassion in the young woman's eyes made Savannah think that maybe all of Tiffy Dante's friends weren't shallow, callous brats.

"I didn't catch *your* name," Savannah said.

The woman extended her hand. When Savannah took it in her own, she noticed how cold and damp it was. "I'm Robyn Dante," she said.

Savannah searched her mental infobanks, trying to recall if the tabloids had ever mentioned Tiffany Dante having an older sister. The name *did* seem familiar, but she just couldn't . . .

"Robyn," she murmured, trying to remember.

"Yes." The woman looked slightly embarrassed and once again, out of place and ill at ease. "I'm Robyn Dante . . . Mrs. Andrew Dante."

Again, her eyes flooded with tears. She blinked and looked away. "You know," she said with a bitter tone, "queen of the castle. The mistress of al-l-l this."

She gave a wide sweep with her arm, encompassing the bright pink room, the garish, raspberry velvet furniture, the enormous painting of her stepdaughter that dominated the room from its place of honor over the fireplace.

Mrs. Andrew Dante sighed, shook her head, and added, "Lucky me."

Chapter 4

"Well, that was a friggen waste of time," Dirk said half an hour later as they left the Dante estate. "That Andrew Dante is a total jerk. Told me nothing. Rich people suck. They just do."

"Ah, Detective Dirk Coulter," Savannah replied, "philosopher, social commentator, orator extraordinaire. And for your information, *all* people suck, not just the rich ones."

Sighing, he said, "Don't hassle me, woman. I'm tired."

He took a small, plastic bag from the dashboard and fumbled with it while he tried to drive.

"Here, let me open that for you before you kill us both." Savannah took the bag from him and unzipped it. Inside were half a dozen cinnamon sticks. She held one out to him. "How's it going?" she asked.

"Like hell." He took the stick and popped it into the side of his mouth. "How do you suppose it's going? Kicking nicotine is worse than going off heroin or cocaine. Ask any junkie who's tried to shake all three."

Savannah made a mental note to question any non-cigarette smoking, former heroin/cocaine junkies she might encounter in the future. And while she was at it, she'd ask them if going cold turkey off those substances was half as miserable as a 1,000 calories a day diet that didn't include chocolate—while you were in the throes of PMS.

Now *that* was suffering!

Dirk had been trying to quit smoking for months. The cinnamon sticks must be working. He was still officially on the smoke-free wagon.

Or maybe it was the nicotine patches on his butt, the ones he didn't think she knew about.

She had found the wrappers among the taco and hamburger litter in the backseat of his car. And she'd checked the following day and found two more—a day when she'd seen him in nothing but a pair of cutoffs.

Never try to fool a detective.

Another one of her mottos.

She turned in her seat and looked at him, studying his face in the one second flashes of headlights from passing cars.

He *did* look tired. And older.

She couldn't help thinking that years ago, when they had first met, Dirk had definitely been a hunk—back when she had definitely been a babe. Now in their forties, they were . . . well . . . a little bit past hunk and babe. Not much past, but a tad.

Too bad we didn't realize how very hunkish and babe-esque we were back then, she thought. *We could have savored that brief time a little more.*

And she thought of something that Granny Reid had told her a few years ago.

Savannah had been looking in her bathroom mirror, frowning at some new lines that were beginning on her forehead.

"Gran, I'm getting old," she said. "Look at these wrinkles."

Granny walked up behind her, put her hands on Savannah's shoulders, and peered at her granddaughter's reflection in the mirror. "Lord have mercy, child. You aren't old. What are you frettin' about?"

"I'm not as young as I used to be."

"Well, glory be, girl. Who is?" She turned Savannah around to face her. Her eyes shone with wisdom and good humor as she reached out with her forefinger and pushed one of Savannah's dark curls out of her eyes and behind her ear. "Savannah girl, if the good God in heaven blesses you with long life, you *will* be old someday. And then, you'll look back and realize how much of your sweet youth was just plum wasted worrying 'bout getting old. Don't even start that nonsense, sugar. It's such a foolish path to walk down."

Looking into her grandmother's face, Savannah thought that she wouldn't have taken away a single line from that sweet countenance. She couldn't imagine changing one thing about this woman she adored—not one wrinkle, one gray hair, one extra pound.

Maybe Gran was right. Maybe worrying about the inevitable and unavoidable *was* a waste of time and energy.

"If you've just got to worry about something," Granny Reid continued, "worry about the child across town who's going to bed hungry tonight or the young mother next door who can't make her rent. That's the sort of thing you might be able to do something about. Don't bother about a little line on your face that don't amount to a hill of beans."

And since that day, Savannah had spent less time peering into the mirror, searching for signs of aging. Instead, she had made a habit of looking deeply into the eyes of the woman in the mirror and saying in a voice that sounded a lot like Gran's, "You're doin' good, sweetheart. You've been through your ups and downs, but you've mostly done your best. You're doin' good."

Old didn't matter so much.

Most of the time.

Savannah rolled down the Buick's window and breathed the sweet, moist night air. "Do you think we're old yet?" she asked Dirk.

He turned to look at her, a surprised expression on his face. "What?"

"Do you think we're old? I mean, I know we aren't old-old yet, but . . . do you think of me as old?"

"You? Hell, no. You're not old, Van. You're no different than you were when I first met you. It's not like you're a guy . . . losing your hair and crap like that."

Poor Dirk, she thought. *Always with the hair.* The world began and ended with The Hair.

Dirk could lose every tooth in his head and gain three hundred pounds, and all he would worry about was whether his hair had thinned in the past two months.

"*I'm* getting older," he said. "I can feel it in my body, especially the day after I've gone a few rounds with some street punk. But you . . ." He shot her a flirtatious grin that, she had to admit, made her heart beat just a bit faster. ". . . you're fresh as a sun-warmed Georgia peach and twice as tasty."

Yeap, the pulse rate is definitely up, she thought. "When you look at me like that," she told him, "you remind me of that guy I met years ago, the one I had to fight off a time or two on stakeouts when we first got assigned together."

He bristled. "Who? Somebody got fresh with you? You should've told me. I would've—"

"I meant *you*, dimwit."

"Oh." He cleared his throat and stared straight ahead, suddenly intent on the road. Finally, he said, "It's been so long since I've tried to get into your knickers that I'd forgotten. And that just goes to show you how old *I'm* getting."

"Naw." She reached over and thumped him on the shoulder. "You're still a virile horndog. You're just tired, run down a little. They've been working you too hard."

"They have been. I've got five cases on my desk already, and now they throw this one at me. I'm telling you, if that girl turns up dead, I'm screwed."

Good ol' Dirk. Always thinking of others, she thought.

"I'll help you find her," she said.

He brightened. "Really?"

"Sure. Sadly, I don't have any clients at the moment. I want to enjoy my visit with Gran while she's here, but I should still have plenty of time to help you track her down."

Breathing a sigh of relief, fatigue, or depression—with him, it was hard to tell which—he said, "So, you think she's all right, this girl? You think she's still alive?"

Savannah thought of how many times Granny Reid had warned her about saying negative things. "A body has to watch what comes out of their mouth," she'd said. "Your words float out into the universe, and who knows where they'll land. You can speak things into being, so be careful what you say."

"Alive?" she said. "Sure. Daisy's still alive. She's just

off somewhere, getting into something she shouldn't, like any other teenager."

Savannah thought of Pam O'Neil, of how her mother's intuition was telling her that something terrible had happened to her precious daughter.

She thought of Kiki Wallace's downcast, guilt-filled eyes.

She thought of Robyn Dante, the so-called queen of the castle, who had answered Savannah's questions with clipped, curt responses. And even those answers had been contradictory.

No, Daisy hadn't been there at all yesterday. Okay, she was there, but not for long.

No, she hadn't talked to her. Well, yes, Daisy had mentioned to her that she was excited about taping the sitcom.

No, Robyn couldn't imagine why Daisy had gone missing. She was sure it wasn't anything bad, though. Couldn't be anything bad.

Dirk jarred her back to the present. "Really?" he was asking. "Do you really think the kid's okay?"

Savannah remembered Granny's "Don't speak evil" warning again, but she also remembered that Gran had taught her not to lie.

"No," she said softly. "I don't think she's okay. After talking to that bunch back there, I don't think she's just off getting into mischief. I think it's a lot worse than that."

Dirk nodded . . . and he *did* look tired . . . and he *did* look old. "Me, too," he said. "I hate to say it, but me, too."

As Dirk turned onto Lester Boulevard and headed toward Savannah's neighborhood, she asked, "Where are you taking me?"

"Home. Don't you want to go home and rest, visit with your grandma?"

She thought about it for a moment: her soft chair,

her big, black cats curled around her feet, a cup of hot coffee, and a slice of the carrot cake that Gran had baked that afternoon. It was tempting.

But then she thought of Pam O'Neil's red, swollen eyes, so full of pain and worry.

"What are you going to do with the rest of your evening?" she asked him.

"I thought I'd drive over to the mom's house and talk to her, maybe get a look at the kid's bedroom. Why?"

Savannah flipped open her cell phone and dialed her house. Gran answered.

"Hi, Granny," she said. "It's not looking good, this case with this girl. We're a bit worried about her."

"I'm sorry to hear that, sugar. Is there anything I can do?"

"Maybe say one of your prayers for her."

"I sure will."

"Are you going to be up a while yet?"

Gran chuckled on the other end. "Just until all my little chickadees are back in the nest," she said . . . the reply that Savannah had heard so many times during her teenage years. "Why? Are you wanting to stay out with your young man past your curfew?"

Savannah laughed. "Just another hour or so. I'd like to go with Dirk to the girl's house before I come home."

"I'll be up quite a while longer. I'm reading my Bible and my new *True Informer.*"

Savannah knew that if her grandmother had a new *True Informer,* she wouldn't be going to bed for two hours. Granny Reid devoured the tabloid from cover to cover, including the classified ads in the back.

"Don't wait up for me if you're tired, Gran. Go on to bed if you've a mind to, and I'll see you in the morning."

"You'll see me when you set foot inside this house," Gran replied. "You go find that little missing girl. Don't you worry 'bout me."

Savannah told her good-bye and snapped the phone closed. "Granny says we can stay out a little longer, but no French kissing and you gotta drive below the speed limit."

"Darn. I guess that means no parking and making out at Lover's Leap."

"Gran's death on parkin', demon alcohol, and chewin' tobacco. She used to threaten me something fierce about partaking of any of those three."

"And did you?"

"Partake?"

"Yeah."

She grinned. "Of course not. I was a good girl. The perfect teenager."

"Yeah, right."

"Okay. Two out of three."

"You partook of two out of three? Or you avoided two out of three?"

She chuckled, reliving fond memories. "That's right. You've got it."

When Dirk called Pam O'Neil to see if they could drop by, she eagerly invited them over. And when they pulled into the driveway of the humble duplex in the working class end of town, she was sitting on the stoop, smoking a cigarette, waiting for them.

"I couldn't believe it when you called," she said as she ground the cigarette out with the toe of her construction boot. "I'm sure glad you did, though. Did you get anything out of Dante or those brat girls?"

Dirk shook his head as he and Savannah followed her into the house. "No, nothing worthwhile. But I'm not done with him or that bunch over there."

"Don't worry," Savannah said, "We're just getting started with this investigation."

Pam led them through the living room with its threadbare plaid sofa, Mediterranean-style coffee table, and plastic, fake Tiffany lamp and on into the kitchen. She offered them a seat at a chrome and Formica dinette table that reminded Savannah of Gran's old set.

"Want some coffee?" Pam asked. "It's fresh. I just made it."

"Sure, thanks," Dirk said.

"Not for me," Savannah said as she looked around the kitchen. Apparently, Pam was into chickens. The wallpaper was a blue and yellow print with chickens of every breed, size, and age doing chicken things: pecking at the ground, crowing from tops of fence posts, and emerging from cracked eggs.

Even the dishtowels hanging on the rack and the canisters on the cupboard were spangled with chickens.

Savannah resisted the urge to judge, remembering her own Unicorn Period. She was so glad she had resisted getting that tattoo on her right breast and spared herself the depressing spectacle of a less than perky unicorn.

Pam slipped a cup of coffee onto the table in front of Dirk, along with a sugar bowl and creamer.

Dirk took a notepad and pen from inside his leather jacket. "We just need to get a bit more information from you," he said. "A description of the car your daughter's driving, the plate number, what she was wearing the last time you saw her, just your standard stuff like that."

"Of course," Pam said. "I want to help any way I can."

"Would you mind," Savannah asked, "if I took a look in Daisy's bedroom? I hate to poke around in your daughter's things, but considering the circumstances . . ."

"Oh, sure. No problem. It's right down the hall there, the door on the right. Help yourself."

"Thank you."

Savannah walked down the short hallway to a closed door that had a plaque on it that said, "Daisy." As might be expected, yellow daisies surrounded the name, and the "i" was dotted with a pink daisy.

When she opened the door, Savannah expected to find a typical teenager's room: posters of the latest rock heartthrobs, garish colors, and stuffed animals vying for space with more grown-up possessions like mountains of makeup, shoes, and purses.

But not this room.

One look told Savannah that Daisy O'Neil was no ordinary teenager.

At first glance, Savannah thought she had stepped into some small tropical paradise. Someone had painted murals on all four walls, surprisingly good murals, of a lush jungle full of exotic palms and greenery, monkeys, parrots, and toucans.

And most impressive of all were the cats. Spotted leopards, black panthers, and ocelots crouched in the trees, while tigers hid in the foliage, their stripes blending perfectly with the tangled vines and thick grasses.

Apparently, Daisy was not only in love with the jungle and its big cats, but she was a talented artist, as well. On one wall, toward the bottom of the mural, Savannah saw the signature, "Daisy O."

The girl was also quite a gifted botanist. The room was filled with all sorts of palms and philodendrons, pothos and schefflera, Chinese evergreens and peace lilies.

The furniture was sparse and inexpensive—a

daybed, one chest, and a desk—but the wicker style fit the jungle theme perfectly. And the bed was neatly made with dark green linens.

Savannah walked over to the desk and sat on the small stool. With practiced deliberation, she quickly but thoroughly examined each book, letter, note, and item both on the desk's top and in its four drawers. Mostly, she found books about wildlife, the Amazon rainforest, ecology, and botany.

One drawer held a small case of makeup: mascara, lip gloss, one color of eye shadow. Apparently, Daisy was a natural beauty. One bottle of clear nail polish, a file, and some clippers were her manicure-pedicure kit.

Savannah thought of Daisy's high maintenance friends and wondered briefly how many bottles of polish and tubes of lipstick were in Tiffany Dante's makeup drawer.

In one of the bottom drawers, far in the back, hidden beneath some folders, was something that caught Savannah's eye.

It was a white bag with a red logo from a local drugstore. And inside the bag was a pregnancy test and a receipt dated September 15th. It was the type that contained two kits in one box. One kit was gone; the other was still inside the box and in its original wrapping.

Savannah stored that bit of information in the back of her mind for future reference, along with the name of the drugstore and date on the receipt.

She returned the kit to its original place in the back of the drawer, deciding, at least for now, to protect any of Daisy's secrets.

As the oldest child in a family of nine kids, Savannah had enjoyed precious little privacy of her own, so she respected others' as much as her occupation would allow her.

She left the bedroom and its exotic decor, returning to the more mundane regions of the house.

At the table, Dirk and Pam O'Neil were still talking.

"Does she have a job?" Dirk was asking. "I mean, something other than this sitcom thing that just came up."

"Yes. Since she graduated this past spring, she's been a cashier at Drug Mart over on Walston Street."

Savannah perked up at the mention of the drugstore, the same one where the pregnancy kit had been purchased. She had noticed that a twenty-percent discount had been applied to the subtotal on the receipt. An employee's discount, perhaps?

"Have you talked to them at the drugstore yesterday or today?" he asked. "Do they know she's missing?"

"I told her boss that she didn't come home last night and asked if he knew anything. He didn't. But he wasn't expecting her anyway. She had asked for the next four days off so that she could . . ." Pam choked and wiped her hand across her eyes. ". . . could do this sitcom taping. I just can't even tell you how excited she was about this."

"And how about a boyfriend?" Dirk asked. "Anybody she's seeing regularly?"

"Not anymore. As I told Savannah, Daisy had a boyfriend that she was really in love with, a guy named Stan. Stanley Crofton. He works there at Drug Mart with her, only he's in the photo department. But Tiffany broke them up a few months ago."

"So it was Stan who ended the relationship?" Dirk asked.

Savannah knew why Dirk wanted to know who had

called it quits. A dumped former boyfriend or husband was always the first and primary suspect any time a female went missing.

"Well, I guess you would say that it was officially Daisy who pulled the plug. She told him to get lost. But only after she found out he was fooling around with Tiffy."

"Did Stan want to keep the relationship together?"

"Sure he did," Pam said, an angry and defiant tone to her voice. "He was stupid enough to fall for whatever Tiffy dangled in front of his nose, but he was smart enough to realize pretty quick what she was up to and that she was no good. He begged Daisy to forgive him, and she did. But she refused to be his girlfriend anymore. And I'm glad she did. I told her she would be an idiot to take back a man who fooled around on her."

Savannah had noticed that although there were many pictures of Daisy and a few of her mother around the house, there was a clear absence of any male faces in those family portraits. Considering the degree of venom in Pam's tone when she talked about wayward men, Savannah wondered if maybe Mr. O'Neil had found out the hard way that Pam wasn't one to keep a philandering fellow around the house.

"So, Stan did *not* want the break up?" Dirk said, clarifying.

"No, I guess you could say he didn't." Pam replied. "Like most men, he wanted to have his cake and eat it, too. Scumbags that they are."

Yes, Pam has a few issues with the opposite sex, Savannah thought, cringing for Dirk, who had chosen to ignore the insult and was scribbling away on his notepad.

"Well . . ."Savannah said, ". . . there just has to be

one or two men on the face of the earth who actually deserve the air they breathe. Present company included."

Dirk stopped scribbling, looked up at Savannah, and grinned. "Naw, she's right," he said. "We're all a bunch of scumbags. She's got us nailed."

For half a second, Pam smiled. It was a pretty smile, and the thought occurred to Savannah that if this mother wasn't worried sick, she'd probably be a nice enough person to be around—sexist attitudes, cynicism, and all.

And Savannah really wanted to return her kid to her and see that tiny smile turn into an enormous one that glowed with joy. She had returned more than one youngster to a distraught parent in her career as a cop, and the experience was one of her very favorite, to be sure. There was nothing as sweet as a happy ending where a child was concerned.

"This guy, Stan," Dirk said, "to your knowledge, was he ever abusive with your daughter? Physically? Verbally? Maybe overly possessive, like jealous of her with other guys?"

Pam O'Neil gave Dirk a long, hard look before she answered. "No. He was not. And if he had been, he wouldn't still be walking around on his own two legs."

"O-o-kay," Dirk said. "So do you have any reason to think he might have harmed your daughter in any way?"

"No. Absolutely not. He's much too afraid of me to do something like that."

Savannah chuckled. "My kind of mamma."

Dirk sighed and flipped his notebook closed. "I'm still going to go have a talk with him. Do you know what hours he works?"

"The evening shift," Pam told him. "They're open over there 24-7. He should be on duty now."

As Dirk rose from the table, Pam stood, too, and picked up his empty cup and saucer. "Go talk to Stan if you want to," she told Dirk, "but I can tell you now, he had nothing to do with Daisy disappearing like this. It's those girls over at that Dante place. You mark my words. They've done something to Daisy."

Savannah walked over and put her hand on the woman's shoulder. "Detective Coulter is just covering all bases," she told her. "He's very good at what he does."

Pam gave Dirk a long once-over before she answered. "Yes, I can tell that he doesn't totally stink at it."

Dirk laughed. "Such high praise. You'll give me a swelled head."

Savannah walked past him and toward the door. "Yes, it is. And you should leave before she gets to know you better."

A moment later, as they got into Dirk's car, he asked Savannah, "Do you really think I'm good at this, or were you just blowin' smoke back there?"

"You? Sure I do. Don't you?"

He thought it over for a moment, then shook his head. "No, I don't. I mean, maybe for a moment, right after I've solved a big case. But usually, I just feel like I'm going through the motions but faking it."

"Eh, everybody feels that way. Don't you think? I'll bet you that even brain surgeons, presidents, and nuclear physicists feel like that . . . like they're faking it. They live in fear that someday, somebody's going to point at them and say, 'I know! I know your big secret! I know you're nothing but a fake!'"

They put on their seat belts, then turned and looked at each other.

"Brain surgeons, too?" Dirk said. "Gawd, I hope not."

Chapter 5

Before Savannah and Dirk arrived at the Drug Mart, Savannah told him what she had found in Daisy O'Neil's bedroom.

"If she's buying and using pregnancy test kits, she's obviously fooling around with this Stan kid or somebody else," Dirk said as he left Pam O'Neil's shabby residential neighborhood and entered a shabby business district.

This wasn't San Carmelita's worst area. That was on the far end of town, where the drug pushers, tattoo parlors, X-rated porn stores, and pawnshops were.

This area wasn't nasty enough to have even the touch of dark side glamour reserved for the worst of the worst. This section was just poor and depressed, like most of the people who shopped there.

Bars covered all the store windows, even on the second floors, and every vertical surface was marred by the ugliness of graffiti.

Unlike the bad side of town, families could walk around in the daylight hours and remain relatively safe. But the minute the sun went down, law-abiding folk were home behind their locked doors and barred windows.

And yet for some reason known only to the corporate powers of Drug Mart, this store was open all day, every day. To be sure, none of those corporate execs would have worked there or wanted their mothers, sisters, or children to.

Savannah could remember all too well having answered a call, back when she was on the police force, to a particularly violent robbery here at this store. A pharmacist had been shot and nearly killed.

"I was just thinking about that Pakistani lady," Dirk said as he pulled into a parking space near the door. "The pharmacist who got shot here that night."

"Me, too," she said.

Long ago, she had gotten over any amazement that they were so frequently thinking the same thing at the same time. After all, they had spent more time together than several married couples combined.

"Let's go see this Stan dude," Dirk said. "Shake him up a little and see what falls out of his trousers."

Dirk had his stern face on, Savannah noted, as he always did when he was dealing with the boyfriend or husband of a female victim.

On one level, she didn't blame him. When a woman was harmed, the perpetrator frequently was her intimate partner. But not always. And sometimes, Dirk forgot that.

If a woman went missing, he went after her man. Every time. With a vengeance.

And Savannah never envied a guy who had Dirk Coulter breathing down his neck.

They entered the store and headed for the photo department near the back, where they found a big, goofy-looking kid leaning over a photocopy machine and reloading it with paper.

Stanley Crofton was huge, well over six feet and

considerably heavier than two hundred pounds. His hair was cut so short that at first glance, he appeared bald. He wore glasses with thick lenses and bent metal frames. His white Drug Mart smock was badly stained with a frayed collar.

In the shabby, depressed neighborhood, Stan fit right in.

"Are you Stanley Crofton?" Dirk asked him as he reached inside his jacket for his badge.

The boy looked up from the copy machine. "Yes," he said tentatively, as though he wasn't sure if this was a good time to be Stanley Crofton or not. "Why?"

Dirk flipped the badge open and showed him the gold shield. "I'm Det. Sgt. Dirk Coulter with the SCPD. I need a few minutes with you."

Stan glanced around, turned a nice shade of pink, and walked over to the counter where they stood.

"Why?" he asked. "Why do you want to talk to me? I haven't done anything wrong."

Dirk's eyes narrowed. "I never said you did. And stop answering my questions with questions."

"Yeah. Okay."

His words were meek enough, and he glanced away, avoiding Dirk's eyes, like a less aggressive male in a wolf pack when confronted by the alpha male.

But Savannah saw a flash of anger behind those thick lenses, and it occurred to her that Stanley might have a nasty side. And that, coupled with his hefty size, might present a problem to anyone who crossed him—even a smaller man, let alone a woman.

She hoped that if Daisy had run afoul of someone, it wasn't this guy. Those huge hands could do serious harm.

"I need to ask you about your ex-girlfriend, Daisy," Dirk was saying. "I guess you know she's gone missing."

Stan's eyes widened. "Missing? What do you mean,

'she's missing'? I just saw her yesterday morning, and she was fine."

"What time did you see her?" Dirk asked.

"I had breakfast with her at the café across the street when I got off work at eight yesterday morning. She was all jazzed about her taping tomorrow. So excited she couldn't even eat. And for Daisy, that's saying something. She and I have that in common. We both like to eat."

A soft, affectionate smile crossed his face just for a moment, and Savannah began to revise her assessment of Stan. Just because a guy was big didn't mean he was a threat. Some of the sweetest guys Savannah had ever known were big mushy teddy bears at heart.

One of them was standing right beside her.

Although if anybody called Dirk a teddy bear to his face, they might get bitten.

Stan had also spoken of Daisy in the present tense. That was always a good sign—at least where his noninvolvement in her disappearance was concerned.

"She had breakfast with you," Dirk said. "So does that mean that you two are boyfriend-girlfriend again?"

Stan shrugged. "I guess. We had a big fight and broke up a couple of months ago, but I think we've made up now. You know how it is with girls . . . sometimes, it's hard to tell."

Both Stan and Dirk chuckled and gave Savannah sideways glances.

"Hey," she said, "don't look at me. A guy always knows where he stands with me . . . in trouble or out of it. No mixed signals here."

"That's true." Dirk nodded. "Very true." He turned back to Stan. "This is Savannah Reid. She's working this case with me and—"

"Case? What case? Do you mean Daisy is a . . . a 'case'!"

He looked genuinely distraught, and again, Savannah dropped him a notch lower on her mental list of suspects.

Stan actually looked like he might start to cry. "You don't seriously think something bad has happened to her, do you?" he said.

It was Dirk's turn to avoid eye contact. "We don't know yet. But she hasn't been seen or heard from in over twenty-four hours."

Savannah added, "For some people, that's no big deal at all. But Daisy's mother says it's unusual for her. Would you agree?"

Stan nodded thoughtfully. "Yeah. That's not like Daisy. She always lets her mom know where she is, what she's doing."

"Her mom is pretty strict with her?" Savannah asked.

"She's not strict like *mean* or anything bad. Pam's a nice lady, and they get along good. Daisy checks in a lot so that her mom won't worry about her. The two of them are close. They're like all they've got."

"I didn't see any sign of a dad around when we were over there just now," Savannah said.

"No, he took off with his secretary when Daisy was just a little kid. Pam's been pretty pissed about it ever since. She doesn't even like me all that much, and I think it's because she doesn't trust men."

Savannah thought better of asking her next question, then decided to jump on in. "Stan, I heard that you and Daisy broke up over Tiffany Dante. Is that true?"

Even as she spoke the words, Savannah thought how ludicrous the whole idea was. She couldn't imagine a shallow, materialistic girl like Tiffany Dante "soiling" her hands with a simple, poor, unattractive kid like this one. If she had, indeed, seduced Stanley Crofton, it could have been for no other reason than to spite her so-called friend.

"I never did anything with Tiffany," Stan said. The indignant look on his face was convincing. "I wouldn't touch that stupid girl. I can't stand her, and I told Daisy a long time ago that she should dump those gals. Pam put that idea into Daisy's mind, or maybe Tiffy did, just to mess with her head. But it's not true at all."

"So, you're serious about this girl, Daisy?" Dirk asked.

"Yeah. Sure I am. I care a lot about Daisy. We've even talked about getting married one of these days. I wouldn't mess around on her like that with anybody, let alone Tiffany Dante."

Savannah leaned across the counter, lowered her voice, and said, "Stan, don't take offense, but . . . I have to ask you. Is there any chance that Daisy could be pregnant?"

His pale complexion blushed dark red. "What? What kind of question is that?"

"A very personal one, I know," Savannah replied. "And I'm sorry, but I have to ask. That's one reason why girls leave home unexpectedly. They're afraid how their family will take it, and—"

"No. She's not. I mean, she said she was . . . you know . . . taking care of it. She told me she's on the pill, and I trust her. Daisy's a smart girl. We both want to go to college and get good jobs before we get married, before we have kids. She wouldn't mess us up that way."

"Okay. Sorry, I had to ask."

Savannah was liking Stan more all the time, but one look at Dirk told her that he wasn't as easily con-

vinced as she was. He was still wearing his Clint East-
wood at high noon look as he evaluated the big kid
in front of him.

Dirk cleared his throat and gave Stan his best
long, stern interrogation look. "So, when is the last
time you heard from her?"

"Yesterday," Stan said, "when I left her after breakfast. We kissed good-bye there in the parking lot, and
she left."

"And you haven't spoken to her on the phone or
heard anything from her since?" Savannah asked.

"No. I called her once tonight, right before I came
to work. But she didn't answer her cell. I left her a
message. She hasn't called me back yet."

Dirk said, "And according to you, you two were on
good terms when you saw her yesterday. She was in an
upbeat mood and didn't mention anything like running away from home or a fight with anybody.
Right?"

"Yeah, she was fine. We were fine."

"So what do you think has happened to her?" Dirk
asked. "What's your best guess?"

Stan thought it over, then shook his head. "I don't
know. I really don't."

"Is there anyone you can think of that we should
talk to?" Savannah asked him. "Any other friends,
people she might have gone to see, phoned, places
she might go?"

"No. Daisy's either home or here at work or out
with those stupid girls, those Skeleton Key idiots.
She's over there a lot. Have you talked to them yet?"

"Yes," Dirk said. "We've talked to them."

"Well, talk to them again," Stan said, and this time
he had an anger in his eyes that made Savannah
think, once again, that this mild kid could be a dan-
ger to the wrong person. "Or maybe I'll talk to them

myself. Because if something bad has happened to Daisy, I can bet you it's got something to do with them."

Dirk reached across the counter and slapped Stan on the shoulder. "You stay away from them for now," he told him. "Let us do our job. And meanwhile . . ." He reached into his pocket and pulled out a card. ". . . if you hear anything at all from Daisy or you think of anything, no matter how insignificant it might seem to you, day or night, you give me a call. Okay?"

Stan took the card, looked it over, then put it into his smock pocket. "Yeah, okay," he said. "Thanks. Thanks for looking for her."

Dirk shrugged. "No sweat. It's my job."

After Dirk walked away, Savannah lingered. She gave Stan a sympathetic look and a wink. "Don't let him kid you," she told him. "He'd do it even if it wasn't his job. And so would I. We'll find Daisy for you."

Stan blinked rapidly a few times, then swallowed hard. "Please do. She's a good kid. A really good kid. Bad things shouldn't happen to good people."

As Savannah walked away, she thought how much she agreed with him. But she knew more than most that fair or not, bad things happened to good people all the time. Sadly, even more often than they happened to bad people.

And it drove her crazy.

"Okay, now I'm bummed. I am seriously bummed," Dirk said as they drove away from the drugstore. "I was just so sure it would be the boyfriend. Hell, it's always the boyfriend."

"Take heart," Savannah told him. "Maybe Daisy's got another boyfriend."

"Yeah, right. Now you're just being sarcastic."

"Well, what would you prefer? A stranger abduction?"

"God forbid."

She agreed with him there. If a stranger nabbed somebody, there was almost never a happy ending. And far too frequently, the case couldn't even be solved.

He took another cinnamon stick out of the bag on the dash and stuck it into his mouth.

"How many packs of those do you, uh, suck a day?" she asked.

"Why? Does it bother you?"

"Not at all. At least with those, I don't have to breathe the secondhand smoke, and you smell like a fresh-baked apple pie, instead of a barroom ashtray."

"Uh, okay. Thanks. I guess." Then he added, "You're the only person I know who can give me a compliment and, at the same time, make me feel like I've just been kicked in the ba—"

"Hey, watch it with the potty mouth. Gran will ask me if the young man I was out with was a gentleman, and I can't lie to her. She can always tell."

He chuckled. "What'll she do? Take you out behind the woodshed and tan your hide?"

"Don't think it hasn't happened. Gran was a sweetheart ninety-nine percent of the time. But if you sassed her or lied to her, heaven help you. She'd take a switch to your hind end and make you dance a jig."

"You don't have to convince me. I'm scared to death of her."

"I'm sure she'd be delighted to hear that, to know that her reputation has spread from coast to coast."

They both laughed.

She noticed that he was headed west. "Are you taking me home now?"

"Yeah. It's after ten. There's not much more we can do tonight, and I want to stay on Gran's good side. I'll go home and grab some sleep and get an early start tomorrow morning."

"And you'll be picking me up at what time?"

"Is eight o'clock too early?"

"Yes, but I'll be ready anyway. In fact, make it seven-thirty, and I'll have hot biscuits and sausage gravy waiting for you."

He gave her a sideways glance that was quick but full of heartfelt affection and soul-deep gratitude. "I love you, Van. Adore you. I worship the ground you—"

"Oh please. You're just a glutton for free food."

"And free, Southern-style, finger-lickin', gum-smackin', calorie-laden cuisine is just part of the glorious wonder that is you." He paused. Rested. Then added, "How's that? Have I kissed up enough to get peach preserves on those hot biscuits?"

"Yeah, I reckon that'll do it. Now shut up already."

"Okay. Cool."

When Savannah entered her house, she found Granny Reid lying on her sofa, sound asleep, her reading glasses on her nose, her Bible on her chest, her *True Informer* folded neatly on the coffee table.

For a deliciously, long time, Savannah stood there, looking at her grandmother, loving this woman who had been grandparent, mother, and best friend to her for so many years.

She shuddered to think what might have happened to her and her siblings if Gran hadn't summoned her considerable strength and decided that she did, indeed, have what it took to raise nine grandchildren.

And now, even though she was more than eighty years old and all of those grandchildren were adults, Gran still felt as though she was on duty. She would consider them all her little chickadees for the rest of her life.

But twenty years ago—maybe even ten years ago—she would not have gone to sleep while waiting for one of them to come home.

Age took a subtle toll, even on as youthful a spirit as Gran's.

For just a moment, Savannah considered waking her grandmother and walking her upstairs to bed. But she knew Gran well, and she knew that Gran's preference was to snooze where she landed. Once she had passed out in a chair or on a sofa, there she stayed until time to rise and shine.

Gently, Savannah reached over and carefully slipped the glasses off her face, folded them, and placed them on the coffee table beside the tabloid. Then she moved the well-worn Bible, too.

She took an afghan, one of her dearest possessions because Gran herself had crocheted it for her, and spread it over her grandmother, covering her from chin to toes. After tucking it around her legs and feet, Savannah reached over and gave her a light kiss on the top of her silver hair.

She stirred slightly and whispered, "Savannah? You home, sugar?"

"Sh-h-h. Yes, I'm home safe and sound."

"Did you have a good time with your young man?" she asked, her voice soft and drowsy from sleep.

Savannah smiled. *Old habits die hard,* she thought. "I was out with Dirk," she reminded her, "looking for that girl who's missing."

"Did you find her?" she asked, squinting up at Savannah.

"Not yet. But we will."

Gran nodded and closed her eyes again. "I know you will, darlin'. I prayed on it. Real hard."

"Thank you." Savannah gave her another kiss, this

time on the forehead. Then she reached up to turn off the table lamp. "Nightie night," she said. "Don't let the bedbugs bite."

But Gran was already asleep. And this time, she was snoring.

The chickadees were safe in the nest—she'd sleep soundly for the rest of the night. But Savannah was pretty sure she wouldn't.

Once upstairs and in bed, she would pray for the missing girl's safety, too. But she didn't have as much faith as Gran.

Sadly, few people did.

Some nights, sleep just would not come. And it was one of those nights for Savannah. Nothing helped.

Her prayers had been said. And her two cats, miniature black panthers named Diamante and Cleopatra, were in bed with her—Diamante snuggled under the covers against her legs, Cleopatra curled inside the crook of her arm. Moonlight was streaming through the lace curtains, throwing filigree shadows across the bedspread. But none of it helped.

"Where are you, Daisy?" she whispered into the night silence. "Are you still with us?"

Or are you already gone?

She didn't speak that thought—not even in a whisper.

Nearly twenty years ago, there had been another girl named Maggie, who had gone missing. And as misfortune would have it, Maggie's case was one of the first that the newly made Detective Sergeant Savannah Reid and her partner Dirk Coulter had been assigned.

Oh, they found Maggie.

Well, actually, they found Maggie's remains. Only hours after the girl had been murdered by a pimp.

Savannah had never gotten over it.

Some hurts, especially those having to do with children, never, ever heal. And from that moment on, any mention of a missing kid re-wounded that injury for her.

When Savannah remembered Maggie, finding her thrown away like so much unwanted garbage in that old citrus packing shed, Savannah felt like she was twenty-something going on nincty. The teenager's young life was ended, and a twenty-five-year-old, freshly promoted policewoman was changed forever.

To Savannah, after Maggie, the world was never quite as good a place.

She lay there, watching the shadows change on her bedspread as the moon made its way across the sky. She did her deep breathing relaxation technique and the hypnosis routine that Tammy had taught her. She watched as the red numbers on her alarm clock changed—one hour of sleep gone, two hours, then threc.

Go to sleep, she told herself. *Just give it up and go to sleep. If you don't, you won't be worth shootin' tomorrow.*

Four hours, and the moonlight was gone.

So were the cats. They liked to go downstairs and sit on their perch every morning just before dawn, waiting to bask in those first rays of sunlight.

Normally, Savannah took this desertion in stride. Cats were, after all, fickle creatures who loved you more than anything in the world . . . except food, pets, and sunshine.

But without the moonlight or the cats' quiet warmth and comfort, she felt especially lonely.

"Don't be like Maggie," she whispered into the dark silence.

Surprisingly, she felt someone, something listening there in the quiet. A presence that she was aware of deep, deep in her soul. Somehow, someone was listening. Someone had heard.

So she said it again. "Daisy, please, please, honey . . . don't be like Maggie."

And finally, her burden shared, she drifted off to sleep.

Chapter 6

The next morning, Savannah's mood was a bit more optimistic. Homemade biscuits and gravy could do that to you. So could having some of the people you loved most in the world seated around your table.

Savannah's favorite thing was cooking and feeding hungry people. And they didn't even have to be hungry. She would happily feed them anyway.

Gran sat at the head of the table—Savannah wouldn't have it any other way—digging gleefully into a generous helping of grits.

Dirk sat at the other end of the table, totally grits free. He'd never actually tasted Savannah's grits. But he had made it clear early in their relationship that even a chowhound like him wasn't going to put something into his mouth named grit.

He didn't know what he was missing.

Tammy sat on one of the side chairs, her laptop on the table in front of her, a fruit smoothie in a mug next to her.

Tammy didn't eat grits either, or anything with saturated fat, processed flour, granulated sugar, preservatives, or artificial anything in it.

And that ruled out ninety-nine percent of Savannah's cooking.

Having breakfast, lunch, or dinner at Savannah's house usually meant that Tammy brought her own bag of "real food," as she called it. And while Savannah would never admit it, over the years she had come to realize the value of a smoothie made from the recently sun-kissed fruits of the earth.

Especially if you threw a big scoop of Ben and Jerry's Vanilla Heath Bar Crunch into the mix.

Savannah got up to replenish the biscuit basket. Dirk was hungrier than usual, having spent most of the night driving up and down San Carmelita's streets, highways, and byways, looking for Daisy's 1991 Honda Accord.

Taking another sip of her smoothie, Tammy studied the computer screen, then said, "According to this, Andrew Dante just married that gal, Robyn. They've been together only a couple of years. It says here that he left his wife for her, and that's why Tiffy hates her."

"Well, I could have told you that," Gran said, reaching for the peach preserves. "I keep up on all that stuff. That Robyn was Dante's travel agent. Any time he went any place, she set everything up for him."

"For his work or when he went away with his family?" Savannah asked.

"Both." Gran took time to savor her first bite of the preserves and biscuit before elaborating. "And then his wife figured out that she was making travel arrangements for him and herself, too. Hanky-panky stuff, if you know what I mean. The kind that'll get your tallywhacker snipped off if you're married to the wrong woman . . . if you know what I mean."

"Yep, we gotcha, Gran," Savannah said, hiding a smile.

Gran prided herself on her subtlety.

Subtle as the Cotton Belt freight train that blew its horn from one end of McGill, Georgia, to the other every Thursday night about eleven forty-five.

"You're not saying much," Savannah said to Dirk when she sat down in the chair across from Tammy and began her own breakfast.

"I'm worn out," he said. "I should have just gone on home early last night and gotten a full night's sleep, for all the good it did me."

"I'm sorry you didn't find the car," she told him.

She could have mentioned that she hadn't slept much herself, but Dirk got irritated if you hogged any of his misery, so she kept it to herself and let him wallow alone.

"Yeah, me, too," he said. "We need that car. If we could find it, we'd at least have a starting place."

"Did you check her credit cards or ATM card yet to see if there's been any activity?" Tammy asked.

"Credit card?" Dirk barked. "What credit card? She's a kid, for Pete's sake. She wouldn't have a—"

"Yes. She does." A light came on in Savannah's brain as she flashed back to finding the pregnancy test in the bottom of Daisy's desk drawer. "I remember seeing a receipt for something she bought at the drugstore there where she works. It had the last four digits of a credit card on it. It's either hers, or her mom lets her use it. Either way, Tammy's right. We need to check that."

Savannah stood, left her food on the table, and walked over to the kitchen wall phone. "What's Pam O'Neil's phone number?" she asked Dirk.

He pulled his notebook from his shirt pocket and read it off to her.

Pam O'Neil answered before the second ring.

Savannah felt a ping of pity for her when she heard the hopeful tone in her "Hello?"

"This is Savannah, Pam. And we don't have anything new, I'm sorry to say," she said, ending the suspense for the poor woman as quickly as possible. "But I do have a quick question for you. Does Daisy have her own credit card?" She smiled and nodded to those at the table. "Can you please give me the number if you know it? We need to run a check on it and see if there's been any activity." She paused. "Sure, I can wait."

A moment later, Pam gave her the long number; Savannah wrote it down on a notepad and confirmed it. Then she asked, "And can you tell me what bank it's drawn from and her pin number? That way we can check it right away without all the legal red tape."

Savannah frowned. "Oh, you don't. Well, let me ask you a few questions about Daisy."

A few minutes later, Savannah was back at the table, notes in her hand.

"Okay, Tammitha," she said, "here's where you get to shine. Hack this account for me, would you? Here's her boyfriend's name, her birthday, her social security number, her favorite color, and the name of her dog."

Tammy took the list and glanced over it. "People are so unoriginal. Luckily for us."

"No kidding."

Savannah wasn't even finished with her first biscuit until Tammy had exhausted the list and still hadn't found Daisy's password.

"I felt sure it would be the dog's name," Tammy said. "People always use their pets' names."

Savannah mentally reran her conversation with Pam. "Yeah, I thought that would be it, too. Pam said that's the second boxer she's had named Oscar. The current one is the first one's son. I saw a picture of

Daisy and one of the dogs there in Pam's living room."

"Hm-m-m . . . he's the second Oscar she's had," Tammy said thoughtfully. "Let me try Oscar2."

Her fingers clicked away on the keyboard. She squinted at the screen. "That didn't work either. I'll try Oscar2nd."

Having no luck, she typed in OscarII.

"Drats," she said. "It's telling me now that if I don't get it right the next time, the security system is going to lock me out for twenty-four hours." She looked around the table. "Any suggestions for my final attempt?"

Gran dumped a second heaping teaspoon of sugar into her coffee and said, "Well now, where I come from, if you name a boy young'un after his daddy, you call him Junior. Yeap, south of the Mason-Dixon Line, we're up to our tail feathers in Juniors."

Tammy brightened. "Okay. Let's try that one."

She typed in OscarJr. And a moment later, Daisy's private financial history was displayed before them in detail.

Tammy danced in her chair for a moment. "I got it! I got it!" But just as quickly, her smile faded, and her enthusiasm evaporated.

"What is it?" Savannah asked.

"It's nothing," Tammy replied.

"What do you mean, 'nothing'?" Dirk wanted to know.

"I mean that she hasn't charged anything or withdrawn a single dollar. Her last purchase was at a local nursery a week ago."

Savannah nodded. "She's quite the botanist. Her room is filled with plants."

"That's too bad," Dirk said. "A person who's spending money right and left is a person who's easy to track down."

"Not to mention the fact that spending money means they may still be alive," Savannah added.

"*May* be?" Granny asked.

Savannah cleared her throat. "Unless the person who's doing the spending stole the card from them and . . . well . . ."

"Yeah." Dirk sighed. "I wasn't going to mention that."

His cell phone went off, and Savannah recognized the personalized tone. It was the station calling.

They all held their breath as they listened to his side of the short conversation.

"Yeah? Where?"

He scribbled in his notepad. "Okay. I'll be there in ten. Have Donaldson secure it. Tell him nobody goes near it."

He snapped his phone closed. "They found her car. It's up at the end of Canyon Park where the hiking trails into the hills begin."

Savannah didn't want to ask, but she had to. "Any DB?"

"No," Dirk said, "thankfully."

They both jumped up from the table.

Savannah started to grab her purse, then paused and turned back to Gran. "I'm sorry, Gran. Here I go off half-cocked, and I didn't even stop to think that you'd like to—"

"Shoo." Gran waved a biscuit at her. "Get out of here, and don't waste time being silly. Go find that girl, and catch me a bad guy."

"Thanks, Gran. I love you."

"I love you, too, sweet cheeks. Make tracks."

Gran waited until Savannah and Dirk had left the room before she leaned across the table and whispered to Tammy, "DB. Does that stand for what I think it does?"

Tammy hesitated a second, then said, "Um . . . it's police code for dead body."

"That's what I figured." Gran nodded and looked self-satisfied. "And we can certainly thank the good Lord for that."

Tammy grinned. "Amen."

Gran reached for another helping of grits. "You said it, Sister Tammy. Tell it like it is."

Most small towns the size of San Carmelita did well to have one nice city park. But San Carm, as the locals called it, had three.

One was downtown in the quaint part of the city, near the old mission. And it was used mostly as a gathering place when the town fathers and mothers deemed it necessary to throw a craft fair, an art show, or any other sort of shindig to raise revenue.

The second was an exclusive hideaway up in the hills, not too far from the Dante estate. And even though it was a city park and therefore open to the public, it was pretty much understood that if you wanted to use the tennis courts, take a dip in the pool, or picnic on the perfectly manicured lawns, you had to behave yourself.

Then there was the third park. A long canyon that stretched deep into the foothills, the park was a stone's throw across and two miles long. And picnickers here were far more likely to be swilling beer or smoking pot than sipping Chardonnay.

Police did patrol the canyon and throw out the rowdiest of visitors, but not enough to cramp anybody's style.

It was pretty well-known that if you wanted to park and make out or blare your boombox and foist your

questionable taste in music onto your fellow park at-
tendees, this was the place to do it.

Savannah decided to give Dirk a break and drove
him to the park in her Mustang. He didn't particularly like being a passenger—typical male thing—but
he was in love with the 1965 'Stang, and she wouldn't
let him drive it. So, on a day when he was tired, she
could sometimes convince him to let *her* chauffeur
him for a change.

And when he didn't try to tell her how to drive,
when he just sat back and shut up and enjoyed the
drive, it went pretty well, and they didn't fight . . . too
badly.

"Why don't you just pass that friggen guy?" he said
as they followed a car that was creeping along at a
mere twenty miles over the speed limit. "We're never
going to get there if you don't—"

"Dirk, do *not* even *start* with me. Or I swear, you'll
be hoofin' it back to my house to get your own
jalopy. Roll down the window, take a deep breath,
and chill, son."

"I'll bet it's a woman driver," he grumbled. "When
they hog the left lane like that and won't get over to
let you pass 'em, it's always a woman."

"It's a man."

"How can you tell?"

"I can see his mustache in his rearview mirror,
and he just about ran off the road looking at that female jogger in the hot pink short shorts we just
passed. Call it a hunch."

"Oh."

"And they gave you a detective's badge?"

"Lay off me, woman, or I'll fly into a blind rage."

"Yeah, yeah. You'd have to gather up your
strength just to spit right now."

He sighed. "That's true."

"Well, don't tell Tammy. She'll start shoving vitamin pills at you."

"No kidding. Great big ones that smell like horse manure. Or she comes at you with those Chinese herbs that taste like frog pee."

Savannah chuckled. He was right. Tammy did have a healing effect on people. People around her tended to remain healthy, no matter what. They didn't dare do otherwise. Her remedies were to be avoided at all costs . . . even if it meant pretending you were feeling dandy when you had a full-fledged case of the whooping, bubonic diabetes.

As Savannah turned off the foothill road and into the park, she saw several teenagers eyeing her car with admiration mixed with envy. She knew she had a hot ride and enjoyed driving the classic car. And although the engine was old and in constant need of some sort of repair, the exterior was cherry. You could see the red Pony SS coming a mile off. And unless you were tailing somebody and trying to blend, or black, smelly smoke was belching out of the tailpipe, driving it around was pretty darned awesome.

As she drove down the narrow two-lane road that ran the length of the park, her anxiety began to build. Maybe there was no DB reported, but that didn't mean the car wouldn't reveal something they didn't want to see.

They passed the sandboxes, the swings, the slides, the picnic tables, and barbecue pits that were pretty much empty. It was a bit early in the morning for the parkers, the potheads, and the frankfurter brigades to be out and about.

The road twisted through the canyon with its steep, wooded hills on either side. And as they drove deeper into the valley, the arroyo became more and more narrow, the trees and brush thicker, the mown lawn more sparse.

And up ahead, at the end was a large gate—the gate marked "No Trespassing," the gate that absolutely everyone ignored and climbed over. Because just beyond the gate were some of the nicest hiking trails in the county.

In the spring, Savannah loved going back there and being waist high in the wildflower splendor. Yellow daisies and sage bloomed in glorious profusion—a feast for the eyes and admittedly, a challenge to the allergic.

Unfortunately, rattle snakes bloomed rather profusely, too, but she carried her Beretta with her, along with a totally unsophisticated Southerner's disrespect for the sanctity of reptilian life.

She might have wept at the sight of a dead bunny rabbit, but she could blow a rattlesnake to smithereens without batting an eyelash.

There would be no nature walk today. At the end of the road sat Daisy's old Honda and next to it, a police radio car, its blue lights flashing.

"Donaldson," Dirk mumbled. "Rookie kid. Always with the drama. I swear, he lights up when he's scooping roadkill."

She grinned, remembering the days when Dirk had used his siren and lights for absolutely any reason at all. And if he was in a squad car right now, he'd have the siren going and lights flashing.

It was a testosterone thing.

They parked the Mustang at least 60 feet from the other two vehicles and walked over to the fresh-faced, eager young cop who was standing guard.

Savannah liked Frank. She couldn't help it. He had been out of the academy two years, but the newness hadn't worn off for him. He was one of those guys who would absolutely love being a cop until the day he died. Unlike most people, Frank had found his passion in life, and he lived it daily. Life didn't get better than that.

Though he was a bit of a fanatic about it and therefore, occasionally, irritating. Especially to someone as irritable as Dirk.

Frank's round, rosy-cheeked face was beaming as he hurried over to them and said, "Hi, Savannah, Detective Coulter. I found it! I just had a feeling I should look down here, and sure enough, there it was!"

"Yeah, yeah," Dirk muttered under his breath. "Fricken Columbo here."

Savannah knew he was irked because during his night of cruising the streets, *he* hadn't thought of checking here. And poor Frank would pay the price.

Sometimes, it was painfully obvious why Dirk was respected but not particularly loved in his own police department.

"Why did you park so close to the vehicle like that?" Dirk barked as they walked over to the Honda. "What if we wanted to check around it for tire impressions or footprints? You probably drove right over anything that was there. Or walked on it."

Frank blushed and sputtered. "Well . . . I . . , tire impressions? Footprints? On asphalt?"

"It rained recently. Ever heard of mud prints?"

"Uh . . . okay."

Poor Frank, Savannah thought. *How dare he find Dirk's possible crime scene before* he *did!*

"So, whatcha got here, buddy?" Savannah asked too brightly. "No sign of the girl, huh?"

"No. Car's unlocked. Keys are gone. No signs of violence inside the vehicle."

Dirk sniffed. "And just what 'signs of violence' were you looking for, Donaldson? Overturned furniture? Broken lamps?"

Frank was an easygoing sweetheart, but this was a bit much even for him. Anger flashed in his pale gray eyes. "No, sir. What I meant was, I saw no blood spatter on the seats or headliner. No brain matter or bone fragments on the windows . . . sir."

Dirk glared at him for a few long, tense seconds, then grinned and nodded. "Okay, Donaldson. Thank you for assessing and securing the scene for me."

He glanced over at the yellow "Do Not Cross" crime scene tape that had been strung in a wide, wide circle around the car and the surrounding area—a much wider area than was necessary . . . even if the secured area did include the young cop's own squad car. "Good job with the tape, too."

Frank grinned. "Thank you, sir."

"Did you start a log?"

Frank produced a notebook and proudly presented it to Dirk. "I did. I found the vehicle at 0900 hours and—"

"Thank you, Donaldson." Dirk snatched the notebook out of his hand, glanced at it, and tucked it under his arm.

As the threesome walked toward the Honda, Dirk told Frank, "Let me give you a couple of tips about how I'd like you to secure my scenes in the future."

Frank perked up, all ears. "Yes, sir. I'd like that, sir."

"First, secure the primary scene itself. The vehicle, the body, whatever. And that area is not to be entered by you, or anyone else, until I, or another detective, arrives. You keep your car, your feet, and your mitts off that area."

"Ten-four, sir."

Savannah repressed a snicker as Dirk rolled his eyes.

"Then," Dirk said, "you string a second, wider perimeter around that, which will provide a secondary containment, protecting any evidence that, say, the perpetrator may have dropped or created making his getaway: footwear impressions, tire impressions, cigarette butts . . . or if they're incredibly stupid, a dropped business card or driver's license. Hey, it's happened."

"I believe you, sir."

"And finally," Dirk continued, "if it's a particularly hot scene, like a murder, and if you have lookie loos or press around, string a third tape wide around the other two, creating a third level of containment."

"Really?" Frank was impressed but mystified. "If I may ask, why a third one, sir?"

"So that you can eat a burger or smoke a cigarette without contaminating your own scene and without some 'film at eleven' chickie-pooh and her cameraman leaning over your shoulder asking you for a statement."

Frank grinned from ear to ear. "Thank you, sir. But what if she's a really hot chickie-pooh?"

Dirk gave Savannah a sideways look and lowered his voice a notch. "Then you put down the burger, step over the tape, and give her an exclusive. Duh, Donaldson. You gotta learn to think for yourself on this job, or you'll never soar to the high ranks of detectivedom."

Savannah cleared her throat. "Uh, can we get on with the business at hand, you two? Or do you want to trade smarmy pickup lines first?"

As they approached the car, she heard Dirk whisper to Frank, "Did they just take you out of the oven, girl, 'cause you are *hot!*"

Frank whispered back, "Hey, all those curves and me with no brakes."

She groaned and added, " 'You're the best-looking woman who's walked through that door in the past twenty years, and I should know. My lazy ass hasn't left this bar stool once in all that time.' That one always did it for me."

When they reached the car, levity ceased, and the looks on all three faces were all business.

With a practiced eye, Savannah scanned the automobile exterior, looking for anything, new scratches, smears, prints, leaves or any other sort of vegetation, debris of any kind . . . and, of course, blood.

The car was dusty and dirty, as though it hadn't been washed in quite a while. It had a few scratches and a couple of fairly deep dents, but they were rusty and old. Nothing fresh.

The tires were free of any extraordinary amount of mud or beach sand.

"Did you open the door with your bare hand?" Dirk asked Frank.

"No, sir. I didn't have any gloves, but I used a clean tissue on the handle so that I wouldn't touch it."

"Get yourself some gloves, and carry them at all times," Dirk said. "If for no other reason than so that you can protect yourself when you're handling somebody who's bleeding. I shouldn't have to tell you that. That's 101."

"Yes, sir. I usually do, but my fiancée took them without telling me to protect her hands when she was dying her hair red last week."

Savannah winced.

Dirk let him have it. "Ask your stupid girlfriend how she'd feel having you bring AIDS home to her."

"Yes, sir."

Dirk pulled three pairs of latex gloves from his jacket pocket and gave one pair to Frank and another to Savannah. When they were all appropriately clad, Dirk carefully opened the driver's door of the Honda and leaned inside.

"Keys are gone," he said. "And Patrolman Donaldson here is right . . . no blood or gore immediately apparent. Nobody got shot, stabbed, or severely bludgeoned in here."

Savannah opened the passenger's door and checked the glove box. She found nothing unusual inside, just the standard registration and insurance cards, a pair of sunglasses, a tube of lip balm, and a packet of mints.

They looked under the seats but saw nothing at all. Not even a gas receipt, a soda can, or a candy wrapper. Compared to the thousands of vehicles they had searched in their day, this one was pristine.

"Hm-m-m," Savannah said.

"Hm-m-m, what?" Dirk wanted to know.

"I was just thinking—the outside of this car is pretty grubby. But the inside, at least up front, is really clean."

"So?"

"It's usually the other way around. Clean cars are usually clean, and dirty ones are dirty—inside and out. But if a car is both clean and dirty, it's usually the outside that's clean and the inside that's dirty. People run it through the car wash for a quickie so that everybody will think they're driving a clean car. And they don't take time to wipe down the dash."

"Okay. And . . . ?"

"And look at this car. It's dirty on the outside and inside, but this area around the driver's seat is spotless. Who would run a car through a wash and only have them clean the front interior?"

"Maybe she cleaned the inside herself at home."

"Maybe. But really, look at this. There isn't a spot of dust on the dash, the steering wheel, the armrests. And yet, there in the back—the armrests, the door handles, dusty and dirty. Somebody cleaned up front and not the back or the exterior."

"Yeah, right. That's not right." Dirk nodded. "How much you wanna bet that we're not going to find a single fingerprint up here?"

Savannah lost that momentary warm feeling she'd gotten when they'd first looked inside and found an interior sans blood spatter.

Dirk took out his cell phone, punched in a number. "Yeah, Coulter here. I need a CSI out here right now. Yeah, in the park. We need this car printed as soon as we can get it. It's a rush."

He hung up, reached down, and fiddled with the trunk release lever. It wasn't working.

He gave Savannah and Frank a troubled look. "We're going to have to get into that trunk," he said.

"I'm pretty good at popping them," Frank volunteered. "I've got this tool in my car that—"

"Get it."

Dirk and Savannah waited for him at the back of the car. Reluctantly, Savannah leaned over, put her face near the trunk lid, and took a tentative sniff.

"Are you smelling for drugs?" Frank asked as he hurried back to them. "You smell pot or something?"

"No," Savannah replied softly.

"She's sniffin' for decomp, you dingbat," Dirk replied far less softly.

"Oh God. You don't think . . ."

"Just open it, would you?"

True to his word, Frank had the trunk open in less than ten seconds.

When she saw the relatively empty interior, Savannah felt a rush of relief so strong that it made her knees weak. The only things inside were a gas can half-filled with gas, a flashlight, a bag of potting soil, and a gym bag with the initials SCHS embroidered on it.

And one other item that was less encouraging.

A well-worn denim purse.

Savannah took it out, opened it, and found Daisy O'Neil's cell phone, her driver's license, a library card, a discount card from a local nursery, an employee's ID from Drug Mart, and the credit card that they had checked less than an hour ago. And three pictures. One of Daisy and Stan, one of her mother, and one of a lop-eared red boxer.

Savannah felt tears well up in her eyes. There was just something about handling a victim's personal items that always got to her, tugged at her heartstrings like little else did.

And what was more personal than a woman's purse?

Immediately, she turned on the cell phone and checked the incoming calls. There were a bunch from Daisy's mother, an old one from Stan, and a flurry of them made in the past few hours that were also from Stan.

The rest of the incoming and outgoing history had been cleared.

"Why is her purse in the trunk?" Frank asked. "That's a weird place to put a purse, isn't it?"

"Not really," Savannah said. "When a female has her purse with her but doesn't want to carry it or leave it in the interior of the car where it might be seen and snatched, she throws it into the trunk."

Savannah looked around her at the thick woods, the dense brush, the hiking trails stretching into the foothills behind them. And she shuddered to think of all the bad things that might be out there, the dangers that could beset a young woman like Daisy.

The rattlesnakes sunning themselves on the paths were bad enough.

But it was the two-legged snakes Savannah worried about most.

"I think she parked here, locked her purse in the trunk, and took a hike," she told them.

Dirk and Frank said nothing, but the looks on their faces showed that they, too, were contemplating what might have happened on that hypothetical hike that might have prevented Daisy O'Neil from returning home for nearly forty-eight hours.

Again, Dirk flipped open his phone and punched in numbers. "Coulter here," he said. "Yeah, I'm at the vehicle. Send me a K9 tracker. Get Don Thornton if you can. And tell him to haul ass."

He hung up. "We have to find this kid," he said, his eyes filled with deep concern, even sorrow. "It's already too late."

"Don't say that," Savannah said. Maggie filled her mind, clutched at her heart. "Damn it, Dirk, do *not* say that!"

Dirk shook his head and closed his eyes for a moment. He swayed on his feet, exhausted. When he opened them, he gave Savannah a long, loving, understanding look filled with defeat. "Come on, Van," he said softly, "Like it's gonna make any difference what I do or don't say." He reached over and put his hand on her forearm.

She shoved it away. "It makes a difference," she said. "You watch your mouth. She's still alive out there. I can feel her. She's waiting for us."

Waiting like Maggie was waiting.

Savannah shook her head. But the thought remained.

She turned away from them and headed for the gate at the end of the road.

"Savannah," Dirk called as he came after her. "Savannah, where are you going?"

"I'm going to start looking for her." She swung one leg over the gate. A piece of rusted metal caught and ripped her linen slacks and scratched her thigh, but she didn't notice. "I'm not going to stand around here waiting. I'm going to—"

"Honey, stop!"

Strong arms wrapped around her waist and pulled her off the gate.

A moment later, her face was pressed against Dirk's warm, hard chest, and he was holding her so tightly that she was pinned against him, unable to move.

Sagging into him, she breathed in the comforting, familiar smell of him—leather, his Old Spice deodorant, and now . . . the recent addition of cinnamon to replace the old tobacco smell.

He reached up and stroked her hair. "You can't go out there and just start running around those hills looking for her, babe," he said. "Wait for the K9. And if that doesn't work, we'll organize a search party."

Savannah fought back tears. "It's just . . . you know . . . she's a kid. Kids are different. They're . . . hard."

He squeezed her a little tighter. "Oh, I know. Kids are the hardest." He reached down, put his hand under her chin, and forced her to look up at him. "This is a new case, Van. It's not her."

She looked into his eyes and borrowed a little of the strength she needed. She bit her lip and nodded.

"Let's take this one minute at a time," he said, "Okay?"

She reached inside and, as Granny Reid called it, gathered up her strength. "Okay. One minute at a time."

Chapter 7

The CSI tech arrived before the K9 unit, but Dirk wouldn't let her begin dusting for prints. "Sorry, Michelle," he told her, "but I don't want anybody walking around the vehicle until the dog's tried to find a scent."

"No problem," the petite blonde replied. "It's time for my morning coffee break anyway. Come get me when you need me."

She returned to the white van with its county logo and the coroner's seal on the side, where she sat and sipped coffee from an enormous Styrofoam cup.

Savannah stood behind the Honda talking on her cell phone, the contents of the SCHS gym bag in her hand. "Yes, Pam," she was saying to Daisy's mother. "The vehicle looks fine. No signs of an accident or anything unusual. Her purse was locked in the trunk, so there's no reason to worry about robbery or anything bad like that."

Just rabid coyotes, rattlesnakes, and sexual predators on wilderness trails, she thought. *Okay, rabid rattlesnakes and coyotes aren't much of a problem. Stop it, Savannah. You're supposed to be logical and comforting here.*

Pam didn't sound all that comforted. "But what could have happened to her! She's been gone so long now! Even if she parked there and took a hike, she would have come back long before now unless something horrible—"

"Not necessarily something *horrible*. It could be something just . . . well . . . a *little* bad or not too bad at all. We may very well find her out there somewhere with a turned ankle, in need of a lift out. Something a lot less awful than all the stuff you're imagining."

Or that I'm imagining.

"But she would have been out there at night, *two nights*, in the dark."

"Yes, but the weather's been very mild. She's a big girl, who, judging from the books in her room, knows a lot about nature. Even if she can't walk out, she could still probably take care of herself. Please try hard not to worry yourself sick."

"A little late for that." Pam sighed, and the pain and misery in the sound went straight to Savannah's heart.

A squad car with a large K9 on the door was coming down the road, and Dirk was motioning the car over to him.

"Listen," Savannah said. "You can help us here. I'm looking in a gym bag that was in the trunk. Inside, there's a red T-shirt with the high school bull-dog logo on it, black shorts, and some gray sneakers. I assume these are Daisy's clothes?"

"Yes, they are." Pam started to cry. "Why?"

"Because we have a K9 unit—a dog tracker—arriving right now. We can use these clothes to help him identify her scent. He might be able to track her down whatever trail she took."

"Oh, good. I'm coming over there right now."

"You don't need to, Pam. Really. We've got it."

"No! I want to! I want to be there. I want to look for her myself."

The last thing they needed was a distraught parent in the middle of what they were trying to do. Just knowing that a worried mother was sitting at home, sobbing her face off was pressure enough.

"Pam, please stay there by the phone. There's really nothing you can do here. Maybe if we get to the point of organizing a search party, then you could help. But for now, you need to stay there. If Daisy phoned you and you weren't there to take her call, you'd never forgive yourself."

There was a long silence on the other end as Pam thought that one over. Finally, she said, "Okay. But would you please call me the second you find anything? Anything at all."

"Of course I will. And you have my number. If you can't stand the waiting, you give me a ring, okay?"

"I'll try not to bother you."

"It's no bother. Really."

"Thanks, Savannah. For everything."

"You're most welcome."

Savannah hung up and hurried over to the tall, slender young officer who was holding an enormous German shepherd on the end of a thick choke chain.

Dirk was greeting him and the dog, who was barking and straining against the chain, eager to get on with his duties. Getting down on his knees, Dirk grabbed the big dog's head in both hands and shook him hard from side to side. "Hey there, Mongo, old buddy! How's my boy?"

Once, when Officer Thornton had gone on vacation, Dirk had dog sat for him. Now Dirk considered himself the Dog Handler Master. He had taught Mongo to fall onto his side and roll onto his back when Dirk fake shot him with his finger.

Dirk didn't realize that Don had already taught

Mongo that trick years before. And Don had been kind enough not to mention it when Dirk had crowed about his accomplishment.

"Is that the vehicle?" Don asked, nodding toward the Honda.

"That's it," Savannah told him. She held out the T-shirt, shorts, and shoes. "And these are her clothes. You're in luck. They haven't been laundered."

Don gave her a broad, proud smile and said, "Even if they *were* laundered, Mongo could pick it up. But he doesn't like lavender-scented fabric softener. Makes him sneeze."

Dirk was pointing his finger at Mongo and saying, "Bang." But the dog didn't respond, only continued to whine and prance anxiously at the end of his lead.

Don chuckled. "If you're finished playing with my dog, we could get down to business here," he said.

"Oh, right. Sorry." And for once, Dirk really did look a bit embarrassed as he got up off his knees. He cleared his throat and donned his serious business demeanor.

They walked over to the car, and Savannah and Dirk watched as Don scented the dog with the gym clothes. A moment later, the dog had his nose to the ground and was sniffing, sniffing all around the car.

Having seen the dog work before, they waited anxiously for his particular alert, his signal that he had found something. Sometimes, he sat on the ground, looked up at Don, and gave an excited bark. Other times, he would just take off, following the trail, his nose to the ground.

But although Don circled the car over and over with him and even the surrounding area, Mongo seemed to be unable to find any trail.

The animal whined and shook his head, looking up at his partner with frustration, obviously as disappointed as they were.

Finally, Don drew him up short and gave him a treat. "Let's give him a minute or two, and then maybe we'll try something else. That's her car, right? Your missing girl?"

"Yes, it is," Dirk said.

"The one she usually drives?"

"Yeah."

"Okay. Let's have him scent off the driver's seat. See if that helps."

Dirk opened the front door of the car, and Don led Mongo over to it. The dog had followed this routine many times before and knew it well. He hopped up and put his front feet on the driver's seat, then sniffed all over it.

Immediately, he dropped to all four feet beside the car and put his nose to the ground. He followed along, smelling, intent and focused. He traced a line from the car door, around the back of the car to the parking space next to it. There he stopped. Sitting on his haunches, he looked up at his handler and gave one sharp bark.

"That's it," Don said. "She walked from one car to here . . . probably got right into another one that was parked here in this spot."

Savannah didn't know whether to be relieved or not. "I guess it's a good thing if she's not up in those hills," she muttered, mostly to herself, "but getting in another car? That could mean anything."

"I guess somebody picked her up," Don said. "Maybe they snatched her, forced her into their car."

Dirk was walking around the spot where the dog had indicated the end of the trail. "But Mongo says the trail ends here, on the left side of this parking space. If the car she got into was nosed into the space the way most people park, she would have gotten into the driver's side. Not the passenger's."

Savannah nodded. "That's true. Some reincarnated gunslingers and gangsters park facing out for a quick getaway, but most people nose in, like you said."

"Maybe somebody drove out here with her," Dirk said, "with the intention of leaving her car here. They pulled in, she got out of the Honda, the other person slid over onto the passenger's seat, she got into the second car and drove off."

"Could be," Savannah mused. "Could be. And that's a cheerier scenario than her getting snatched and shoved into the passenger's seat."

Michelle, the CSI, sauntered up to them and gave Don a flirtatious smile. "My coffee break is way over, and I can only justify so many games of sudoku on the taxpayers' time," she said. "Can I start dusting yet?"

"Yeah," Dirk said, "you might as well. It looks like it's been wiped down, though. Good luck."

She grinned. "Oh, those are the fun ones. I just lo-o-ove a good challenge."

As she walked back to the van to retrieve her kit, Officer Don watched her backside with avid male interest.

Savannah leaned close to him and whispered in his ear, "Um . . . isn't your wife the one who threw a beer bottle at you at the Fourth of July picnic because you were checking out some gal in a tight halter top?"

He snapped out of it instantly. "Yeah, right," he said. "Come on, Mongo. Let's go get you an ice cream cone."

An hour later, Michelle was still inside the Honda, sitting in the driver's seat, swirling fingerprint dust with a thick, soft brush onto the dash.

Savannah watched as she worked, dropping the dust, placing sheets of tape onto the area, peeling it off, and then attaching the tape to white evidence cards.

"Anything yet?" Savannah asked, standing by the open driver's door, trying to see what she was doing.

"Nope. Nothing. Dirk wasn't kidding when he said it was wiped clean. I've covered just about every surface up here. And I haven't found one print, even a partial."

That small bit of hope that maybe there was a nonsinister explanation for Daisy's disappearance evaporated. There was simply no good, honest reason why a person would remove their fingerprints from a car . . . or anywhere else, for that matter.

"That Officer Thornton," Michelle said as she dusted. "He's a hottie. Is he married?"

"Yes, absolutely married," Savannah told her.

"Happily?"

"I'm not sure, but you don't want to go there. Trust me."

"You a moralist or something?"

"Let's just say if you're a survivalist, you'll steer clear. She's got a temper and a half. Very jealous. Prone to violence."

"That bad? Really?"

"Clocked him in the head with a beer bottle in front of at least fifty off duty cops at a picnic. I heard it took nine stitches to close up the gash. He bled all over the potato salad. Ugly. Very ugly."

"Oh, okay. Gotcha."

Dirk walked over to the car, opened the passenger's door, and stuck his head in. "How's it coming?"

"Lousy," Michelle said. "Nothing. And I'm about done."

He grunted. "Don't forget to do a Night Stalker."

"Yeah, yeah . . . telling me how to do my job again. None of us *ever* forget to do a Richard Ramirez."

Dirk left them and wandered away. Savannah

could tell he was getting tense, just waiting around. To Dirk, wait was a nasty, obscene four-letter word.

Savannah watched as Michelle carefully dusted the back of the rear view mirror, applied the tape, and ripped it off.

Years ago, the horrific murder spree of serial killer Richard Ramirez, the so-called Night Stalker, had come to an end because the cops had found a single fingerprint on the rearview mirror of a car he had driven.

And as a result, any CSI tech worth their brush and dust checked all sides of a vehicle's mirror before the job was done.

"Oh my God, I don't believe it!" Michelle said, staring at the white card where she had affixed the tape. "I've got one. It's a partial, but I'll bet it's enough for a match."

"Hey, Dirk," Savannah called out to him. "Come back here. She's got one."

It took him only five seconds to return to the car and snatch the card out of Michelle's hand. One look, and a big grin spread across his face.

"Fantastic!" he said. "Michelle, consider yourself kissed, kiddo!"

He handed the card back to her and said, "Sign it and fill it out. I want to get that over to the lab right now so they can process and run it."

Michelle began to write on the card, filling in the necessary information to properly document it. Then she slipped it into a manila envelope and sealed and signed the envelope as well.

She handed it to Dirk and started to get out of the car.

"Wait." Savannah put her hand on the tech's shoulder and pushed her back into the seat. "Hold on a minute. I want to see something."

After looking down at Michelle's legs and feet, she said, "Did you move this seat?"

"What?"

"Did you adjust the seat, move it forward or back?"

"No, of course not. Why?"

"How about the mirror? Did you adjust it, or was that the position it was in when you first got into the car?"

"No. I didn't move it. I'm really careful about that kind of thing." Michelle looked confused and more than a little defensive. "Why are you asking me this stuff? I know how to—"

"Sh-h-h. I know you do." Savannah reached into her purse and pulled out the pad where she had been jotting notes since she had first talked to Pam O'Neil at the Dante estate. "Michelle, how tall are you?"

"Five-two," she admitted reluctantly, "not that it's anybody's business."

"And your feet reach the pedals just fine there, right?"

"Uh . . ."—she looked down—". . . yeah."

"And when you look in the rearview mirror, it's in a good position for you?"

She glanced at the mirror. "Yes. Why?"

Savannah checked her notes. "Because Daisy O'Neil, our missing girl, is five feet, ten inches."

Dirk had been on his cell phone, alerting the lab that he was on his way in to see them, but all of a sudden, he was interested in the point Savannah was making.

"That's right," he said, checking out the position of Michelle's body in the seat. "Daisy would have had the seat a lot farther back than that if she was the one at the wheel."

"Somebody else was driving Daisy's car," Savannah said, wondering what the significance of that might be. "They may have dropped this car here, got out, hopped into another car, and driven off in the second one."

"That would be my guess, too." Dirk nodded thoughtfully. "And whoever was doing the driving wasn't nearly as big as Daisy . . . or that boyfriend of hers, either."

"Nope. Petite. A very short man or a small woman."

Savannah's eyes met Dirk's, and they exchanged knowing looks.

"I guess I know whose prints you're going to run a comparison on first," she said.

"Yep." Dirk slipped the envelope into his inside jacket pocket. "In less than an hour, I'll know if it's Miss Tiffy's."

Savannah crossed her fingers.

If she'd thought it would've done any good, she'd have crossed her eyes, toes, and legs, too.

Savannah drove Dirk to her least favorite part of town, the industrial area. Not all that many years ago, this land had been covered with orange, lemon, and avocado groves and strawberry fields—blooming, bearing fruit, cleaning the air, and perfuming it with the intoxicating scent of blossoms and fresh citrus.

Now it grew nothing but more and more gray steel and cement.

Progress.

Los Angeles had arrived.

And in the middle of the boring and soulless maze of windowless concrete block buildings with steel garage doors was an equally unremarkable windowless building with a small, white door with the Great Seal of California emblazoned on it.

They parked, hurried up to the door, and Dirk punched the doorbell button.

A moment later, a voice spoke from the intercom speaker mounted over the door just below a security camera.

"What do you want?" asked a pseudo-gruff female voice. "Whatever you're selling, we've got enough."

"Open this door, Eileen," Dirk barked back. "I got something that's gotta be processed right away."

"What else is new?"

When the door opened, a sixty-something woman with long, curly silver hair was standing there, her hands on her hips. She wore a crisp white lab coat, blue jeans, and sneakers and a broad smile on her face—for Savannah.

Eileen Bradley had been head of the lab since Savannah had been a cop, and she ran the place with impressive efficiency and frightening despotism. But in Savannah's opinion, Eileen was a good egg . . . as long as you weren't foolish enough to cross her.

"Hey, girl," she said, giving Savannah a warm hug. "I don't see nearly enough of *you* around here." As she turned to Dirk, the smile dropped off her face. "*You*, on the other hand, I see far too much."

Ignoring the insult, Dirk reached into his pocket and pulled out Michelle's envelope. "I've got a latent here that I need run ASAP."

Eileen turned to her other techs, a middle-aged Latino and a freckle-faced young miss, who were both sitting at computers, their noses practically on the screens. "Hear that?" she asked them. "Detective *Coulter* has something that *has* to be processed *right away*. Drop everything, run over here, grab his evidence, and kiss his ass."

Savannah cringed and gave Dirk a sideways glance. She half expected him to explode. And maybe with anyone else, he might have. But Eileen had the upper hand, gold shield or not. She could make him WAIT. And in Dirk's world, that gave her rank and stature.

"It's important, Eileen," he said in a far softer tone than Savannah might have expected. "A kid's missing and—"

"And another kid's dead," Eileen interjected. "Shot four times, twice in the head. Do you mind if we process his *bullets* first before we get to your *latent*?"

For a moment, Dirk looked confused and a bit chagrined. Then he flared, "Who? You mean that damned gangbanger who got himself popped Monday night? Give me a break. My kid's an innocent civilian. That punk was asking for it."

Savannah winced. "Dirk . . . don't . . ." she whispered as she waited for Eileen to slap him.

But Eileen didn't. She balled her fingers into fists but kept them at her sides as she glared up at Dirk. "I don't believe you said that," she told him in a low, deadly even tone. "He was seventeen. He had a family who's mourning him. What the hell's the matter with you, Coulter?"

Savannah reached over and gently took the envelope from Dirk's hand. "Why don't you, uh, go out and wait for me in the car," she told him under her breath. "Okay?"

Dirk's face flushed, and she knew he was furious. But to her surprise, he turned around and left the room.

And to his credit, he didn't even slam the door behind him.

"I'm sorry," she said to Eileen and the other two techs, who were now all ears. "He's really worried—

we both are—about this girl. She's a good kid who's been missing for forty-eight hours now, and that's too long, *much* too long. It's not looking good at this point."

Eileen's face softened a bit, so Savannah continued. "I know you guys are swamped. You always are. And it's a terrible shame about the kid who was murdered. But he's already gone. If you can run one print, and I'll even give you a possible match for it, it might point us in the right direction. Maybe we could save this other kid."

Savannah held out the envelope, along with her most beguiling, pleading, half smile.

Eileen shook her head and sighed as she took the envelope and opened it. She pulled out the card, held it up, and gave it a long look. Finally, she said, "Okay." She turned to the young woman behind her. "Cindy, drop what you're doing there, and take care of this for me."

Turning to Savannah, she added, "ASAP."

Savannah smiled. "Thank you. Eileen, you're the best."

"No, I'm second best. *You* are the best. You not only do your job, but you also have to do it with *him*. When you get outside, remind that numbskull of that."

"I will. Oh, I will."

Chapter 8

"You didn't have to do that, you know. I was handling the situation just fine back there," Dirk complained as she drove him back to her house to pick up his car.

"You were not." Savannah stared straight ahead, trying not to grip the steering wheel so hard she'd break it in two. Classic Mustang steering wheels didn't come cheap.

"I was, too." He huffed and puffed a bit. "I'm not as stupid as I look. I know how to talk to people."

It occurred to her that if anything, Dirk looked smarter than he was. But she decided to keep that to herself and simply replied, "Do not."

"Wha . . . what?" he sputtered. "How can you say that? Aren't you the one who's always been happy to hand your suspects over to *me* to interrogate them?"

"You're good at *scaring* people, not at talking to them. You pretty much suck at that. Most of the time, you don't have a clue what to say to get what you want out of folks."

"Oh yeah? Says who?"

"*Me.* And to prove my point—you're sitting there yelling at me when you should be thanking me that your print is getting processed right now. Instead, you should be sweet-talking me, telling me what a great gal I am and how grateful you are to have a sparkling gem like me in your life."

"I should kiss up to you after you embarrass me like that?"

"Absolutely. You should be smooching hiney big-time, boy."

"Give me one good reason why."

"Because it's lunchtime, and you're on your way to my house."

Dirk thought that one over a long time before he cleared his throat, donned a repentant face, and said, "Thanks a million, Van. You really came through for me back there. I appreciate it. Bigtime."

She grinned. "You're welcome."

They drove a bit farther. "What do you want for lunch?" she asked.

"You got any of that fried chicken left over?"

"I think so."

"Good. That and a big helping of your potato salad should do it." He reached into his jacket, pulled out his cell phone, and flipped it open. "I'm gonna call Eileen and tell her to get a move on with that print. She's had it for twenty minutes now. What are they doin' over there, making plaster of Paris volcanoes with their chemistry sets?"

Savannah sighed. "Right, Dirk. And you be sure to mention that when you talk to her."

"Oh, I will! Don't you worry. I will!"

"When do you think you'll get the results on that print?" Tammy asked as she helped Savannah lay odds and ends of leftovers onto the table.

Savannah rolled her eyes. "God only knows. It's a long, sad story."

They could hear Dirk in the living room, harassing somebody on the phone, and Gran was upstairs, taking a nap.

"How can I help with this?" Tammy said as she took the lid off a jar of kosher dills. "It's nice having your granny to myself, but she and I both have been itching to do *something* on this case."

"Thanks, sugar. I can't think of anything right now, but if I do . . ."

"How about her computer? Doesn't she have a computer I can be rummaging through, reading old e-mails, stuff like that?"

"Her mom told Dirk that it quit working a few weeks ago. The hard drive's fried or whatever. They donated it to some charity or something."

"Darn. How about her cell phone?"

"I already looked it over. The incoming and outgoing calls have been erased. The only ones showing are the ones she's missed the last couple of days—her mom's and her boyfriend's."

"Hm-m-m . . . you should ask her mom if she normally does that. Most people don't."

"Except cheating boyfriends."

"Let's not be sexist now."

They both added in unison, "And cheating girlfriends."

"Dirk, come in here and eat your lunch before it gets cold," Savannah called out.

Tammy giggled. "It's already cold. It's straight out of the refrigerator."

"Like he would notice."

As they sat around the table, Tammy munched on her salad, Dirk devoured a chicken leg, and Savannah downed a ham sandwich.

"Is Granny still napping?" Dirk asked in midchew.

"Yes," Tammy said. "I wore her out this morning, taking her to the old mission. She spent hours there."

Dirk looked confused. "But the mission is Catholic. I thought she's a Baptist or something Southern like that."

"She is," Tammy replied. "But the mission has the biggest thrift store in the county. It's right next door."

"Ah." Savannah nodded. "No wonder she's exhausted. Gran loves a bargain." Turning to Dirk, she said, "Any word from Eileen yet?"

"Several words," he grumbled. "Several nasty, totally uncalled-for words."

"Imagine that. But no print ID yet?"

"No. She made it pretty clear that *she* will call *me* when she's finished." He took a bite of potato salad. "That woman needs to take a few anger management classes."

"Go figure."

Tammy had been sitting quietly for a few moments, apparently mulling something over. Suddenly, she brightened. "Ah . . . I know something I can do!"

"What's that?" Savannah asked.

But Tammy was already halfway to the living room.

"What's the bimbo up to?" Dirk asked under his breath.

"Don't call her that."

"Why not? She can't hear me."

"Because I don't let *her* call *you* names around me, and I don't want you to—"

"She calls me names? What does she call me?"

"Nothing. Forget I mentioned it."

Tammy came back in, several papers in her hand, and sat back down at the table.

"Do you call me names behind my back?" Dirk demanded to know.

Tammy looked up from the papers, confused for a second, then said, "None that I don't call you to your face. Just Dirko, Pee-Pee Head . . . stuff like that."

"Oh, okay."

"What have you got there?" Savannah asked, eager to change the subject.

"The printout of Daisy's bank statements for the past six months. I see here that she pays for her cell phone by check. That's a good thing. Or at least, potentially a good thing."

"How?" Dirk asked. "Why would that matter to us?"

"Because it means she may not have set up an account to pay her bill online."

"And . . . ?" Savannah prompted.

Tammy gave her a sly grin. "That means that . . . um . . . 'Daisy' could still do that. And if she did that, she'd be able to look at all of her incoming and outgoing calls. Even the ones that have been deleted from her phone."

"And let me guess," Dirk said. "Sometime this afternoon, you're going to do her the big favor of going online and doing that for her."

Tammy nodded, looking very pleased with herself.

"And what are you going to use for a password?" Savannah asked. "OscarJr?"

"No way. If I'm going to do this for Daisy, I'm going to do it right. The second worst thing people do when setting up their passwords—after choosing one that's just way too obvious—is using the same one for everything."

"So what are you going to use?" Dirk asked.

Tammy's smile disappeared, and for a moment, she looked quite sad. "I know what I'd like to use," she said. "I'd like to use FoundSafe&Sound."

"Don't we all," Savannah added. "Don't we all."

Dirk's phone began to play "Funeral March of a Marionette," the theme song from the old TV show *Alfred Hitchcock Presents,* one of Dirk's very favorites . . . next to *Gunsmoke* and *Bonanza.*

Everybody at the table brightened.

"It's Eileen!" Savannah said.

"Yeah?" Dirk answered, ever the smooth talker.

He listened, then grinned broadly. "I love you, Eileen. Have I ever told you that? You're a queen among women, a real—"

He stopped talking, took the phone down from his ear, and stared at it. "She hung up on me! Can you imagine that? I was being nice to her, and she had the nerve to—"

"Dirk!" Savannah reached over and slapped him on the shoulder. "Damnation! What did she say?"

"It's a match," he said. "The latent is a match to the thumbprint on Tiffany Dante's DMV record."

The table erupted in cheers.

Dirk pushed his only half-empty plate away and stood. "I think I'll go lean on a certain little spoiled brat. I think I'll see if I can't scare her . . ."—he looked at Savannah—". . . since I've been told on good authority lately that I'm good at that. You wanna come?"

"And watch an artiste in action? Of course."

She turned to Tammy. "Do you mind staying home and checking those phone records for us?"

Tammy smiled. "Hey, as long as I'm sleuthing, I'm happy."

Savannah reached over and patted her friend on the top of her shiny blond head. "And that's why we love you, Nancy Drew. Give a holler if you get anything."

"Will do."

A minute later, Savannah and Dirk were gone, swirling away like a Kansas tornado, and Tammy was sitting alone. She glanced over at Dirk's plate and said, "Wow, old Wind in His Pants really *is* eager to solve this case! He left *free food* behind! Like Granny Reid says, 'Wonders never cease!'"

When Savannah and Dirk pulled up in front of the Dante mansion, she thought she had suddenly been plunged into hell itself. The exquisite grounds were littered with dismembered, rotting corpses, coffins and tombstones, and every conceivable sort of monster, and cobwebs were strewn over every bush and hedge.

"Oh, gross," Dirk said as they got out of his Buick and walked around the circular driveway to the front door. They passed a ravaged torso, a severed hand with the bloodied knife lying beside it, and a disembodied head, who looked surprised and displeased to have been separated from his other body parts.

Workers were still setting up, spreading more Halloween "cheer" on other parts of the lawn. One fellow was dumping a dark red liquid into the fountain. A moment later, the four tiers began to flow with "blood."

"Ew-w-w," she said. "They've got a real Dante's Inferno here." Savannah glanced over at a coffin to the right of the door and saw that it was occupied by a vampiress dressed in Gothic dominatrix attire. "And you say that *I* overdecorate for parties," she told him.

He shook his head in disgust. "I'll never mention it again. Your bowls of spaghetti brains and vats of grape eyeballs are understated elegance compared to this crap."

After ringing the doorbell, they waited, and waited, and waited.

Finally, the door opened, but instead of the maid who had greeted them before, the person on the other side was a young man on his way out, weighed down with a dozen or more hangers full of costumes.

As he sailed by, Savannah saw everything there from the Bride of Frankenstein to a bloody-fanged Easter Bunny.

"I feel like Alice in Wonderland on a really bad LSD trip," she said.

"I hear ya. And this is in the daylight. Can you imagine what this is going to look like tomorrow night?"

"Scary thought what money can buy." She looked inside the still open door and saw at least five or six more people scurrying around with all sorts of equally disgusting props.

"Let's go on in," Dirk said.

"Uninvited?"

"That guy with all the stupid outfits, he invited us in. Didn't you hear him?"

"Sure. I believe his exact words were, 'Walk right in, folks, and make yourself at home.'"

"Yep, that's what I heard, too."

As they walked through the door and into the glorious foyer, Savannah nearly ran into a life-sized Grim Reaper dressed as a pirate. As she walked by him, the skeleton brought the blade of his scythe down in a chopping motion, nearly hitting her on the head.

"Watch it, you bag of bones," she told it. "I'm armed myself, and a gun beats a sickle any day of the week."

They walked through the house down a hallway that was now a gallery of serial killers. Jeffrey Dahmer's holographic portrait hung between Ted Bundy and John Wayne Gacy, Jr., and above Henry Lee Lucas and Ed Gein.

Savannah was sure that this was meant to be funny. But having seen firsthand what misery and suffering they caused, she didn't find this display the least bit humorous.

"Am I just getting old and boring, or is all of this in really bad taste?" she asked Dirk.

"Oh, it's just gross to be gross," he replied. "Whatever happened to plain old Frankenstein, ghosts, and werewolves like we used to have?"

"I guess with all the gruesome movies around now, it takes a lot more to scare people than it used to."

They entered the great room, which was now a combination wedding chapel and funeral home. Near the fireplace stood a skeleton bride and groom and an equally emaciated priest waiting to officiate. The happy couple and their wedding guests sported three-inch-long bloodied fangs and Gothic vampire attire. Most of the guests were lying in coffins, lined up from one side of the immense room to the other, like parishioners in church pews.

Four perfectly alive and unbloodied workers were going up and down the rows, adjusting this, rearranging that.

Dirk walked up to one of the least harried of the women and asked her, "Do you know where Tiffany Dante is? Or her father?"

The woman rolled her eyes and nodded toward the door. "Last time I saw them, they were in the library." She lowered her voice and added, "And that's why I'm staying out of there, if you know what I mean."

"I know exactly what you mean," Dirk told her. "Thanks."

She turned to Savannah. "Well, what do you think?" she asked, indicating the room with a vague wave of her hand.

"Honestly?" Savannah asked.

"Sure."

"I'd say it's grotesquely overdone, grisly, and . . . well . . . frankly . . . deeply disturbing."

The woman smiled and said, "Good. Then Miss Tiff should love it. That's exactly what she says she wants."

Dirk and Savannah left the decorators to their artistic endeavors, and Dirk led the way to the library, which was at the end of a long hallway toward the rear of the house.

But even before they reached the room, they could hear raised voices, the sounds of an argument.

"I think it's Tiffy and her dad," Savannah whispered to Dirk as they stopped outside the door and listened.

Dirk glanced up and down the hall, but no one was watching. They could eavesdrop unobserved.

"You do love her more than me! You do! And it's just so sick!" the young woman shouted, crying.

"Tiffy, stop this right now. I do not! You're my daughter. My own flesh and blood. What makes you think I would ever put anyone above you?"

"Because you do! It's so obvious! She gets a fantastic vacation to Amsterdam, and then you tell me that I have to watch my budget here with my party, a party I've been planning and looking forward to for months!"

"Oh, give me a break. You're already way over budget here, and you know it."

"Well, I want the best, and I deserve it. You always wanted me to have the best until *she* came along and spread her legs for you, and now, to hell with me and what *I* want!"

Savannah cringed. For half a second, she tried to imagine what would happen if she or one of her siblings were to utter such a thing in front of Gran. But the mental image wouldn't even form in her head. Some things were just unthinkable.

"Shut up! I mean it, Tiffy! Shut your mouth! I'm not going to discuss her with you."

"I don't blame you for not wanting to talk about her. You couldn't keep your zipper closed, and you ruined our family. Mom is never going to be the same after what you've—"

"This conversation is over. Get out of here right now!"

"No! Not until you tell me that I can have the sword and fire dancers, too. I'm not going to cut back on my party just so that you can send her on a long trip to—"

"All right! Hire your damned dancers. But get the hell out of here so that I can work."

Savannah shot Dirk an uh-oh look. They retreated as quickly as they could from the door and ducked into an alcove halfway down the hall.

They weren't a moment too soon because Tiffy came sauntering out, to their surprise, with a big, happy self-satisfied smirk on her face.

Walking right by them, she didn't even notice them standing there. And she was equally clueless when they fell into step behind her and quietly followed her toward the front of the house.

She tossed out orders right and left to the workers as she made her way through the Dante's Nightmare, criticizing this, demanding that, much to the irritation of those she commanded.

Savannah knew exactly why Dirk hadn't called out to her or caught up with her yet. And she grinned, confident of what was coming next.

And she was right.

When Tiffany reached the front of the house and was standing in the foyer, demanding that more blood be added to the Grim Reaper's scythe blade, Dirk walked up to her, his open badge in his hand.

He stuck it under her nose and said quietly but firmly, "Ms. Dante, I'm Detective Sergeant Dirk Coulter, and I need you to come with me right now."

"What? You're kidding, right?"

"Not one bit, Ms. Dante. I am very, very serious. Come along now."

"What? Wh-where?" she sputtered, indignant, incredulous.

"The police station. You and I have to talk right now."

He gave a quick glance down the hallway, and Savannah knew he was keeping a lookout for Andrew Dante.

Tiffany was no longer a minor, so Dirk could take her in and question her without her parent being present. But Andrew was, undoubtedly, more legally savvy than his daughter, and Dirk didn't need anybody reminding Tiffy about the folly of speaking to law enforcement without legal counsel present.

"What the hell is this?" Tiffany shouted. "Are you telling me that you're arresting me? You're arresting *me!*"

A hush fell over the busy household as those whose job it was to spread artificial murder and mayhem stopped to watch the exchange.

"No, you aren't under arrest," Dirk told her, keeping his voice low as he reached over and grabbed her upper arm. "But you are going to have to come with me to the station. I have to ask you some questions."

"To hell with your questions." She jerked her arm away from him. "Just in case you're blind or stupid, I'm getting ready for a party here, and I do not have time to mess with you or any idiot questions about—"

Dirk grabbed her again, apparently much more firmly than before, because she winced and cried out. "You don't understand," he told her, his voice still low but deadly serious. "You have no choice, Ms. Dante. You can come down to the station right now voluntarily, or you can come involuntarily. But either way, you're coming. This isn't open for discussion."

Five seconds later, he had her across the foyer and out the front door. Half his size, she dangled from his hand like a limp chicken. Savannah followed close behind, trying to hide her amusement while keeping watch for any angry fathers who might come charging to the rescue.

The workers they passed on the way to Dirk's Buick didn't bother to hide their delight. Most snickered, and a few guffawed outright to see the princess of the castle removed so ignominiously.

However, one more chivalrous fellow stepped forward and blocked the walkway. "Hey, what's going on here?" he asked. "Miss Dante, are you all right?"

Before she could answer him, Dirk flashed his badge. "She's fine. Step aside," he told the guy, who promptly did as he was told.

When they arrived at Dirk's old Buick, a new look of horror crossed Tiffany's face. "Are you *nuts?*" she shouted. "There is *no way* that I'm going to get into that rust heap. I wouldn't be caught *dead* in a car like that!"

Savannah decided to help a bit. She stepped forward and leaned her head close to Tiffy's. "Sh-h-h," she said. "He's very sensitive about his ride."

Tiffy gave him a quick sideways look. He nodded and said, "Very. Very sensitive. Watch it."

Savannah added, "He could call for a radio car, and it would be here in maybe two minutes."

"What's a radio car?" Tiffy wanted to know.

"A real, honest-to-goodness cop car," Savannah said, "with a cage in the back and everything. Just think about how that would look on the front of the *True Informer* if we run into any paparazzi."

Without another word, Tiffy allowed Dirk to deposit her in the back of the car. And no sooner were Savannah and Dirk in the front seat than Savannah's warning seemed to materialize out of thin air.

A car pulled up near the Buick, and a woman with a large camera in her hand jumped out and ran toward them.

"Oh my God!" Tiffany yelled, ducking her head and trying to cover her face with her long hair. "It's Anna Petroski! She's always stalking me! And if she gets a shot of me in this junk heap, I'll never live it down!"

"So duck, dummy!" Savannah reached back, grabbed her by the shoulder, and shoved her down onto the seat. "Dirk, let's make some tracks outta here. Get a move on."

Dirk sped away, leaving the frustrated photographer standing in the middle of the street, a tired, grumpy look on her face.

"Oh my God!" was the plea again from the backseat. "Oh, like, just gag me! What *is* all this? Oh, this is just so . . . so . . . gro-o-o-os!"

Savannah laughed—she couldn't help herself—and turned to Dirk. "See, it's not just me. I keep telling you, once in a while you've just gotta clean out the garbage back there. All those disgusting taco and hamburger wrappers, the empty chicken buckets, the greasy pizza boxes—it's a friggen health hazard."

"There is some really nasty junk back here. It's like, blue and green! I think I'm gonna puke!" came another plaintive cry from the rear. "Can I get up yet? Is she gone yet?"

Savannah glanced around. The reporter was far out of sight; they had the road all to themselves.

She looked over at Dirk and gave him a wink. "Naw," she said. "She's right behind us. You'd best stay down there a while."

Chapter 9

As Dirk drove Tiffany Dante to the station house, it occurred to Savannah that this was a golden moment, possibly the only opportunity they would have to question her without benefit of an attorney. Fortunately, Tiffy didn't have a cell phone on her, and therefore, she couldn't be reached by her father. No doubt, by now, someone had told him that his daughter had been nabbed by the cops. And just as predictably, there would be an attorney en route to the station.

"It's going to take us a while to get to the police station," Savannah said over her shoulder to Tiffany. "Are you okay back there now?"

"Of course, I'm not okay!" was the angry reply. "I'm going to sue you both for . . . for kidnapping and police brutality and . . . and . . . .my dad is not going to stand for you doing this to me. He knows the mayor! He knows people on the City Council! You are in so much trouble, you . . ."

And on and on it went.

Below the dash, Savannah made a squiggly round and round motion with her forefinger so that Dirk could see it and Tiffy, who was now sitting upright, could not.

He looked confused for a moment, then grinned and nodded ever so slightly. At the next intersection, he turned from the direct route they were on and took a detour along the foothills.

Yes, it would take a long time to get to the police station.

Savannah turned in her seat and looked at their furious passenger. She was sitting sideways, her legs and feet on Dirk's backseat, as far as possible from the landfill that was his floorboard.

She really couldn't blame the girl. But safety first.

"Turn around and put your seat belt on," she told her.

"No."

"Yes. Or I'll have him stop the car, and I'll come back there and put it on for you. Tight."

Tiffy didn't budge.

"I mean it. *Really, really* tight."

Shooting death rays from her eyes, Tiffy complied.

"Thank you," Savannah said. Then she decided to dive right in. "The reason why you were picked up . . . it's quite simple. We just need to know a couple of things."

"Then why didn't you ask me back there at my house?" Tiffy said, tossing her hair back over her shoulder and rolling her eyes. "I told you, I have a party to put together. The biggest Halloween party ever in this stupid little town. Even *Entertainment Tonight* and *Inside Edition* are going to be there."

"Yes," Savannah replied evenly, "but your friend is missing, and for all we know, she may be dead. So unless you want to look like a coldhearted, totally selfish brat, you'll give us a few minutes of your precious time. Right?"

Tiffy replied with more deadly glowering.

Savannah returned the stare and said, "After all, what those tabloids say about you being shallow and stupid and spoiled, it isn't true. They just tell those lies to sell papers. You have feelings like anybody else, right?"

To Savannah's surprise, Tiffany Dante's eyes instantly filled with tears. Ah, so she *did* care what people thought of her. That was a plus.

"And you won't mind just answering a couple of quick questions if it might help bring your friend home, maybe even save her life, huh?" Savannah continued when there was no reply.

Finally, Tiffany said, "What do you want to know?"

Savannah leaned a little further over the seat and said, "We need to know why you drove Daisy's Honda to Canyon Park the other day and left it there."

Bingo.

Tiffy was a pretty good poker player, but Savannah caught the slight widening of the eyes, the small intake of breath.

"I didn't drive Daisy's rust heap anywhere," she said, messing with her hair again. "I wouldn't touch that horrible car, let alone drive it."

"You didn't? You weren't in it?"

"No! I was *not!* That's what I said. I said I wouldn't touch it. You'd have to *touch* it to get *in* it, now wouldn't you? Duh."

"Yes, you would," Savannah said. "You definitely would. And you're saying that you've never, even once, long ago, been inside Daisy's Honda."

Tiffy gave her a condescending look. "Boy, for some sort of investigator, you aren't very sharp, are you? I said, 'No.' No. No. No."

Savannah smiled. "Well, it just so happens that you aren't as smart as you think you are either. Because in spite of the fact that you gave it a good wipe down, you missed a print. You left your fingerprint, Tiff. Clear as day."

"I did not! I mean . . . I couldn't have. I wasn't in it."

Raising one eyebrow, Savannah turned to Dirk and said, "So, now we know two very valuable bits of information. Tiff here drove the car and—"

"Do not call me 'Tiff.' Nobody calls me that! Nobody!"

"And we know that she wiped the car down thoroughly or had somebody do it," Savannah continued, ". . . and now she's lying about it. So that means she was up to something unsavory."

Dirk nodded solemnly and studied his backseat passenger in his rearview mirror. "Yep. Unsavory. No doubt about it."

"And that means she's involved in this disappearance. Probably even totally responsible for it," Savannah continued.

"Do *not* talk about me like I'm not even fricken here!" Tiffany interjected. "I will *not* be ignored!"

Savannah turned back to her. "For someone who's the number one suspect in a kidnapping, maybe even a murder, you've got a lot of petty rules, young lady. If I were you, I'd ditch the attitude and get real here. Otherwise, this guy sitting beside me is going to be the one questioning you in a six by eight–foot interrogation room with no windows and no air conditioning. And we'll see how you like that!"

"Yeah," Dirk said, "and I'm not even half as nice as she is."

"Now," Savannah continued, "if you don't want to miss that party of yours altogether, not to mention having the press feast on this juicy story about your missing Skeleton Key girlfriend, you had better start telling the truth. You were in the car. You drove it there, and you got into another car and drove away.

Was Daisy with you at that point, or had you already gotten rid of her?"

"Gotten *rid* of her? You mean, like *killed* her? You think I *murdered* my friend? You're crazy. I'm not talking to you anymore."

Savannah reached across the back of the seat, grabbed a handful of her silk mesh top, and pulled her forward. "If you think that you can hurt Daisy and get away with it, *you* are the one who's crazy, little girl. She's got a mother who's going out of her mind, worrying about her daughter. If you know where Daisy is and what's happened to her or if you've hurt her in any way, God help you. Because I will personally take you apart piece by piece. I don't care if your father is the King of Siam. You got me?"

She knew she had struck home when Tiffany turned a sickly shade of pale and began to shiver just a little. "I don't know where she is," she said. "Or what's happened to her. Honest. I saw her the other day when she dropped by to go over her lines with us. But we were busy planning this party, and I told her to get lost. She seemed a little bummed about it, like her feelings were hurt or whatever. And she left. That's all."

"How did your fingerprint get in her car, and how did the car wind up in Canyon Park?"

"I don't know how it got there. Honest, I don't. And my fingerprint . . . I don't know. Maybe I did drive it once, a long time ago, and I just forgot. Yeah. I think I *did* drive it one night about a month ago when we went out partying and Daisy drank too much. I drove her home. Yeah. I remember now. That's what happened."

"Bull," Savannah told her. "You're lying. You know it, and so do we. You've got a lot of explaining to do."

"I'm not saying any more. Aren't you supposed to let me call a lawyer or something?"

"That's if you're under arrest. You aren't."

"So I could leave if I wanted to, right? I could get out of this car right now, and you couldn't stop me."

"I'm going forty-five miles an hour," Dirk told her. "I certainly wouldn't advise it."

"But what about a lawyer? I want my dad to call me a lawyer. I don't want to talk to you two anymore. You think I did something awful. You think I'm a terrible person. I don't like you."

Tears began to flow, and she looked like a petulant kindergartner.

Savannah didn't buy it. "Sure, you can have a lawyer present when you're questioned," she said. "And you're sure going to need a good one because we're going to nail you with murder. If you think the tabloids gave you a hard time when the cops busted that sex–drug party of yours last year, wait until they get a load of *this!*"

"I didn't kill anybody!"

"Then tell me why you dumped that car there at the park."

Tiffany crossed her arms over her chest and sat there, "snorting like a bullfrog on a hot sidewalk," as Gran would say. Finally, she said, "Look. Daisy's fine. Nothing bad has happened to Daisy, okay?"

"No. Not okay. Not without more details, that is not okay. Where is she?"

"I don't know. But I'm sure she's all right."

"Did she tell you she was going somewhere?"

"No. But she needed to."

"What is that supposed to mean? Why did she need to go somewhere?"

"Because she was irritating everybody around her. She was so full of herself, getting that stupid little part for TV. And it was just so wrong that she got it. She's nothing. She's stupid and ugly and fat! Maybe she went away to a fat farm to get rid of some of that

ugly blubber she was carrying around. She was a disgusting pig, and if she's gone for a while, good. I didn't
want her at my party anyway. She would have ruined
it, somebody like her showing up and saying she was
a friend of mine."

Suddenly, Tiffany seemed to realize she had said
more than she intended. She leaned far back in her
seat and lowered her head until her hair fell over
her eyes. "That's it," she said. "I'm not saying another word until I get a lawyer."

Okay, Savannah thought. *Go ahead and clam up if
you want. I got what I wanted out of you anyway.*

Besides, they were pulling up to the front of the
San Carmelita Police Station, and she recognized
the bald guy sitting in front of the station in a Mer-
cedes that Tammy would have described as "honkin'
big." It was Phillip Neilson, one of the area's most
prominent defense attorneys. He had spotted them,
too, and he was getting out of his car and coming toward them with a no-nonsense look on his face and
an unmistakable determination to his stride.

A Knight of Swords in a pin-striped suit, coming
to rescue the nobleman's daughter.

And neither Savannah nor Dirk needed him to
stick his head into the Buick and say it. They knew—
the Tiffany Dante interview was over.

When Savannah returned home, she found
Tammy at the rolltop desk in the corner of the living
room, working at the computer, as usual. And
Granny Reid was sitting in Savannah's big rose chintz
chair, talking on the house phone.

Gran looked annoyed, and Savannah knew the
look all too well. Gran was talking to one of the more
bothersome of the nine siblings.

Savannah's guess was Vidalia, the one with not

one but two sets of twins. She and her long-suffering husband, Butch, were frequently on the outs.

Though it could be Marietta, who was now between husbands and never at her best when single. Looking for Hubby Number Four in all the wrong places could be a nerve-wracking task.

She shot Tammy a questioning look. Tammy replied with an eyeball roll and a head shake.

" 'Lanta," Gran said, "this little conversation of ours is over, darlin'. The day's just never gonna dawn that I shell out a thousand dollars for a pair of cowboy boots. Land's sakes, girl! That's more than I used to spend all year on clothes for all nine of you young'uns when y'all were growin' up. I've got groceries to buy and property taxes to pay."

Ah, Atlanta, Savannah said to herself. The youngest one, the perpetual teenager who was now well into her twenties. The last chickie who kept returning to the nest.

Every one of them but Savannah kept trying to sneak back in from time to time, demanding room and board from their softhearted, octogenarian grandmother.

But Gran had gotten better and better at booting them back out.

At the moment, Atlanta was in Nashville, chasing the dream of being a country singing star. And having convinced Gran a few months ago that a rhinestone-studded denim jacket with jeans to match was a wise business investment, she was apparently after another installment.

" 'Lanta, honey, I can feel my blood pressure risin' now, so I'm gonna tell you good-bye. If you've just gotta have those fancy boots, then I suggest you go out and earn the thousand dollars yourself. Then you'll just appreciate them so much more. Bye-bye, sugar. I love you."

Gran looked quite sad for a moment, then she said, "Well, I'm sorry that you don't feel all that lovin' toward me right now. But what I said stands. So you can just get happy in the same britches you got unhappy in. Bye."

She hung up the phone and sighed, for a moment looking her age.

Savannah felt her temper flare. How dare that spoiled brat Atlanta!

"I'm sorry, Gran," she said. "She's got a lot of nerve asking you for something she knows you can't afford."

"Oh, I reckon I could afford it. I could go without a few things and . . ."

"You've gone without long enough. Don't even think about it. She doesn't need thousand-dollar boots."

"Well, she says she does. Says it's for an audition she's got next week. Could lead to her getting some more backup singer jobs in the recording studios there in Nashville."

"Since when do backup singers have to wear thousand-dollar boots? That's the stupidest thing I've heard today." She thought back on her interview with Tiffy Dante. "And that's saying something."

"Did Dirko get anything out of Tiffany?" Tammy said. "Did he squeeze her? Put her in the hot seat?"

"No. We were debating between the rack and the iron maiden on the way to the station house. But her attorney was waiting for her when we got there. So even the Chinese water torture was a no-go."

"Darn. I hate it when that happens." Tammy grinned. She motioned for Savannah to come over to the desk. "But maybe after you see what I've got for you here, you'll feel a little better."

Savannah glanced over at Granny, who was thumbing through her Bible, looking peaceful enough. But Savannah detected a trace of sadness remaining on her face.

She debated which of her two tasks at hand to deal with first.

"Want a glass of lemonade, Gran?" she asked.

"No, thank you, sweetie. I'm fine," came the less than perfectly fine reply.

Savannah said to Tammy, "Let me go upstairs to the little girls' room and powder my nose. Then I'd be very happy to see what you have there."

She took her purse with her and once behind the closed bathroom door, Savannah dialed her sister Atlanta's number.

When the youngest Reid kid answered, she was crying.

" 'Lanta, what the hell's the matter with you?" Savannah snapped.

"I'm . . . I'm . . . I'm very upset!" was the whiny reply.

"Well, get over it. Right now! 'Cause you upset Gran, gettin' all huffy with her over those danged boots, and you're going to call her right now and apologize to her and tell her you love her."

"I am not. Gran's the one who got pissy with me, telling me to get happy in my britches."

"Atlanta Reid, don't you ever use Gran's name and a cuss word in the same sentence!"

"Cuss word? What cuss word?"

"You know what word: *pissy*. I tell you, I won't abide this kind of disrespect toward Granny. Now you call her and apologize for even asking her for such a big, expensive, ridiculous thing. And, while you're at it, tell her you're sorry for your crappy tone—don't use the word crappy—and you be sure to tell her you love her. I mean it, Atlanta! You make it right with her, or I swear, I'll land on you like a duck on a June bug."

Savannah hung up, and sure enough, less than a minute later, she heard the downstairs phone ring. Smiling, she took her time, washed her hands, brushed her hair, and eventually strolled back downstairs.

"Ah," she said. "Much better. Trying to get Dirk to stop at a service station . . . forget about it."

She glanced over at her grandmother, who was off the phone, still sitting in the rose chair. But she had a smirk on her face. "Your sister just called back," she told Savannah.

"Oh? Did she forget to ask for a thousand-dollar cowboy hat to go with the boots?"

"No-o-o. She was calling to apologize to me for the other call. Imagine that." She chuckled as she gave Savannah another little sly grin. "She buttered me up like a hot breakfast biscuit. She even told me she loves me."

"Good. I'm sure she does."

"She said something else, too, just before she hung up."

"What's that?"

"She said, 'Tell my big, bossy sister that she can kiss my . . . um . . . foot.'"

Savannah laughed. "Well, as long as she said, 'foot.'"

"I told her she shouldn't call you that."

"Why not? I'm big, and I'm bossy. Never claimed to be anything else." Savannah walked over to the desk and pulled up a chair beside Tammy. "So, kiddo, show me what you've got there."

"I have Daisy's phone records for this past month."

"Including right before she went missing?"

"Absolutely."

"Good girl!"

Tammy brought the appropriate screen up on the

computer's monitor and began to show Savannah the most pertinent calls.

"She talks to her mother a lot," Tammy said. "And her mom calls her frequently, too. They don't talk long, just two or three minutes."

"Just touching base."

"Exactly." Tammy pointed to the screen. "This number is the Dante house. Daisy calls there pretty often, too. They never call her."

"Why doesn't that surprise me?"

"This is Tiffy's cell phone number. Daisy calls it at least once a day. Tiffany doesn't call her. Although the afternoon that Daisy went missing, she called Tiffany once . . . here . . . at 3:39. And then Tiffany called her back an hour later."

Savannah squinted at the screen. "Actually, Tiffy called her three times that afternoon—at 4:30, 5:03 and 5:15. That seems a little odd—a flurry like that from somebody who ordinarily never bothers to call."

"Look," Tammy said, pointing to another number. "Daisy called Tiffany again at 4:59."

"Those calls were flying back and forth pretty fast and furious for a while there."

"And that's exactly when you figure she went missing."

"That's right," Savannah said. "Pam told us that Daisy left the house about four to go to the Dante estate. And after I twisted their arms a little, Tiffy and company admitted she came by for a little while, supposedly to have them help her with her lines for the sitcom taping."

"Which they say they refused to do."

"Yes. They say she dropped by, but they told her to get lost and she left. Supposedly."

Tammy tapped her fingertip on the screen. "Well,

it looks like maybe she *did* leave. It wouldn't make much sense for Daisy to be calling Tiffy and vice versa if Daisy was at the estate."

Savannah mulled over the possibilities in her mind. "So, why the calls back and forth?"

"They were arguing? Fighting about something. Maybe one hung up on the other or . . . ?"

Gran stirred in Savannah's chair. "Or maybe they were meeting somewhere. When I go home after I visit you here, Waycross picks me up at the airport, and if it weren't for our cell phones, I don't know how we'd ever find each other. You call back and forth like that sometimes when you're trying to find each other."

Savannah considered that one for a while. "You might be right, Gran. Like if they were both driving around, trying to meet up somewhere?"

Tammy nodded. "Maybe they did meet somewhere. And took a drive in Daisy's car."

"With Tiffany at the wheel? Why would that happen?" Savannah said. "Or maybe they met somewhere, and after Tiffany did whatever she did to her, she decided to move the car to another location . . . to the park where we found it."

"I don't like the sound of that," Gran said.

"Me, either," Tammy added.

Savannah shook her head, trying to imagine how a tiny, petite woman like Tiffany could have controlled the big, stout Daisy.

"Good work, Tam. Can you print that out for me, and one for Dirk, too?"

"Sure."

"And one more thing . . ."

"What's that?"

Savannah didn't even want to say the words. Certainly didn't want to picture the scenario in her mind. But . . .

"Find out if the Dante family has any gun permits."

Tammy gave her a startled look. "Wow," she said softly, "okay."

"Thanks." Savannah glanced at her watch. "Now, if you ladies will excuse me, I have to go call a worried mom and tell her that we still have no idea where her daughter is."

Chapter 10

Over a dinner of chicken and dumplings, Savannah, Dirk, Tammy, and Gran tried to have a normal conversation. But try as they might, the topics kept changing from the weather, the beaches, the fine art of kite flying to the missing girl.

Savannah couldn't help noticing that Dirk was all but gulping down his meal—unheard of for him. He was far more of a savor every bite kind of guy, which was the main reason why she liked feeding him.

But she had to admit that she didn't have much of an appetite. She found herself wondering if Pam was eating, trying to take care of herself and keep her strength up. She hadn't sounded so good earlier on the phone.

Also, Savannah couldn't help wondering if Daisy was eating dinner somewhere . . . anywhere. Would Daisy O'Neil ever eat at her mother's table again?

"What's the matter, puddin'?" Gran whispered, leaning over and laying her hand on Savannah's forearm. "You're worrying yourself sick about that girl, aren't you?"

Savannah laid down her fork. "Well, not exactly

sick yet, but I'm concerned." She looked across the table at Dirk, who had abruptly stopped an argument with Tammy to listen in. "We're all pretty worried about her," she added.

"In fact," Dirk added, "as soon as I'm done here, I'm going back to the Dante place."

"You'll be shot," Savannah told him. "Tammy checked. They've got everything from deer hunting rifles to antique dueling pistols over there. And now that Dante knows what you did to his little darlin'—"

"You mean, what *we* did."

Savannah shrugged. "Okay, what *we* did . . . he'll probably slap a lawsuit on you."

"Or just plain slap you with a glove or something," Gran added, "and challenge you to a duel with those old pistols of his."

Dirk gave her a borderline flirty grin. "I think you hotbloods down there in Georgia go in for that dueling stuff a little more than we do here in Southern California. But if I see him getting out a pair of white leather gloves, I'll duck."

"You'd better," Gran told him. "That name Dante sounds Frenchish. He could be part Creole, and then you'd have real problems on your hands."

"Thank you, Mrs. Reid. I'll certainly keep that in mind," Dirk told her.

His cell phone went off and after listening to his caller for only a few seconds, he jumped up from the table and ran to the living room.

"What's the matter?" Savannah hurried after him.

He rushed to the TV and turned it on, then hung up his phone. He grabbed the remote and turned to the local news.

"Oh, no!" Savannah said as she saw footage of herself and Dirk escorting Tiffany Dante down the walkway of her father's mansion to Dirk's Buick. "Who took that?"

"It's fuzzy, not a very good picture," Dirk said, watching himself drag the unhappy heiress along against her will. "Looks like maybe somebody shot it with a cell phone camera."

"Unfortunately, the picture isn't fuzzy enough. Look at that." Savannah groaned as the Dirk on the screen shoved Tiffany into the backseat of his car. "If Andrew wants to sue you, that film would certainly help his case."

"Let him sue me," Dirk said. "She's obviously resisting there. Sh-h-h, what are they saying?"

"Socialite Tiffany Dante was taken into custody today by a deputy of the San Carmelita Police Department . . ." the reporter was saying.

"Deputy?" Dirk was incensed. "I'm a detective sergeant, you big-haired bimbo! Get it right!"

"She was questioned by the deputy in connection with the disappearance of one of her closest friends, Daisy O'Neil, a member of Tiffany's exclusive Skeleton Key Club."

"How about a picture of the missing girl instead of that idiot bimbo?" Savannah said. Then to Dirk, she said, "Didn't you guys get a picture to them of Daisy? I gave you the one her mother—"

"Yes. I gave it to Shelly. She scanned it in and sent it to the LA stations and asked them to cover the story."

"Well, looks like they are all over it," she replied sarcastically.

Tammy and Gran joined them, and all four watched the footage of Savannah, Dirk, and their captive making their getaway, Buick tires squealing.

Dirk cleared his throat. "Um . . . did I really peel out like that? Hm-m-m."

"Video doesn't lie," Savannah said. "Jurors just love videotape."

"Oh, shut up." Dirk headed for the front door.

"Where are you going?" she asked him.

"To the Dantes'. I'm going to wave Tammy's phone records under their noses and scare the sh—" He looked over at Gran. "—the crap out of them."

He disappeared out the door.

After a couple of profoundly silent seconds, Tammy said, "It might take a little more than a telephone bill to terrify Andrew Dante."

"True," Savannah replied. "So true. I'll go with him."

When Savannah and Dirk pulled up in front of the Dante estate, they had to fight their way through a crowd of paparazzi that made the Pasadena Rose Parade look poorly attended.

And they realized it was a mistake to be arriving in Dirk's Buick, which was now a celebrity in its own right. The moment the camera-toting professional stalkers spotted them, they were swarmed.

But neither Savannah nor Dirk had a problem with the press.

"Get the hell out of my face, or I'll arrest every one of you for obstruction of justice!" Dirk roared, holding his badge above his head.

A tiny bubble of camera-free space appeared around him. But twice as many tightened around Savannah until she thought she was going to suffocate.

After sleeping with at least three or four siblings at a time growing up, she had developed a bit of claustrophobia. And finding herself besieged by shouting people, her eyes blinded by their flashes, the phobia exploded inside her.

"Get off me!" she yelled. "The next person who touches me gets clobbered. Back off! I mean it!"

To her surprise, they actually complied, and miraculously, a narrow path opened between them and the house. Dirk plowed through the crowd like an offensive lineman, with Savannah following in his wake.

This is one of those moments for the mental scrapbook, Savannah thought as she worked her way through the bizarre scene of photographers, coffins, dismembered bodies, and monsters, all illuminated by the surreal flashes of their cameras.

"Are you here to arrest Tiffany Dante?" one reporter shouted.

"Did she murder Daisy O'Neil?" another cried out, a note of hysteria in her voice.

"Nobody's dead that we know of," Dirk yelled. "Just settle down. There's nothing to report here. Really."

"Sheezzz," Savannah added, "don't you people have homes to go to?"

When they reached the front door, fortunately, it was ajar, so they darted inside and closed it behind them.

"Holy cow," Savannah said, checking herself to make sure she still had everything she'd come with: a full set of clothing, all of her limbs, her purse, her Beretta in its holster beneath her jacket. "If Tiffy has to run gauntlets like *that* all the time, maybe it *isn't* much fun being her."

They glanced around, but the only one in sight was the Grim Reaper with his newly bloodied scythe. At least, he was the only one who was still intact. A few headless corpses were propped against one wall, and someone had tossed some dismembered body parts around Grim's bony feet.

"A nice touch," Savannah said.

For once, it was Dirk who decided to be a bit cautious. "I don't think we should just go walking around in here," he said, "until we see somebody and get invited, or at least tolerated. Dante's gotta be really pissed. I don't want to give him any good reasons for those lawsuits he's talking about with his attorneys."

"No kidding." Savannah listened, but the house seemed strangely quiet without all of the chaos that had been swirling through it only a few hours before. Apparently, the Murder and Mayhem Crew had gone home, and only the inhabitants of the house remained . . . along with their ghoulish rubber and plaster "visitors."

"Can you imagine sleeping in a house with all this mess tonight?" she said, looking around and shuddering.

"Not really. I actually avoid sleeping in the middle of gory crime scenes. And to think of the money that must have been paid for all this."

"More than you can imagine," said a quiet female voice behind them.

They turned to see Robyn Dante coming out of the great room, a sad but resigned look on her pretty face. She was wearing loose gauzy pants and a simple crocheted top, the picture of delicate feminine beauty.

"None of Tiffy's parties are cheap," she said as she walked over to them. She looked up at the Grim Reaper, who was more than a foot taller than she was, and shuddered.

"It's amazing," she continued, "how much you can pay for tasteless garbage. But that's what my stepdaughter loves . . . demands. Expensive, tasteless garbage."

Savannah was a bit surprised that she would say anything so blatantly critical of Tiffany. That sort of talk couldn't go over well around Daddy Dante.

"You're the ones who took Tiffany out of here today," she said, looking them up and down. "I saw your story on TV." A small grin lit up her tiny face, and her blue eyes sparkled with mischief. "Andrew's not going to be happy about this when he gets home."

"Gets home?" Dirk said, a bit of relief in his voice.

"He left tonight for London . . . a business trip."

Savannah resisted the urge to dance an Irish jig. This was good news, no matter how it was told. 'No Andrew' might mean better access to the Dante mansion and the people in it.

Especially if they were on the good side of the mistress of the manse.

Moving a few steps closer to Robyn, Savannah glanced around and said softly, "It couldn't be much fun for you having to deal with . . . well . . . all of this."

"You have no idea. You marry for better or for worse, but when you're saying those words, you think it's your mate's better and worst. You don't count on his family's worst."

"That's true, very true. And you two haven't been married that long, right?"

"We'll be celebrating our second anniversary on New Year's Eve."

Savannah looked into Robyn's big blue eyes and saw some doubt there. Apparently, Mrs. Dante wasn't that sure she'd even make it to the end of her second year.

"I hear you were his travel agent," Savannah said.

"Yes." For a moment, the young woman smiled a sweet, reminiscent smile. "I was working for World Travel International, and he walked in and . . ." Her smile disappeared. "And the rest, as they say, is history. It was splashed all over the tabloids how I took him away from his wife, Tiffy's mom. They didn't bother to report that she had left him and had been living in Switzerland with a lover for two years before I ever met him."

"Well, that's not as juicy," Dirk said. "Wouldn't sell as many papers."

"That's right." Robyn looked grateful for a sympathetic ear. "And the truth doesn't play as well for Tiffy, either. It's to her advantage to think of me as the evil stepmother who tore her family apart."

"I can imagine," Savannah said.

"Andrew's a sucker for guilt where she's concerned," Robyn continued. "He's always spent a fortune on her, but now . . . it's crazy how she works on him."

"Like this party?" Dirk said, waving a hand to indicate the room and all its gruesome props.

"Oh, this party is only one of many, many of her extravagances. And it isn't just the material stuff. It's what he lets her get away with. She's wild! She does exactly what she wants, with whom she wants, to whom she wants. She has no accountability whatsoever."

"Which brings me to why we're here," Dirk interjected. "We still haven't found Daisy O'Neil, and we have concrete evidence that Tiffany was involved in her disappearance."

Robyn didn't look surprised. "I figured that's why you came and got her today. I assume you had a good reason for wanting to question her."

"We did."

"And I'm equally sure that she never would have gone with you without you forcing her to," she added.

"We're committed to finding Daisy O'Neil," Dirk said "No matter what we have to do."

"Good. She's a sweet kid. I hope you do."

Savannah glanced around again and asked, "Is Tiffany here?"

"She's out back by the pool, inspecting the new cemetery we have back there now." She sighed. "It's just lovely."

"I'll bet it is." Savannah pushed aside the mental images of "bodies" floating in the pool. "And how about the other Key girls? Are they here, too?"

"Oh, they've been here all day, helping her ... which means waiting on her hand and foot. Those girls are nothing but slaves to Tiffany. She uses them terribly. Uses us all, for that matter."

Savannah turned to Dirk. "I'd love to have a few minutes alone with Bunny or Kiki, if that's possible."

"I could probably arrange that," Robyn said. "Which one would you like to talk to first?"

Carefully, Savannah considered her answer. Bunny, the cocky, self-assured brunette who was obviously trying to be a Tiffy clone? Or Kiki, the black-haired, exotic beauty with the haunted almond eyes?

"Kiki," she said. "I'd love to have some one-on-one time with Kiki."

Robyn crooked a finger, beckoning them to follow her, and led them to the rear of the house and the kitchen. "Go in there," she told Savannah, motioning to the glassed-in breakfast nook. "I'll see if I can get her to join you."

Turning to Dirk, Robyn said, "And how can I help *you*?"

Dirk smiled a nasty little smile. "Oh, I want to talk to Miss Tiff again. And since Mr. Dante isn't at home, all I need is your permission to be here on the property."

Robyn laughed an equally nasty little laugh. "Oh, you have my permission to stay as long as you want." She waved an arm wide. "Search if you want. Search everything and anything. In fact, I believe that Tiffany's bedroom, the one with the bright pink door on the second floor, is *my* property."

"I like how you think," Dirk told her.

"Go for it. As far as I'm concerned, you can search her lingerie drawers if you want."

"Well, I don't think that'll be necessary," he said, "but it's nice to have your blessing. In fact, maybe I'll put off talking to Tiffany for a little while."

"How long do you figure it'll take you to toss her room?" Savannah asked.

But Dirk was already on his way upstairs.

Not a lot of opportunities passed by Detective Sergeant Dirk Coulter. He was a grab the moment sort of guy.

"Go," Robyn said. "Sit down in there behind that big fern so they won't see you from the pool. I'll see if I can get her to come in alone."

Savannah did as she was told. She went into the breakfast nook and took a seat at the table behind a giant fern, making sure she was well-hidden from anyone outside.

Robyn left her, and Savannah could hear her shout from the back door, "Kiki! Ki-ki! Could you come help me a minute?"

"She can't. She's busy helping me!" came the indignant reply.

"Just for a minute," Robyn said. "The workers left some boxes here in the kitchen, and I need somebody to help me move them so that I can make myself some dinner."

Savannah smiled. Robyn was no dummy. With the threat of physical labor looming on the horizon, what were the chances that Tiffy herself would come rather than sending one of her flunkies?

A few minutes later, she heard Kiki come inside and say, "Okay, where are they?"

"The boxes? Yeah . . . well, come in here with me."

When Kiki entered the breakfast nook and saw Savannah, she looked startled and not at all happy she was there.

She whirled around to Robyn, who was behind her, and said, "What is this? What is *she* doing here?"

"She just got here and asked to speak to you for a moment. I'm sure you'd like to help her find Daisy."

"So there aren't any boxes to move?"

Robyn shrugged. "Oh, I can move those myself. You go ahead and talk to Ms. Reid." She gave the girl a long, hard look. "After all," she added, "it's the very least you can do for your friend, right?"

Kiki looked back at Savannah, a look of pure misery in her beautiful almond eyes. "Sure," she said with absolutely no enthusiasm whatsoever. "Why not?"

Chapter 11

Ten minutes later, Savannah realized that, even though Kiki gave the appearance of at least pretending to cooperate, she was no more informative than her friend Tiffany.

"So, you're saying that you didn't even see Daisy at all on Tuesday, the day she went missing."

The girl sat across the table from Savannah, staring down at her hands, which were demurely folded in her lap. Her long black hair hung like a dark privacy curtain around her, concealing much of her beautiful face.

"That's right," she said softly. "I didn't see her. I wasn't here."

"Where were you?"

"When?"

"All day but specifically, Tuesday afternoon, say between five and six."

"I was driving around, doing some errands for Tiffany."

"What kind of errands?"

Kiki shrugged. "Oh, I dropped some clothes at the cleaners for her, and I picked up her party costume from the seamstress in Twin Oaks and stuff like that."

"Then why did other people tell me that they saw you here Tuesday afternoon?"

"Who said that? Who told you that?"

Savannah decided not to cause Robyn any trouble since she had become her newest best friend. "It doesn't matter who. But you *were* here. So why are you lying to me about it?"

To Savannah's surprise, the girl burst into tears and covered her face with both of her hands, sobbing into them.

Quickly, Savannah rose from her chair and knelt beside Kiki. She put her hands on her shoulders, forcing her to face her. "Kiki, honey," she said in her most comforting, maternal voice, "I don't want to upset you. I want to help you. Please talk to me."

Instead of replying, the girl continued to cry, her face covered.

"You know what happened to Daisy, and I think you feel really, really bad about it. If you tell me what happened, I can help you get through this awful thing. Really, I can."

"I can't," was the muffled, tearful response. "I can't tell you anything. Please don't ask me."

Savannah reached up and gently pulled Kiki's hands from her face. "Look at me, sugar. And listen to me. Whatever it is, I'll just bet that you're not the one responsible for it. Someone else is, and we know who. We already know that it's Tiffany."

Kiki's eyes widened, and she gasped. "You do?"

"Yes. We have solid physical proof. We know most of it already. We just need you to fill in the blanks."

"Please, ask somebody else. Ask Tiffany or Bunny."

"We already questioned Tiffany. She told Detective Coulter that it was you and Bunny who did it."

Another gasp. "She did not!"

"She did. She didn't say exactly what was done to Daisy, but she implied very strongly that it was you two, not her, who did it."

Okay, so my tongue will turn black and fall out from lying, she thought. *The end justifies the means and all that. Not that Gran would agree with the fine points of my theology, but . . .*

"Tiffany said that Bunny and I did it?" Kiki was saying, her hair and her hands away from her eyes as she searched Savannah's face. "Are you kidding me? She said it was *us?*"

"Yes, but I didn't believe her for one minute. You seem to me like a much better person than she is. I knew that the other night when I first met all three of you. You aren't like her and Bunny. I could tell that you're genuinely upset by what happened to Daisy."

"I am! It isn't fair! It's an awful thing to do to somebody, and I don't care what Tiffy says—it's because she was jealous of Daisy over her getting that part on the TV show."

"I know it is. She's just jealous."

"She's like that. So spiteful! She'll pretend to be your friend, but if you cross her in any way, she gets back at you."

"Like she did Daisy."

Kiki nodded. "Yes. And even though she has everything, *everything,* if you get anything she wants, she hates you for it. And she'll find some way to punish you."

"Like she did Daisy."

"Yes. Like this thing with Daisy."

Savannah's heart was pounding so hard she could hardly hear what the girl was saying for the pulse throbbing in her ears. This was it. She had her right where she wanted her.

"It wasn't fair, what she did to Daisy," Savannah prompted her. "Daisy didn't deserve it."

"No, she didn't. I told Tiffy, 'That's not funny. It's no joke. It's an awful thing to do to somebody' but she said—"

"What's going on in here?"

They both jumped and turned around to see Tiffany standing in the doorway, her hands on her hips and Old Testament wrath on her face.

It was all Savannah could do not to swear and reach for something to smash . . . like Tiffany Dante.

So close, she thought. *Hell-fire and damnation! I was so close!*

"What are you doing in my home again?" she demanded of Savannah. And to Kiki, she said, "And what are you telling her? A bunch of stupid, filthy lies about me?"

Tiffany ran across the small room and grabbed Savannah's arms. "Get out of here!" she shouted as she pulled Savannah to her feet. "Get off my property this very minute! How dare you after what you did to me today! Kidnapping me! Dragging me out of my house like that! And in front of *cameras,* too! You made a fool out of me. Get out! Get out!"

She kept tugging, yanking, her nails digging into Savannah's hands and arms.

Savannah didn't budge. For her, it was like being attacked by a small, bothersome child.

The nails were getting a bit irritating, though.

Calmly, she said, "Take your hands off me this minute, or I swear, I will lay you out on this floor. And you won't be getting up without help. Do you understand me?"

Apparently, Tiffany did understand because she instantly released Savannah and stood there, huffing and puffing from the exertion.

Finally, she recovered her breath enough to yell, "This is my house! Get out of my house, or I'm going to call the cops on you!"

Savannah decided not to mention that there was already a cop on the premises, one who was upstairs, probably going through her closets at that very minute.

"Let's be accurate with our facts here," Savannah said. "Technically, this is not *your* house. It's your father's house and your stepmother's. And I have permission to be here, so—"

"You do not have my father's permission! No way he would let you in here. He's going to hate you when he finds out the things you did to me in that old car. As soon as his plane lands in London, he'll pick up his phone messages, and he's going to hear the awful, hateful things you accused me of. How you threatened me with physical violence and—"

"Whoa, whoa! Hold on there. What threats of physical violence?"

Tiffany stammered and sputtered for a moment, then flipped her hair back over her shoulder and said, "Well, you know, the seat belt thing."

Savannah laughed at her. "Oh, right. I did threaten to physically restrain you with a seat belt in a moving vehicle. I'll probably get the needle for that one."

"Well, you shouldn't have insulted me like that. My dad is going to sue your asses off the minute he gets back from London, or maybe even before. Nobody treats me the way you two did today and gets away with it. You just wait and see what happens to you!"

Tiffany turned on her friend, who was still sitting at the table, crying, her hands over her eyes. "And what were you telling her just now? You're just a filthy, ungrateful, rotten liar. That's what you are! If you were telling her lies about me, my dad's going to sue you, too. After all I've done for you, and you turn on me! You're going to get it, too."

Kiki didn't reply but continued to sob uncontrollably.

"Yeah, yeah, we'll see what horrible fate befalls those who dare to ruffle *your* feathers," Savannah said.

Her flippancy enraged Tiffany that much more. "I'm calling the cops. That's all there is to it," she said, spinning around and stomping back toward the kitchen.

But Robyn was standing in the doorway, blocking her. "They have my permission to be here," she said softly but firmly. "I invited them in."

Tiffany exploded. "Oh, you did, huh? Well, that just figures! My dad leaves, and what do you do? You—"

"Act like the mistress of my own home. Yes. I did." Robyn locked eyes with her stepdaughter, and it occurred to Savannah that maybe Robyn Dante wasn't the meek little mouse she appeared to be at first glance.

"And you," Robyn continued, "will settle down and answer this woman's questions about your missing friend or—"

"I will not! She—"

"Or leave this room. Now. Which is it going to be?" Robyn stepped to the left, clearing the doorway should Tiffany decide to make an exit.

But before Tiffany could make her move, they heard a scream—a loud, terrible scream—coming from near the pool.

And then another and another and another.

"Oh my God!" Robyn said. "What is that?"

Even Tiffany froze in her tirade.

Kiki stopped crying and jumped to her feet.

Savannah ran for the door that led to the patio, flung it open, and raced outside.

She had heard screams like that before. Quite a few times, in fact. And she knew a shriek like that meant one of two things: either somebody was dead, or someone was about to be.

Automatically, her hand went to her Beretta, but she didn't pull the weapon. She scanned the scene, trying to take in everything at once.

The kidney-shaped swimming pool, dyed blood-red like the fountain, was in front of her. The pool lights shining through the red liquid gave the whole scene a sinister, surreal crimson glow.

And surrounding the pool on all sides were more grotesque displays, like the ones in the front yard and the rest of the house: bodies, monsters, coffins, and assorted torture devices.

But the only moving figure was the one on the opposite side of the pool.

It was Bunny.

Dressed in a bright pink halter top and shorts, she was jumping up and down—indeed, like a rabbit—waving her arms wildly, and screaming, screaming screaming.

Savannah ran around the pool, weaving her way through the gore, until she reached the distraught girl.

She grabbed her by the upper arms and turned her to face her. "What is it?" she said. "Bunny! Stop it. What's wrong?"

The girl kept flailing her arms and shrieking hysterically. "Oh my God! Oh my God! Oh my God!"

Savannah was aware of the others behind her. Of Robyn asking what was wrong. But she had her hands full with the unhinged teenager.

She shook her hard, then put her hands on either side of Bunny's face to force her to look at her.

"Bunny! Calm down, sugar! Settle down! Stop! Stop screaming!"

The girl focused for a moment and seemed to hear her. She was shaking violently.

"What is it?" Savannah asked, forcing her voice to be soft and soothing, even though she felt like shaking the girl's teeth out. "What's wrong, darlin'? Tell me what's the matter."

Finally, Bunny turned and pointed to a nearby display of vampire gore. Two coffins, laid side by side, held male and female vampires. Dressed in traditional Gothic finery, the Dracula wannabe and his bride were lying in not so sweet repose, hands folded demurely, fangs sufficiently bloodied. And of course, the obligatory stakes driven into the centers of their chests.

Savannah wondered why this exhibit would strike such terror in Bunny's heart when all around, there were far more gruesome displays.

"Okay," Savannah said, thinking briefly that maybe being in these sordid surroundings had unbalanced the girl's mind. "What's the big deal about them? They're—"

"Real! It's not fake! It's real!"

"What?"

"It's not fake. It's a real body!"

As Savannah ran to the coffins and knelt beside them, she had time for a hundred thoughts to race through her mind. But uppermost, hope that Bunny was wrong and these were dummies like all the rest. And wrestling with that hope, fear that they had found their missing Daisy.

She knelt beside the coffin and looked at the female form inside. It was a woman in a black leather corset, laced in the front with burgundy ties, and a long black velvet skirt.

Her black hair was divided neatly in the middle and flowed down past her waist.

Savannah studied her features carefully. Her face was gaunt, pinched, with sunken cheeks, and she had a pronounced widow's peak.

"This isn't Daisy," she said as relief, mingled with confusion washed through her, making her knees weak.

She looked at the "wound," the deep hole in the chest through which the wooden stake had been thrust. Reaching out, she touched the darkened area next to the wood, then looked at her fingertip. Nothing. It was dried paint. "This is a dummy," she told them.

"No! Not that one!" Bunny cried. "It's him!" She pointed to the male in the adjacent coffin.

But Savannah was already looking at the male figure, her heart in her throat.

Even in this dim light, she could see the difference in this body and the female's. The features were far finer, more realistic. The hair was real, not a phony wig. The hands, the fingers, and the nails were all too beautifully detailed to be fake.

As before, she dabbed her finger into the dark area around the stake, and this time, she felt the telltale wetness. Blood. The real thing.

Savannah knew what she was looking at, but her mind refused to take it in. She didn't want to believe that the big, handsome blond man in the coffin was Dante. But it was.

Whether she wanted to admit it or not, Andrew Dante was lying there beside his own swimming pool in a coffin—with a wooden stake through his heart.

She had seen some pretty bizarre stuff in her years in law enforcement, but this was the strangest yet.

Someone gasped behind her. She turned to see that Robyn had also realized the grim truth. The woman cried out and clapped her hands over her mouth.

"What's going on?" Tiffany said as she elbowed the stunned Robyn aside and pushed past her to get closer.

Savannah reached for her to prevent her from seeing what would undoubtedly scar her soul forever. "No, honey, don't," she told her, trying to turn her away.

But Tiffany would not be deterred. "Get out of my way. I want to see it. I—oh my God! Daddy?"

She fell to her knees beside the coffin, leaned over, and put her hands on the corpse's face. "Daddy! Daddy!" she screamed, shaking him as though to wake him.

Again, Savannah reached for her, but the girl fell forward, collapsing face-first into the coffin.

Savannah grabbed her and lifted her up and away from her father's body. She tried to sit her down on the ground a few feet away, but Tiffany folded like a card table with lousy leg supports.

It wasn't until Savannah laid her down and stretched her out that she realized Tiffany was unconscious. She had fainted dead away.

But not as dead as Daddy.

She glanced over at the stake that was sticking up at least a foot and a half out of his chest.

Nope, they didn't need a doctor to pronounce Andrew Dante or a coroner to determine the cause or manner of death.

Death by impalement.

And highly suspicious, to say the very least.

Chapter 12

"Everybody move back," Savannah said. "I'm sorry, but you can't be here. We can't be this close to the bo...I mean, him. Come on. Come with me back into the house, please."

She turned to Kiki and Bunny, who seemed the least distraught at the moment, and asked them, "Would you two please help Mrs. Dante into the house? I'll get Tiffany."

They did as she asked, and Savannah helped the recently revived Tiffany to her feet. "Come on, sugar. There's nothing we can do for him now. Let's just get you and your mom...er...your stepmom into the house."

Once inside, she convinced them all to go into the living room and sit down. She coaxed Tiffany and Robyn to lie on the sofas.

After running to the kitchen for glasses of water and distributing them, she raced upstairs.

"Dirk!" she shouted as she hurried along the upstairs hallway. "Dirk! Get out here, boy! Dirk!"

He stuck his head out of a bedroom door. "Why? Is she coming?"

"What?"

Then she realized he meant Tiffany. He was rummaging through her room and thought that Savannah was there to warn him.

"Get down here," she told him. "We've got a body."

"A body? Oh, damn."

She could tell by the stricken look on his face that he thought she meant Daisy. "No, not her," she told him. "You're not going to believe this, but it's Dante, Andrew Dante is lying down there by the pool with a wooden stake through his heart."

He stared at her blankly, then shook his head and said, "I don't believe that."

"I told you you wouldn't. You have to see this! It's bizarre!"

"A stake?"

"Through his heart. He's dressed up like Dracula, lying there dead as a doornail, a wooden spike sticking out of his chest."

"Holy crap!"

As they raced down the broad spiral staircase together, Dirk said, "I thought he was supposed to be in London."

"Me, too. Or at least on the way there."

Savannah paused at the bottom of the stairs and lowered her voice so that no one in the living room could hear her. "By the way, did you find anything up there in her bedroom?"

"Not really," he said, "but I wasn't exactly looking for wooden stakes or a bloody hammer."

"No garlands of garlic or giant crucifix, either, I suppose," she added as she rushed him through the kitchen and out the back door.

"Sick joke," he said.

She looked at the pool with its red blood, the

coffins, bodies, and occasional tombstone. "Grave-yard humor," she said. "It's sorta like gallows humor."

"What is this?" he asked, looking around. "Hell's waiting room?"

"No kidding. And wait till you see the body. Who-ever did it dressed him in this weird Goth vampire getup and put him into a coffin and everything. Now *that's* sick."

She took him around the pool to Dante's resting place, which from this moment on, would be consid-ered a crime scene.

As he bent over the body, studying it, he said, "It's so damned dark out here. We're going to have to light this up bigtime."

"Dr. Liu's CSI crew will have plenty of lights. Or we could just tell the paparazzi in the front yard about this, and they'll be all over it with floodlights."

"God forbid!" He shuddered. "Can you even imagine what a disaster that would be? In fact, when I call for the coroner, I'll ask for some backup to do crowd control out there."

He looked at the rugged stake protruding from Dante's chest and shook his head. "This is so ugly," he said. "And the press is going to eat it up. What a mess."

"Oh, this is going to be huge. Tiffany Dante's Daddy Mega bucks dead, Dracula style. Film at eleven."

Dirk shook his head and wiped a hand across his face. "And the most depressing part of it all, at least for me . . ."

She knew what he was going to say, so she said it for him. "All this . . . and we still haven't found Daisy."

He nodded wearily. "She could be lying out there somewhere with one of these—"

"Don't say it."

He looked up at her and gave her a sweet, under-standing look. "It could be true, Van," he told her, "no matter what I say."

"Still, don't say it."

I don't want to hear it, she thought. *Daisy's been missing too long. Much too long.*

Together, she and Dirk had recovered many, many kids. Most had wandered away from home, away from playgrounds, away from their moms in shopping malls and grocery stores.

But out of all those kids, none had been missing this long and been found alive. Not a single one.

That was something else she didn't want to think about. Because if she did, she'd crumble inside.

And broken, crumbled people weren't worth a damn at anything. Especially at finding missing kids.

"All right, listen up," Dirk told the crowd gathered in the foyer: patrolmen, crime scene investigation technicians, coroner's assistants, and the county coroner, Dr. Jennifer Liu herself. "You've got literally hundreds of cameras and microphones out there, everything from your everyday paparazzi to CNN and the BBC. And this will spin totally out of control if we don't keep a lid on it. *Anybody* who asks you *anything*, your reply will be 'No comment.' If I hear that even one of you has breathed a word of anything to anybody, you'll answer to me personally for it. No phone calls to your wives or boyfriends. Mouths shut about this one! Got it?"

Some mumbled, "Yes," and others, "Okay." A few just gave a perfunctory nod.

"And," he added, dropping the drill sergeant tone, "I'm going to thank you all for what will undoubtedly be a long and trying night. You're the best. And I appreciate your efforts on this case."

Savannah would have leaned over and given him a kiss on the cheek for being unusually gracious, but of course, he would have died on the spot and never forgiven her.

There was nothing Dirk hated more than being caught in the act of being a nice guy.

Fortunately, it didn't happen often enough to be a problem.

Dirk continued to dispense his orders—instructions to the patrolmen about how he wanted the crowd outside contained, along with admonitions to the forensic collection team that since they didn't know exactly where Andrew Dante had been murdered, the entire enormous estate was their crime scene.

Once the troops were dispersed and immersed in their own duties, Dirk turned to Savannah, shook his head, and said, "Man, oh man, Van. Where to even start with this one! The dude was supposed to be on his way to London, and he's out back, dead? What the hell's going on in this house?"

"Well," she said thoughtfully, "I'd start with the two women of the house and then go from there. I'll help you out. I'll take one of them."

"Thanks." He brightened considerably. "You take Tiff—"

"In your dreams, sugar. *You* take Tiffany. I'll take Robyn."

His smile disappeared. "I thought you said you were going to help me out."

"You wanna do them both while I go home and put my feet up and have a nice cup of hot chocolate and visit with my granny?"

He grumbled something under his breath, the

swear words encoded just enough to convey his an-
noyance without getting himself slapped.

Together, they returned to the living room where
Robyn and the three girls were still as they had left
them.

Tiffany was sitting, curled into a ball around a
cushion. Her face was pressed into the pillow, and
she was crying.

Bunny and Kiki sat close to each other on a love
seat. Kiki had her arm around Bunny's shoulders
and was whispering to her in low, comforting tones.
Robyn stood near a window, looking out, her arms
crossed. She was shivering.

Savannah scooped up a silk fringed throw from
one of the chairs, walked over to her, and draped it
around her shoulders.

A quick glance out the window revealed what
Robyn had been staring at. The window overlooked
the pool . . . and her dead husband's body.

"I'm so sorry," Savannah told her.

Robyn's face was strangely blank as she turned to
Savannah and said a simple, "Thank you."

She didn't seem as distraught as most recently wid-
owed women Savannah had dealt with over the years.
Savannah decided to give her the benefit of the
doubt, at least for now, and chalk it up to shock.

Glancing over her shoulder at Dirk, Savannah saw
that he was down on one knee beside Tiffany, his
hand on her arm, and he was speaking to her softly.

Yeah, yeah, big, bad dude, she thought, sending him
a little love. Dirk could be rude and obnoxious, but
he always came through in a pinch.

Sometimes, it had to be a really *tight* pinch, but . . .

She turned back to Robyn. "I'm sorry to have to
intrude at a time like this," she said to her, "But I really do need to talk to you for a while. Is there some-
place private we can go?"

"What?" Robyn shook her head slightly and seemed to come back to full consciousness. "Oh, sure. Um . . . let's go into the library. We can shut the door and . . ."

"That's fine. Thank you."

Robyn looked once more out the window, a long, strange look. Then she glided across the room—the gracious queen of her castle—and led Savannah through the foyer and down the hall to the library.

It was the same room where she and Dirk had stood near the doorway and overheard Tiffany arguing with her father.

What a difference only a few hours could make.

Robyn flipped on the lights, illuminating what had to be the quintessential gentleman's library. From the glowing mahogany paneling to the massive oak desk to the rows and rows of leather-bound books, this room reflected all the grace and dignity that an enormous amount of money could buy.

And it was purely a man's room. Not a hint of pink anywhere.

Something told Savannah that Andrew Dante spent many of his at-home hours here in this room. And that made it the perfect room to begin an investigation.

"This was Andrew's favorite room," Robyn said, echoing Savannah's thoughts. "He would lock himself in here for hours, even days . . . when he was actually home."

She looked sad and lonely when she added, "Andrew traveled a lot. I used to go with him, but lately, he preferred to go alone."

Robyn walked over to the enormous desk and ran her fingertips over the leather blotter, the lapis world globe, and tortoise shell fountain pen.

When she sat down in the executive leather chair and looked up at Savannah, there were tears streaming down her face. "At least," she said, "I think he's been going alone. But with Andrew, who knows for sure?"

Savannah thought of all the times Granny Reid had warned her girls about getting involved with married men. "If they'll cheat *with* you, they'll cheat *on* you. You'll never really be able to relax and know that your man is true to you."

But Savannah wasn't going to judge the woman in front of her too harshly. She could certainly understand how appealing a handsome, wealthy, powerful man might be to a young travel agent. And even with Granny's admonitions, Savannah wasn't sure she could have resisted such a temptation in her late twenties or early thirties.

It took a while to get smart. And she was still working on it.

"Do you have any reason to suspect him of infidelity?" Savannah asked as she sat down on an accent chair beside the desk.

Robyn reached into the desk and pulled out a box of tissues. "Sure," she said. "Don't all wives suspect? I mean, you'd be stupid not to suspect, wouldn't you?"

Savannah thought of Grandpa Reid, his devotion to Gran and the grandchildren he helped her raise, his commitment to leading a noble life. No, she didn't suspect Pa. And to her knowledge, Gran hadn't either.

"I don't know," Savannah said. "I've never been married. Have you ever seen any evidence that he was being unfaithful to you?"

Robyn wiped her eyes. "A few months ago, he started being secretive about his cell phone, taking it into the bathroom with him, especially when he shaved and showered. And sometimes, he would look at the caller ID and not take a call, then sometime afterward, find a reason to go into another room."

Oh yeah, Savannah thought. *My antennae would go up, too.*

But it wasn't court-admissible proof.

"So, did you get your hands on it once in a while and check it to see who he was calling?"

For a moment, Savannah thought Robyn was going to deny it, but finally, she nodded. "A few times."

"And?"

"He'd deleted everything."

"Ouch."

"Yeah."

"Anything else?"

Robyn sniffed and dabbed at her face with the tissue. "In the bedroom. There were changes in our love life. I could tell that he just didn't want me anymore. He'd lost interest." She bit her lower lip and fought for composure. "We were so passionate at first, and even during our first year of marriage. He couldn't keep his hands off me. When he was out of town, he either took me along, or he called me ten times a day just to tell me he was thinking about me, wanting me. Andrew was a very romantic, loving man."

"But not so much lately?"

"No. And it was really abrupt, too. He took a trip to Amsterdam, and when he came back, things were different. Very, very different. It all changed in just a few days."

"When was this?"

"Four months ago. In the middle of June."

Savannah mulled over what possible connection there might be to Andrew's trip to The Netherlands in June and the reference to Amsterdam she and Dirk had overheard earlier that day when they were eavesdropping outside this room.

What was it Tiffany had been complaining about? Her father giving somebody a luxury trip to Amsterdam?

"Were you planning any trips abroad yourself in the near future?" Savannah asked.

Robyn shook her head. "No, of course not. With the way Tiffany's been acting out lately, somebody had to stay home all the time. The last time Andrew and I left her and went to Copenhagen for three days, we came back to find that she'd had a wild party here, lots of guys, drugs, you name it. The police had been called, and the house was trashed—thousands of dollars of damage. After that, Andrew told me there had to be an adult at home at all times. And of course, that meant *me*, because he has . . . I mean, had . . . to travel for his work."

"You must have resented that enormously."

"Oh, you have no idea." Robyn blew her nose and wadded the tissue into a tight ball in her clenched fist. "That brat has ruined our lives, destroyed our marriage. She thinks of absolutely no one but herself, her posh lifestyle. I wouldn't be surprised if she wasn't the one who killed Andrew. I wouldn't put it past her at all."

"But why would she do that? He's the source of her income, the support for her lifestyle."

Robyn shook her head. "That doesn't matter. Andrew has already made more money than even Tiffany could possibly spend in one lifetime. And now that he's gone, it's all hers. Every dime of it. She's going to be one of the wealthiest young women in the country, if not the world."

"*Every* dime? But you're his wife."

"I signed a prenup." She shrugged. "I know, dumb. But I was in love and eager to prove to him that I wanted him, not his money."

"Do you seriously think Tiffany could kill her father, especially like . . . that?"

"I wouldn't put anything past her. She's really a bad kid, growing up to be an awful woman."

"Other than Tiffany, did Andrew have any enemies? Anybody who wished him ill?"

"Andrew was a very successful businessman, and he didn't get that way by being a softie. He's stepped on some people and made them mad over the years, sure."

"But has anyone actually threatened his life?"

"Nobody but his ex-wife."

"Where is she now?"

"She was in Switzerland, but I heard she'd moved to Argentina with some polo player."

Savannah ticked off the possibilities on her mental checklist. "Any gambling? Possible drug problems?"

"No. Andrew wasn't into any of that. He led a pretty clean life, actually. Except for women."

Savannah was at the bottom of her list, and she wasn't feeling particularly excited about anything she had heard from Andrew Dante's wife. Savannah had hoped for at least a red flag or two to show her where to start looking.

"I'm really sorry, Robyn," she said. "I can't imagine how you feel right now. It's a terrible loss."

The compassionate words seemed to lift the lid off the woman's emotions. She collapsed in wracking sobs and nearly fell out of her chair.

Savannah stood and hurried over to her, gathering her in her arms and rocking her, much as she had her younger brothers and sisters for as long as she could remember.

Big sisters got good at that sort of thing. Being

oldest wasn't all just babysitting and being bossy about chores.

"There, there," she murmured, holding the young widow's face to her shoulder and stroking her hair. "You're going to get through this, Robyn. I know it's awful, but you'll get through it. And we're going to find out who did this to Andrew. I promise."

Abruptly, Robyn pulled away from her and stared at her blankly for a moment. Savannah wasn't sure how to read that reaction. Most victims' families welcomed a promise of justice for their loved one.

Savannah made a quick note to herself not to totally exclude this young woman from her list of suspects. After all, it had only been four months since her husband's affections toward her had changed, and she admitted that she believed he was being unfaithful.

Maybe it was more than a belief. Maybe she'd found proof.

She wouldn't be the first wife to put an end to a cheating husband's philandering in a violent way.

Although a stake through the heart was a pretty strong statement, even for a scorned woman. Savannah couldn't imagine a big, hunky guy like Dante just sitting calmly by and allowing a woman half his size to drive a wooden spike into his chest.

"There's just one more thing I need to ask you," Savannah said. "Why did you think that Andrew was in London?"

"What?" She looked genuinely confused.

"Earlier, you told us that your husband was on his way to London, and obviously, he wasn't. What led you to think he was?"

"He told me. I mean . . . he left me a note."

"A note? He leaves to go overseas, and all you get is a note?"

Robyn nodded. "Actually, I thought it was a little

weird, too. But I told you, he's been a little strange lately, especially when it comes to his travel plans."

"Does he often leave so abruptly like that?"

"Not often, but sometimes he does."

"And he leaves you notes instead of telling you good-bye in person or on the phone?"

"No. That was the first time."

"Where was the note?"

"It was on the refrigerator. That's where everybody leaves notes. Andrew, Tiffany, her friends, even the servants. We all stick them on the fridge."

"What did it say?"

"I don't remember every word, but it was something like, 'Babe, I'm off to London to meet with Peter. Last minute thing. I'll call you when I land.'"

"Where is the note now?"

"I threw it into the garbage."

"In the kitchen?"

"Yes. Into the compactor."

Oh, goody, Savannah thought. *Is there anything less pleasant than going through garbage looking for evidence?*

And of course, she knew the answer to that one. Looking for a decomposing body in a Dumpster or a landfill. At least there wouldn't be a zillion seagulls swarming over her head in the Dante kitchen.

Yes, it could be a lot worse.

"Let's go look for it," she said.

Slowly, Robyn rose from her chair, but Savannah noticed that she was a little unsteady on her feet.

She walked over and slipped her arm around the woman's waist. "And while we're there," she said, "we'll pour you a glass of something stronger than water."

"I think there's some Johnny Walker Blue in there."

"Yep. That should do it."

Chapter 13

Robyn took Savannah to the kitchen where Savannah poured and served Robyn the promised shot of the expensive Scotch. And even though Savannah knew that her teetotaler grandmother would never approve, she had seen how the well-timed alcoholic beverage could calm down a distraught person . . . and occasionally, loosen a suspect's tongue.

Not that Robyn Dante was any higher on Savannah's suspect list than anybody else. But like Dirk, she always kept the spouse, the former spouse, or any love interest high on that list.

At the moment, Savannah had her solidly in the number two slot, right beneath her stepdaughter. Not that she had any particular evidence against Tiffany. But in any investigation, Savannah had her favorite, the one she hoped against hope was the perpetrator. And it was usually the person she disliked most as a human being.

It was so much easier to bust and send away someone you didn't like. In fact, she had found it to be one of life's most satisfying pleasures . . . along with dark chocolate and fine brandy.

In fact, she promised herself a square of a good 90% cacao bar and a snifter of a *nice VSOP* Cognac if she ever got to go home again and put her feet up. And, of course, if Gran was sound asleep in the guest room.

She kept reminding herself of that treat, holding the chocolate and brandy out in front of her mind's eye as she stood in the Dantes' kitchen and transferred every piece of trash, bit by bit, from their compactor to another garbage pail.

The latex gloves she was wearing helped to make the job a little less queasy. But the fact that someone had eaten salmon and some sort of chocolate mousse for dinner and thrown the leftovers into the trash didn't help at all.

Halfway through, she decided to pass on the chocolate once she was home.

"You say the note was written on yellow paper?" she asked for the third time. She was examining everything from lipstick-smeared napkins to used and wadded tissues, but she wanted to be sure.

"Yes," Robyn said. "Pale yellow with a large D watermark on it."

Robyn was far less distressed and more than a little tipsy, having downed the Scotch in only a couple of gulps and then consumed half of another just as quickly. But she strolled on unsteady feet over to the opposite side of the room, pulled open a cabinet drawer, and took out a tablet.

She plopped it down on the island where Savannah was working and pointed to it with the studied deliberation of someone who was totally soused.

"There," she said. "It was written on a sheet of that. It's the house stationery. We all write our notes on that."

"Okay. Thanks." Savannah held up a coffee-sprinkled, salmon-enhanced banana peel. "It helps to know for sure what I'm looking for. Although I'm beginning to have my doubts that it's in here. When was the last time this thing was emptied?"

"Oh, the housekeeper takes it out at least once a day. Although today was her day off, so I guess the trash was taken out yesterday."

Savannah had reached the bottom of the barrel, so to speak, and had decided that she might never eat again. Now would be the perfect time to start that diet she'd been threatening to go on for the past twenty years.

"Are you absolutely sure that you put it in here?" Savannah asked as she removed the last item, an empty yogurt container, and tossed it into the nearby garbage can.

"Yes, I'm sure," Robyn said after giving it much consideration. "I'm absolutely sure. I took it off the refrigerator, read it, and then threw it in there. Yes. Positive."

Her eyes were glazed, her speech slurred, but Savannah didn't doubt her honesty. At this stage of intoxication, she wouldn't have been capable of fabrication.

"And what time was that?"

Again, it took Robyn a few extra seconds to get the brain cells popping. "Um . . . it was when I came home from the spa. Let's see. About five forty-five or six."

"So, when was the last time you saw Andrew?"

"This afternoon when I left for the spa. It must have been a little after one. My facial was at one-thirty, so . . . yes. About one or one-fifteen."

"What spa was this?"

"Euro-Spa in Twin Oaks."

That would easy enough to verify. So far, Suspect Numero Dos had an excellent alibi.

But where was this note she claimed to have found? And why wasn't it where she said she'd put it?

One of the crime scene techs passed by, and Savannah called out to her. "Melinda, would you please dust the outside of this compactor for latents?"

"Sure." The tech hurried over with her kit and set about searching for fingerprints. Even though Savannah was no longer on the police force, she had made a lot of friends there, and many of them were still furious that she had been unfairly terminated all those years ago.

"We miss you, Savannah," the woman said as she expertly swirled her brush. "It's just not the same, having to deal with Dirk and no Savannah around to dilute the acid, if you know what I mean."

"He's not so bad," she replied with a snicker, "if you box him upside the ears every Friday night and keep him in line."

"You're the only one who's ever been able to do that and survive. He'll take it from you, not from the rest of us."

"Dirk's crusty, but inside, he's a marshmallow."

At that moment, Dirk's bass voice roared through the house. "Come on, people! We've got a lot of ground to cover here, and I don't want it to take all friggen night! Let's move!"

Melinda shot Savannah a look. "Oh yeah?" she said. "A real sweetie pie, that Dirk Coulter."

"You just have to get to know him."

"No, thanks. Not into rude dudes."

Dirk paused as he passed the kitchen door, looked in, and saw Savannah taking off her rubber gloves. "Dr. Liu," he said gruffly, "is getting ready to bag the

body. You wanna watch her do it or keep playing with
your garbage there?"

"You wanna watch your tone or become a suspicious smell in an attic?" Savannah tossed back.

He looked moderately surprised for a moment,
then gave her a big grin and a wink and continued
on his way.

"See there," she said to Melinda. "Coulter's not so
bad. You just have to smack him around once in a
while."

After helping Robyn Dante to her bedroom and
tucking her into her four-poster bed, Savannah went
back downstairs to watch the official bagging of the
body.

When she stepped out the back door and onto the
patio area, she was struck with how very different
everything looked fully illuminated. The spooky, surreal red glow from the pool was lost in the harsh lu-
minance from the CSI floodlights. Mounted on
six-foot-tall telescoping poles, the portable units cast a
bright, shadow-filled light over the whole scene, re-
vealing the stark reality of the crime that had been
committed.

Under the unforgiving white lights, the fake
corpses looked fake, the faux blood and gore looked
faux. And the very real body of Andrew Dante in his
strange resting place looked depressingly real.

Savannah walked over to the area around the
body that had been cordoned off with yellow tape in
a ten- or twelve-foot circle around the coffin. She
stopped at the tape and waited for Dirk and Dr. Jennifer Liu to look up from their task and acknowledge
her.

Dr. Liu saw her first. The Asian beauty smiled the

moment she spotted her, rose, and hurried over to embrace her as well as she could, considering she was wearing bloody gloves. "Savannah," she said, "so good to see you."

"You, too, Dr. Jen."

Savannah glanced down at the sequined miniskirt that stuck out only a couple of inches below the coroner's white lab smock. And below that were black fishnet stockings and a serious pair of black stilettos with four-inch heels.

"Caught you out partying, did they?" Savannah asked with a grin.

"Don't they always?"

"Either you party a lot or they have lousy timing."

Dr. Liu smiled a naughty, mischievous little smirk. "Or maybe a bit of both." She nodded toward the body. "You want to see?"

"I already saw, but sure. Let's have another look now that we have lighting."

Savannah ducked under the tape and walked over to the coffin and its unfortunate occupant. Dirk was squatting next to it, also wearing gloves. He was gingerly lifting the fabric that covered the body's blood-soaked chest with two fingers and looking beneath it.

"Get a load of this," he told them.

Both women hurried over to him and knelt on either side of the coffin, Savannah next to Dirk.

"What is it?" she asked.

"These clothes . . . the vampire getup," he said. "He's not actually wearing it. The stuff's lying on him."

"What?" Savannah looked closer.

Dirk lifted the edge of the burgundy velvet vest that covered Dante's midriff area. "These weird Dracula clothes. Somebody must have laid them on top of the body. Look. Here are his regular clothes underneath."

Sure enough. Beneath the costume was a simple, pale blue polo shirt. Under the black pants was a pair of jeans. And he had a pair of Nikes on his feet that were covered by a small piece of black velvet.

"That's weird," Dr. Liu said as she bent over and began to peel the fabric back herself. "Charles," she called out to one of the photographers, who was standing nearby taking pictures of the pool area. "Come here, and get some shots of this."

The young man walked over to them and stepped inside the perimeter tape.

He shuddered when he saw the body. "Wow," he said. "That's a pretty grisly one. Rough way to go."

Dr. Liu crooked her finger, beckoning him. Reluctantly, he came closer.

"Zoom in tight on this," she said as she pulled the vest and white shirt away from the blue polo shirt.

After he had taken several shots, she pulled it further away, and he took more.

Then she laid it back down. "I'll wait till I get him home to take it off. I don't want to lose anything in the way of hair or fiber that might be on it." She looked around them at the palms, which were dancing in the night breeze. "It's a bit too windy out here tonight for my taste. Something good could blow away."

Dirk didn't reply. He had stood and was staring down at the body, looking perplexed.

"What is it?" Savannah asked him.

"I'm still wondering . . . He's a big guy. Bigger than me. And he was in great shape, too. How do you figure he stood still for somebody to ram that thing into his chest? Anybody who would come at me with something like that, I'd go crazy on them. Why didn't he?"

Savannah knelt and looked at the body's hands. "Good point. No defense wounds that I can see. Not a single skinned knuckle, not even a tiny cut." She turned it over in her mind for a moment or two, then said, "Postmortem, maybe?"

"Maybe," Dirk said, nodding. "Which would mean that the stake may not even be our murder weapon."

Dr. Liu had finished directing the photographer and was instructing some of her assistants to lay out the body bag next to the coffin. But she was eavesdropping on their conversation.

"That would make sense," she said. "That wound just doesn't look right to me."

"Well, no, a gruesome wound like that, what's right about it?" Savannah looked down at the sticky red gore in the middle of the victim's chest.

"Oh, it's gross all right," the doctor agreed. "But what I mean is, the wound itself, at least what I can see of it here in this lighting with the body still dressed, it doesn't look right to me. The edges around the wound are very ragged. I'm thinking the stake might have been inserted postmortem. And I'm not totally convinced he was killed here. He may have been, but . . ."

"What do you mean?" Dirk asked her. "You don't think he was killed here?"

"I don't know, and I won't until I get him on my table. But I have my doubts."

Dirk and Savannah watched as the coroner and her team unfolded a white sheet and laid it on top of the open, unzipped body bag. Then the four of them lifted the corpse from the coffin and laid it onto the sheet.

Dr. Liu filled out an evidence label and scribbled pertinent information on a toe tag, as well. She removed Dante's tennis shoe and slipped the tag onto his toe.

Savannah smiled—it was a pleasure watching her high level of professionalism. Some coroners waited until the body was in the morgue to put on the toe tag. But years ago, Dr. Liu's predecessor had temporarily mixed up a couple of bodies in the morgue. And since that was one of the main reasons he had lost his job and Dr. Liu had gotten hers, the good doctor was particularly cautious about that sort of thing.

The two men and two women were out of breath by the time they had the body moved, properly bundled in the sheet, and placed into the body transport bag.

Dirk turned to Savannah and said, "If this guy wasn't killed here and somebody moved him—"

"It must have been more than one person who moved him," she finished for him.

"No kidding," Dr. Liu said, smoothing her long black hair back and retying it with a silk scarf. "He's a handful. Several hands full."

"Dr. Liu," one of the techs said, "what are we going to do about that?"

He had zipped the bag as far closed as he could, but the stake sticking out of the chest prevented him from closing it all the way.

"Yes, that's a bit of a problem," she said. "I don't want to remove that until I get him on the autopsy table. I want to properly examine and document the angle and all that."

"You can't take that out the front door with a crowd of paparazzi waiting," Dirk said. "Can you imagine? They'd go crazy!"

Dr. Liu gave him a withering look. "I'm ten steps ahead of you, Detective, as usual. But my concerns are more legal than media-oriented. This is a homicide—I can't leave that body bag unsealed."

Dirk returned the nasty, condescending look. "Well, in spite of you grossly insulting me, as usual, I'm going to help you out. And then, when you see what a brilliant solution I have to your problem, you can apologize to me properly."

With a cocky strut, he walked away from them, around the pool, and back into the house.

"*Apologize?* To *him?*" Dr. Liu said with a chuckle.

"Oh, yes. And *properly,*" Savannah added.

"O-o-okay." She shook her head. "That'll be the day, when Coulter rises to brilliant."

"Hey, he can surprise you. Dirk's not just a pretty face, you know."

While Dirk was gone on his mysterious errand, the coroner's team brought in a gurney and placed it beside the body bag. After carefully lifting the bag and its strange burden onto the gurney, they raised the stretcher to waist level.

By then, Dirk had returned with his treasures—a roll of duct tape and a white plastic garbage bag.

"Voila!" he said, presenting both items.

"Voilà?" Dr. Liu said. "I don't see a voilà in front of me. No 'There you are!' in sight."

"Do I have to do everything myself?" Dirk said with the sigh of the well-practiced martyr.

"Apparently so," Savannah told him.

With much flourish and a style that was lacking in polish but rich in drama, Dirk tented the garbage bag over the stake, tore off a long piece of the tape, and began to seal the edges around the garbage bag onto the transport bag.

A few minutes later, his creation was finished. A true example of functional art.

He pulled a permanent marker from his pocket, handed it to Dr. Liu, and said, "There! Sign it, your signature running over the seam, and then . . . you may offer me your apology and see if I will accept it."

Dr. Liu stared at him for a long time. And Savannah held her breath.

Of all the many qualities, the myriad virtues that

made up Dr. Liu's character, humility wasn't among them. Jennifer Liu was highly intelligent, successful, strong, and beautiful. She didn't really have a lot to be humble about. So she didn't bother.

She stepped up to Dirk, and in her four-inch heels, she was eye to eye with him. And when she leaned forward, they were literally nose to nose.

"You, Detective Sergeant Dirk Coulter, are, indeed, brilliant," she said with only a modicum of sarcasm. "You are a man among men, a prince among thieves, a diamond among the rough, a tribute to your gender. I bow before your austere magnificence and pay homage to your—"

"All right, enough." Dirk stepped back and crossed his arms over his broad chest. "Is there an apology in there somewhere, or are you just trying to bore me to death with all this crap so that you won't have to admit that I'm smarter than you?"

"Smarter?" Dr. Liu threw back her head and laughed. "Get real, Coulter. The day you're smarter than me, I drink an arsenic milkshake and wind up on my own autopsy table. But . . . in this particular circumstance, you've proven yourself a wee, tiny, smidgen bit more resourceful than I."

Dirk stood there, breathing hard, arms still crossed, staring at her. Finally, he grinned, dropped his arms, and slapped her on the shoulder. "That'll do," he said. "I'm happy with that."

He left them and walked over to a group of CSI techs who were combing the area around the pool. In no time, he was arguing with them, waving his arms, gesticulating wildly, obviously telling them off about something.

Dr. Liu shook her head and gave Savannah a sympathetic smile. "How do you stand him?" she said.

Savannah looked across the pool at her old friend and thought of how kind and respectful he was to

Granny Reid. She remembered how he took the time to scratch behind Diamante's ear, just the way she liked it, for as long as the cat wanted. She considered that he had never once said, "I don't have time," when she was troubled and needed to talk at three in the morning. She recalled how he had held her head and soothed her when she was sick and throwing up during that stakeout—after he had fed her a tuna sandwich and forgotten to tell her it had been in the glove box for three days.

With a soft sweetness in her voice, she said, "Hey, what's not to love?"

Chapter 14

"I'm so sorry, Gran," Savannah said into her cell phone as she apologized yet again for leaving her grandmother alone at home. "But there's been a murder here at the Dante mansion and—"

"Oh, I know!" Gran replied on the other end. "I'm sitting here right now, watching it on the television. They've got live coverage of the front of the house! In fact, you should come to the front door and wave to me."

Savannah suppressed a chuckle as she walked around the pool and into the back door of the house. "I don't think I'd better do that, Gran," she said. "Those reporters are a bunch of wild hyenas out there. If I were to open that front door, I'd get trampled in the stampede."

"Well, don't do it then. But I have to know . . . the dead body . . . it's not that little Daisy girl you've been looking for, is it?"

"No, Gran. Thank goodness it's not."

"Is it Tiffany Dante herself?"

"No. Tiffany's okay."

"Then who is it?"

Savannah nearly told her, but since she was on a mobile phone and for miles around, they were surrounded by trucks and vans full of all sorts of fancy audio equipment, she decided against it.

"If you're still up when I get home, I'll tell you then."

"You'll tell me everything?"

Savannah laughed again. "Yes, Gran. I'll tell you way more than I'm supposed to."

"Good. I'll wait up."

"It's going to be late."

"Who cares? I'm old. I can lay abed in the morning if I've a mind to."

"You certainly can. I'll even bring you breakfast in bed if you've a mind to have it. I'll see you later. I love you, Gran."

"I love you, too, Savannah girl. Be careful around those murderers and reprobates."

"Oh, I'm keeping an eye peeled for reprobates, degenerates, and miscreants. Don't you worry about me."

As Savannah entered the kitchen, she found Dirk having a hot debate with a woman she had never met before. The lady was well-dressed in a pale jade silk blouse and matching trousers, and her hair was cut in a sophisticated, shoulder-length bob.

She looked somewhat familiar to Savannah, but she couldn't place her until Bunny came running into the room and fell into her arms, sobbing. The family resemblance was strong. No doubt, this was Bunny Greenaway's mother.

"There you are, sweetheart!" the woman said, holding her daughter tight. "This policeman said I couldn't take you home yet, but I told him—"

"All right, all right," Dirk interjected. "Take her home. But I'm not finished interviewing any of the girls yet, so do *not* leave town." He took his notebook from his pocket and a pen and said, "But before you do, I want your home phone number and address and everybody's cell numbers. I *will* be calling you, and I'm not going to have the time to track you down."

Mrs. Greenaway did as she was told, but the moment she had finished writing on his pad, she shoved the paper and pen back at him and said, "I'm not going to forget how rudely you treated me and my daughter. My husband is on the City Council, and I am a major contributor at the Annual Police Benefit Ball. Don't think I won't remember this when I make out my check in December."

Dirk gave her a deadpan look as he stuck his notepad back inside his bomber jacket. "Dear me," he said. "Whatever shall I do this Christmas without my Greenaway donation stocking stuffer? Oh, I know . . . the same as I *always* do because I never even *see* your stinkin' money, let alone *get* any of it, and furthermore—"

Savannah stepped up and grabbed his arm. "Uh, Detective Coulter," she said, "they need you out back by the pool. Right away."

She didn't think it would work. Dirk could usually tell when she was blatantly lying. But he was tired, and his BS detector wasn't finely tuned.

"Oh, all right," he said, then disappeared.

"He's very tired," Savannah offered as a feeble excuse. "He's been working on the Daisy O'Neil case night and day, and now this . . ."

"Well, he didn't have to be so ill-mannered and curt with me." Mrs. Greenaway continued to hug and soothe her daughter. "I just want to take my baby home. She's had a terrible experience here and needs to be with her family."

Savannah glanced down at Bunny, who continued to cry against her mother's shoulder, although there did seem to be a shortage of actual tears streaming down her face, considering the amount of boohooing that was going on.

"Yes, she has had a dreadful shock," Savannah said. "A terrible thing, finding a homicide victim."

Mrs. Greenaway raised one perfectly plucked eyebrow. "We are a *good* family," she said. "We don't allow things like this to happen in *our* family. Girls going missing and people getting horrible things stuck in them—it's just so, so low class."

Savannah nodded and kept a straight face when she said, "It is a bit tacky, to be sure."

Mrs. Greenaway waved an arm, indicating the enormous kitchen with its luxury appointments. "They may have all of *this*, but I have to tell you, for all their money, I don't approve of their lifestyle around here. I've had my doubts about the influence Tiffany and her friends have had on my Bunny."

Bunny pulled back from her mother's embrace, a nasty scowl on her face. "What is that supposed to mean? It's an honor to be one of the Skeleton Key Three."

"Oh, phu-u-ush, it is not. I don't even like the sound of that name—Skeleton Key. I worry about you developing an eating disorder like Tiffany has."

"Mom, I told you we do not have any kind of disorder. Oh my God, you drop a few pounds and—"

"You're bingeing and purging again."

"I am not!"

"You are, too. I heard you last night in your bathroom, and you were—"

"Ladies, ladies!" Savannah interrupted them. "Please. The past few hours have been stressful for all of us. Mrs. Greenaway, maybe it would be a good idea if you took Bunny on home and put her to bed.

Some rest would do everyone good. I'm sure we'll all feel a little better in the morning."

Both mother and daughter seemed to agree with her because they allowed her to usher them through the house to the foyer. Savannah was debating the wisdom of taking them directly out the front door and fighting a path through the press or trying to sneak them out a back door when the front door flew open.

Two young uniformed policemen were escorting a distraught woman, who appeared to be both fighting them and clinging to them at the same time.

"Pam," Savannah said, leaving the Greenaways and hurrying over to Daisy's mother. "What's wrong? What is it?"

"What do you mean, what's wrong?" she asked. "I turn on my TV, and they're saying that there's been a murder here, that you've found a dead body!"

"Oh, you poor thing." Savannah shooed the policemen away with her hand and took hold of Pam O'Neil herself. "It isn't Daisy, honey. We haven't found her. It's someone else."

Pam swayed against her so suddenly and unexpectedly that Savannah nearly lost her balance.

"Whoa," she said. "Steady, sugar."

One of the cops stepped forward to help, but Savannah gave him a soft, "Thank you," and shook her head. "I've got her. But if you guys would see these two ladies to their car, I'd appreciate it. And please be sure that nobody bothers them with any irritating questions."

The older of the two gave her a nod and a wink. "No problem, Savannah. We'll make sure it's a quick, smooth trip."

A moment later, Bunny and her mother were being escorted out the door and into the mob.

Savannah started to lead Pam O'Neil over to the staircase, thinking to sit her down there, but she realized they would be directly under the scythe of the Grim Reaper. And that would be just too creepy.

So she took her on into the great room and seated her on a sofa. Although, since the skeleton wedding was still set up near the fireplace, it was equally eerie. "I'm really sorry, Pam," she told her as she sat down beside her. "I should have called you, but it was a real shock, finding the body like that."

"I understand," Pam said. She was still shaking, and her normally suntanned face was disturbingly white. "I just heard that news broadcast on the TV, and I was so sure that it was Daisy."

"That's perfectly understandable. And so is the fact that you were so upset. I would have been, too."

"I tried to call you on your cell phone, but you didn't pick up. I thought you weren't taking my call because it was Daisy and you didn't want to tell me so on the phone."

Savannah took her cell phone out of her pocket and saw that, indeed, she had missed a call. "It was pretty noisy out back where they're processing the scene. I guess I didn't hear it ring. Again, I apologize."

Pam reached over, grabbed Savannah's hand, and squeezed it. "You have nothing to be sorry for. I know you've been doing your best for Daisy and for me. I'm sure you have your hands full."

"It's pretty hectic. That's for sure. A missing person and now a homicide. It's a full plate."

"Do you think they're connected, my Daisy disappearing and the murder?"

"We don't know yet. I suppose we have to assume they could be."

Savannah heard heavy footsteps coming through the foyer and toward them. Even before she saw him, she knew it was Dirk, and he wasn't happy about something.

He charged into the room, but when he saw that she was talking to Pam O'Neil, his brusque manner softened instantly.

"Oh," he said. "I was looking for you, Savannah, but if you're busy, I . . ."

"She isn't busy," Pam said as she stood, tucked her shirt into her jeans, and adjusted her collar. "I know you guys have a lot to do. I don't want to get in your way. I just had to know."

"She heard the news and was worried that it was Daisy we found," Savannah told him.

"Those damned reporters," he said, shaking his head. "They report whether they have anything to report or not, and that just stirs everybody and everything up. I hate 'em."

"Yeah, well . . . whatever." Savannah patted Pam on the back and walked her to the door, Dirk following behind. "Are you going to be okay going through the gauntlet again?" she asked her.

"Sure. The reporters didn't bother me," Pam said. "I don't look like anybody, if you know what I mean. Nobody asked me anything. It was the cops who were trying to stop me from getting in."

Savannah chuckled. "Well, if you got in, you shouldn't have any problem getting out. Again, I'm sorry you weren't able to get in touch with me. Hopefully, it won't happen again."

"And if it does," Dirk said, pressing one of his cards into her hand, "call me. Between the two, you should be able to get one of us."

Pam thanked them both again warmly and then left.

Savannah turned to Dirk. "What did you want me for?"

He looked disgusted. "I'm going crazy trying to

question that Tiffany twerp. I swear I'm losing my patience. I'm about to strangle her."

"Go right ahead. I don't care."

"I'd get in trouble. Big trouble."

"I don't care about that either. Forget it. You're not saddling me with that brat."

"Ah, come on, Van."

"No way. That's why you get paid the big bucks."

"I'll give you a quarter. I'll be your friend forever."

"You're already going to be my friend forever."

"But the quarter? Fifty cents? A buck?"

"No."

"Tiffany, I know you and I haven't gotten off to the best start," Savannah said, trying her best to sound like she didn't want to just reach across the kitchen table and slap the girl silly.

It wasn't easy.

"But I do feel terrible for you," she continued, "losing your father this way, not knowing where your close friend is. It must be just awful."

"Don't lie. You don't care about me," Tiffany said, then took a swig of soda from the can in her hand. "You don't give a damn about me. Nobody does . . . now that my dad's dead."

There was a sorrow in the girl's voice that touched Savannah's heart, and she actually felt guilty for disliking the kid so much. After all, she was only a product of her indulgent upbringing. Any child who had never heard the word no and had been given everything she asked for would have turned out the same way.

"Okay," Savannah said. "I admit I didn't like you very much when I first met you. But I do care about you. And I do feel bad for you, considering this horrible thing that's happened. I'm not lying about that."

Tiffany lifted red, swollen eyes to Savannah's and stared at her for a long time. It was a searching look, as though she was truly considering whether she could trust her or not.

She seemed to decide Savannah was being honest with her, and she dropped a bit of her hostility.

"So are you going to find out who killed my father?" she asked. "Or, maybe I should say, are you going to nail that bitch stepmother of mine and make her pay for this?"

"Why do you think Robyn killed him?"

She gave a disdainful sniff. "Oh, pleeez. Like we don't all know she did it."

"*I* don't know that she did it. Do *you?*"

"Of course she did."

"Why? Why would she kill your dad?"

Tiffany hesitated, then said, "Because he was fooling around on her. My dad was a good guy, a great father, but he was a lousy husband, unfaithful and all that. It's not like that's a secret."

This time, the hurt in the girl's eyes, mixed with shame, was so strong that Savannah felt it wash all the way through her.

Besides, Savannah knew what it was to have a father who chased women and to have everyone around you know it, too. It was a shame she and her eight other siblings had borne their whole lives.

Everyone in the little town of McGill, Georgia, knew that Macon Reid, Sr., had girlfriends who rode across the country with him in his eighteen-wheeler. He would stash them in a fleabag hotel when he came home a couple of times a year. And when he would leave to go back on the road, he took his latest squeeze with him and left his wife at the local bar to drink away her anger and loneliness.

And this young woman sitting across the table lived with the same shame. Only, thanks to the tabloids, the whole world knew about her father.

"I'm really sorry for your troubles, Tiffany," she said. "I can understand why you don't like your stepmother. My dad finally married one of his girlfriends. I'm not very fond of her, either."

Tiffany looked surprised. Either that she and Savannah shared a life experience or that Savannah would tell her about it, Savannah didn't know which.

"Are you sure your dad was fooling around on Robyn?" Savannah asked her.

"Yeah, I'm sure. I know how he acts when he's got somebody new. We went through this about every two or three years when I was growing up. I know the symptoms. He gets all happy . . . and giggly . . . and worried about how he looks. And sneaky."

"Do you know who he's been seeing?"

Tiffany stalled, sipping from her soda can, playing with her hair, before she finally said, "No."

Savannah didn't believe her. "Do you have any other reason to believe that Robyn did it?" she asked her. "Did you overhear them fighting about another woman, or anything else, for that matter?"

"Not really. Dad wasn't home enough for them to fight much. He'd be home a day or two, and then he'd leave again. Probably to be with *her*."

"The girlfriend."

"Yeah."

"The girlfriend you don't know."

Tiffany shot her an unpleasant look. "Yeah. The one I don't know."

She downed the rest of her soda and stood up. "Are you about done with me now?" she said. "Because I'm really tired, and I want to go lay down. You let Robyn go to bed. I want to go to bed."

"Sure." Savannah stood, too. "I just have one more question. When you got out of Detective Coulter's car there in front of the station and your attorney picked you up . . . did he bring you right back here?"

"Yeah. He did."

"And was your father here then? Did you see him?"

"No. I mean . . . he wasn't in the house. The house was empty. I guess he might have been already out there, but I didn't see—"

She choked on her words and started to cry.

Savannah reached to touch her, comfort her, but she flinched and moved out of reach.

"Okay, thank you," Savannah told her. "Go on upstairs, and get some rest. I appreciate you talking to me. If you need anything, let me or any of the rest of us know."

Tiffany shot her a bitter look and said, "Yeah, right. All of you can go screw yourselves." Then she left the room.

Savannah stood there in the middle of the kitchen, shaking her head and muttering a short prayer. "Lord, give me patience," she said, feeling too tired to breathe. "Because if you give me strength, I just might slap that girl into next Tuesday."

"I wish I'd gotten another chance to talk to Kiki Wallace," Savannah told Dirk when he finally took her home at nearly three in the morning. "I swear she was just about to tell me something about Daisy when Tiffany came in and put a halt to it. And then Bunny found Dante, and all hell broke loose."

"Yeah," he said as he turned down her street. "Her

mother came and got her, too, and I couldn't really hold her any longer. You were talking to Tiffany, and I figured that was more important."

"As it turns out, not really. She says she thinks Robyn killed him. But I think that's wishful thinking on her part. I'm sure nothing would make her happier than to see her wicked stepmother go away for it."

"But the kid gets the old man's money either way, right?"

"According to Robyn, yes. I'd check it out though, just to be sure."

"In my spare time."

"Yeah, in your spare time."

They both sighed, exhausted.

"I'm sorry that you have to drive home," she said. "I'd let you crash on my sofa, but . . . well . . . Gran."

"No way. I'm afraid of your grandma. She'd think I was up to no good for sure."

"She would. She truly would."

They drove a few more blocks through the silent, moonlit neighborhood. The only sounds were some yipping coyotes in the foothills beyond. The cool October night air smelled of citrus and eucalyptus as it rushed through the car's open windows.

Dirk reached over and took a cinnamon stick from the dash. Sticking it into his mouth, he said, "I felt bad for that O'Neil gal. Must be hell what she's going through."

"I can't even imagine. It's got to be a fate way worse than death."

Savannah reflected back over the conversation she'd had with Daisy's mother earlier. "There's just something that's sorta bothering me," she told him.

He drew a long breath through the stick. "What's that?"

"She came rushing over there because she was afraid that the body we'd found was Daisy's, right?"

"That's what she said. Why?"

"Well, we talked for a while, for several minutes . . ."

"Yeah? And . . . ?"

"We talked, and she left." Savannah ran her fingers through her hair and massaged a spot that was starting to ache right in the middle of her forehead. "And she never once asked me who it was that we found."

Dirk shot her a quick look. "Oh yeah?"

"Yeah."

They rode on in silence a little while.

Then Dirk said, "I would have asked. I mean . . . she may have just been really upset and worked up about it being Daisy and was so relieved to hear that it wasn't her. And she's probably really tired and hasn't slept."

Again, a prolonged, tense silence. Finally, Savannah said, "I don't know for sure because I'm not her, but I think I would have asked."

Dirk nodded, took the cinnamon stick out of his mouth, and tossed it out the window. "Me, too," he said. "Me, too."

Chapter 15

This time, when Savannah walked into her house, she found Granny sitting in her comfy chair and wide awake.

"Well, look at you," Savannah said, peeling off her jacket and removing her weapon and holster, "all bright-eyed and bushy-tailed in the wee hours of the morning."

Gran chuckled. "Hey, I've got a chance to find out something juicy even before the *True Informer* does! How many chances in a lifetime does a body get to do that?"

Savannah kicked her loafers off and tossed them into the bottom of the coat closet. Then she put the Beretta in its off duty resting place on the top shelf of the closet under a folded windbreaker.

"Dirk gave us strict instructions not to say *anything* to *anybody* about what happened over there today," she told Gran as she walked through the living room and into the kitchen. "On pain of death, not one single word."

Gran followed right behind. "So, that means you're only going to tell me half of it?"

"Oh, no. I'm going to spill it all. There's no way I could keep anything like this all to myself. Besides, I remember what you told me about the definition of a secret."

Gran smiled. "A secret is something a body tells to one person at a time."

"That's it. Tonight I tell you. Tomorrow I tell Tammy."

"And who do I get to tell?"

"Certainly not the *True Informer!* You make any phone calls to them, and we'll all be in deep doo-doo."

"What if I call Martha Phelps, and she calls them? Then we could split the money they pay."

Martha had been Gran's best friend for more than seventy years, and she was sure that whether she gave Gran permission or not, Martha would know every grisly detail before sunrise.

And since the two dear ladies were living off meager pension checks and were both born blabber-mouths, why interfere with the normal processes of nature?

"I don't want to know anything about anything having to do with Martha or the *True Informer*," Savannah said. "Not a word."

Gran's eyes twinkled. "You won't. I'll be the soul of discretion."

"Yeah, right." Savannah reached into the refrigerator and took out the pitcher of sweet tea. "Want a glass?" she asked.

"No, thanks. It would keep me up all night."

Savannah glanced up at the clock and said, "In case you haven't noticed, the night's pretty much gone already."

"You sure are burning the midnight oil on this one."

Savannah took a long drink of the iced tea, then stood still, eyes closed, waiting for the sugar and caf-

feine to hit her system, for the cold refreshment to
do its work and refresh her tired body.

But nothing happened.

"You look plum worn to a frazzle, sweet pea,"
Gran said. "If you don't get some rest, you're just
gonna fall down in a dead faint."

"I know. I'm going to go to bed and try to get
some sleep pretty soon. I'm sure tomorrow's going
to be a doozy. Just looking for Daisy was enough, and
now this murder on top of it."

"There's nothing new at all about the girl?"

"No, nothing. For a moment tonight, I thought I
was going to get something out of one of the girls in
their little club, but then the body was discovered
and . . ."

Savannah dumped the rest of the tea into the sink
and put the glass into the dishwasher. "That's the
worst part," she said. "Not that I don't feel terrible
about Andrew Dante getting murdered, but—"

Gran gasped. "It's Andrew Dante who's dead!
Lord have mercy! I figured it was one of their servants or somebody working on the party there."

"No, it's the master of the house himself. And all
the media coverage is just going to make things
worse, not to mention the pressure from folks in
high places." She ran her hand over her face and
through her hair. She was too tired to even focus anymore. "I just feel so bad for Daisy and her poor
mother. Andrew's dead and of course, we have to
catch the killer, but Daisy . . . Daisy's the one who's
going to keep me awake tonight. I feel guilty even
going to bed when she's still out there somewhere."

Gran reached for her, took her in her arms, and
gave her a hearty hug. Holding her close, she patted
her back and said, "My sweet, brave Savannah. It's always about the kids for you, isn't it, darlin'? Always
has been about the kids your whole life."

Savannah looked into her grandmother's dear face and remembered the years and years of sacrifice that she had made to raise her and her siblings. "You're somebody to talk," she said, giving Gran a kiss on the nose. "You softie. You still spoil them rotten."

The pat on the back turned to a playful slap. "I do not. I'm gettin' downright ornery in my old age."

"Yeah, yeah. That'll be the day."

She took her grandmother's hand and said, "Okay, come on into the living room, and I'll fill you in on all the gory details. But there are a few things that you can't even tell Martha because they're confidential facts of the case. You're going to have to keep it straight, what you can repeat and what you can't. Got it?"

Gran swelled up, moderately indignant. "Listen, young lady, I may be old, but I'm not the least bit senile. I'm fast as a tack and sharp as a whip."

Savannah sighed. "That's what I'm afraid of."

By the time Savannah arrived at the county morgue the next morning, Dirk was already there. She saw his Buick in the parking lot when she pulled in and parked the Mustang beside it.

Normally, he might have waited for her in the lot to see if she had brought him any biscuits left over from breakfast. The fact that he had gone on inside without her, risking the possibility of having hot biscuits get cold, showed that he was in a highly agitated state.

She laid the tin containing the fresh bread on the black dash of her car in the sunshine. The biscuits would still be warm, even if it was hours before they returned.

She left the car and walked up the pathway to the

brick building, thinking that she'd rather go to the dentist or the gynecologist.

Too many sad things occurred inside this building for it to be one of her favorite places. She had witnessed one too many next of kin having to identify the remains of their loved ones inside these walls.

Walking through the front doors, she saw the other reason why she hated to come here: the desk attendant, Officer Kenny Bates.

"Savannah!" he exclaimed the moment he saw her. "Hey, girl, you're looking good today!"

She and Kenny had a love-loathe relationship. He loved her; she loathed him, the ground he plodded on, the air he breathed.

Especially the air he exhales, she thought as she caught a whiff of something that smelled like a toxic mixture of garlic and licorice.

Yeap, there were dill pickles and licorice whips on his desk.

She tried to breathe through her ears as she wrote on his sign-in sheet, Ida Spize U.

"I was wondering," he said, leaning over the counter, trying to look down her blouse. "Do you wanna—"

"No. I do not."

"Go to Las Vegas—"

"No!"

"With me—"

"Never."

"For a long, romantic weekend?"

"I'd rather die. No, wait. I'd rather that *you* died."

"We can take in some of those topless shows and get massages together, maybe get our naked bodies painted with chocolate while the other one watches."

She looked at his metal-framed glasses, the lens of which hadn't been cleaned for years. She watched as he licked his lips with a black, licorice-stained tongue. She noted the shirt wet with green pickle juice and the way it gaped open over his gut between the buttons, letting some of his belly hairs stick through.

"I'll bet that'd put you in the mood, huh?" he said. "I'd even lick the chocolate off you if you want me to."

The way he waggled one scraggly eyebrow at her made her fantasize about vats of hot, flaming oil being poured from castle parapets down onto deserving pervert, peasant desk attendants.

"Someday," she told him, "I'm going to just say, 'Screw it,' and shoot you dead where you stand, Bates. Or maybe I'll stab you in the eyeballs with your own pen over a hundred times and let Dr. Liu decide if it was overkill."

He chuckled. And as she walked away, she heard him say, "I love all this sexual tension between us, Savannah. But we just have to take it to the next level. Reconsider that Las Vegas offer, okay."

"Go to hell, Bates. Do not pass Go. Do not collect two hundred dollars."

At the end of the long hallway with its shiny, hospital-type linoleum, she came to a pair of large swinging doors.

Opening one of them a couple of inches, she peeped inside and said, "Yoo-hoo. Anybody here? Dr. Jen?"

"Yeah, Van, come on in," replied a masculine voice.

She opened the door the rest of the way to find that Dirk was there with Dr. Liu, both of them looking down at the body stretched out on the autopsy table.

"Sorry I'm late," she said.

"You aren't late," Dr. Liu told her. "This guy is just rushing me."

"Who? Me?" Dirk looked highly offended. "I'd never rush anybody."

"Oh please." Savannah shook her head. "You've offered to push little old ladies with walkers to get them out of your way."

"That only happened once! *Once,* and now you're never gonna let me live it down "

"Sh-h-h. Can't you tell when I'm teasing you, boy?"

Out of habit, Savannah went over to a cupboard, opened it, and took out a paper smock, cap, booties, and a pair of surgical gloves.

Once she was appropriately dressed, she walked up to the table where Dr. Liu was in the middle of Andrew Dante's autopsy.

"See," Dr. Liu told Dirk. "Savannah wears the disposable protective gear like I ask her to."

"Yeah, and she crosses streets at the corners, inside the little lines, too. She's a nerd, so—ow-w!"

He grabbed his arm and rubbed the spot where Savannah had slugged him. "And for a nerd, she's got a pretty good right jab, too," he said with a chuckle.

"What have y'all got here?" Savannah asked, looking down on the body with the detachment of a professional and only a little of a layman's queasiness.

"What we have," Dr. Liu said, "is a very interesting case."

"That's for sure," Dirk added. "Wait'll we tell you what killed him."

"What killed him?" Savannah looked down at the grievous wound in the chest, which had been incised even further open. "The stake didn't do it?"

"Nope." Dirk grinned, enjoying the suspense. "The stake didn't do it. Remember Dr. Liu said at the scene that the wound didn't look right to her, didn't look like your average stabbing with a foreign object."

"The stake was inserted postmortem," Dr. Liu said.

"For effect, I suppose." Savannah shook her head. "And whoa! What an effect! What was it that actually killed him?"

"Manner of death, homicide," Dr. Liu told her. "Cause of death, gunshot wound of chest."

"Gunshot? Get out!"

"She's dead serious," Dirk said. "Can you roll him over, Doc, and show her?"

"No, but if you suit up, I'll let you roll him over," Dr. Liu said with a grin.

Grumbling, Dirk went to the cupboard, got the disposable protection gear, and put it on. When he returned to the table, Savannah snickered and said, "You didn't have to put the cap on. That's to keep your hair from dropping on the body."

"Shut up."

"We could do a hair count before and after you look at him," Savannah continued, undaunted. "If you start out with eleven and end up with eleven, no problem."

"I said, 'Shut up.' There are some things you just don't tease about. And the hair is one of them."

He walked around to the opposite side of the table, put one hand on Dante's shoulder and the other under his hip, and rolled him onto his side. "Are you going to stand there smarting off about my lack of hair, or are you gonna check this out?"

"I'm checking. I'm checking."

Savannah hurried around the table to stand next to him. One look at the back of Andrew Dante's shirt told the story all too clearly.

In the center of his pale blue shirt—high, only a few inches below the neck—was a neat black hole burned into the fabric. A small amount of blood had oozed onto the fabric around it. But even with the

bloodstains, she could see the telltale stain of gun-
powder residue.

"Oh, wow," she said. "And this is the entrance wound.
Which means that awful thing on the front . . ."

"The exit wound," Dr. Liu added.

"High caliber, too," Savannah said, thinking out
loud. "Neat hole here in the back, a major blowout
in the front." She turned to Dr. Liu. "I can see why
you didn't think the wound looked like a stab there
at the scene."

"Yeah, well . . . before you toot my horn too
loudly, I have to admit, I was wrong when I said I
doubted he was killed there. Now, I'm pretty sure he
was."

"Oh, really? Why?"

"Roll him back over, Dirk, and I'll show her."

Dirk did as he was told, and Dr. Liu lifted the vampire costume carefully off the body.

Immediately, Savannah could see the gruesome
evidence. A disturbing amount of gore was all over
the front of the pants, basically in the victim's lap.

"Mercy," she said. "That's pretty ugly."

"Yes, it is." Dr. Liu pointed to the chest wound.
"The bullet entered his back high up between his
shoulder blades, went through his heart, and exited
right here, slightly below center."

"So the shooter was slightly higher than he was,
aiming downward?"

"I think so," Dr. Liu said. "I'll know the exact
angle by the time I finish the autopsy."

Dirk got a sick look on his face. "The guy could
have even been sitting down when he got hit, like sitting there in that coffin when somebody shot him
from the back."

"That's a pretty grim way to go," Savannah added.
"I wonder if he knew it was coming."

"He must have figured something was up if he was

already sitting in a coffin." Dirk shuddered. "I mean, you couldn't be too cheerful, sitting in a casket, maybe waiting for somebody to shoot you in the back."

"He couldn't have known it was coming, not for sure," Savannah said, "or like you said at the scene, he would have fought like a maniac. Andrew Dante was a big guy, and I'm sure not a shy one, considering all he'd accomplished in his life. You don't get to the level of success he had by being a pushover. I can't imagine he'd go peacefully."

"Or maybe it was somebody he trusted," Dr. Liu suggested. "Maybe someone was threatening him with a gun, but it was someone he loved, and he didn't really believe they would hurt him."

Dirk chuckled—a hard, bitter laugh. "Well, if that was the case, he must have been pretty friggen surprised."

Savannah groaned. "Hopefully, he wouldn't have lived long enough to be unhappily surprised for long."

"No," Dr. Liu said, "it wouldn't have been long at all. He would have bled right out, gone unconscious very quickly."

"Well, that's good," Savannah said without enthusiasm. "I guess."

"It still sucks," Dirk muttered.

"Yeah. It sure does."

Savannah pictured it: Andrew Dante sitting in that ridiculous prop casket, someone he may have loved and trusted—at least at one time—threatening him with a gun. Him hoping, believing they'd never actually do it. Then . . . bang! Surprise!

"Yeah," she repeated, "that really does stink—a rotten, rotten thing to do. Let's get 'em."

Chapter 16

"Try to be a little nicer to Eileen today, would you?" Savannah asked Dirk as they pulled into the forensic lab's parking lot. "No arm twisting, no pushy crap, no name-calling, hair pulling, groin kicking, eyeball gouging . . ."

He laughed. "Boy, you sure know how to cramp a guy's style." Giving her a wink, he added, "I'll be good. I'll be sweet. I'll be so nice to Eileen that you'll get jealous."

"Jealous? Me?"

"Yeah, you."

She sniffed. "That'll be the day, *you* make *me* jealous."

As they got out of the car and walked up to the door, Savannah gave it a little more thought and got moderately irked. "I do not get jealous of you, ever. That's just your overinflated ego talking, boy."

He punched the buzzer button with his thumb. "You do, too. Every time we go to the Patty Cake Donut Shop and I flirt with that little cutie, Sherry, you get pissy."

"No way!"

"Uh-huh. Not enough to kill your appetite for maple bars, but you do give her dirty looks."

"I give *you* dirty looks for buttering her up just so that you can get an extra large coffee for the price of a small one. It's about you being cheap, not me being jealous."

"Yeah, right. I know what I see."

"See this!"

She started to make a gesture that was definitely not on Granny Reid's list of approved hand signals for Southern ladies. Then she realized they were on camera, the one mounted over the door. And that was another rule: if at all possible, never behave badly on videotape.

The door opened, and a cranky Eileen filled the space. Eileen was a big girl who seemed to expand when her mood turned ugly.

"If you're here about those clothes your victim was wearing," she told Dirk, hands on hips, "turn around and march right back to your car. We just got them, and I haven't even had time to open the bag."

Dirk lifted both hands in absolute surrender, a sheepish look on his face that Savannah knew darned well was totally fake, but Eileen might buy it. "Please, Eileen, forgive me for the other day. I've been informed by somebody who knows a lot more about being polite and courteous than I do . . ." He cut a sideways look at Savannah. ". . . that I was a jerk to you last time I was in here. And I'm really sorry. Can you find it in your heart to forgive me?"

Eileen gave him a sustained drop-dead look, then shook her head. "Oh, please," she said, "like I'm going to buy a ton of crap like that. I'm busy here. What do you want?"

Dirk dropped the repentant sinner façade in an instant. "To look at the coffin," he replied, equally acerbic.

"That's it? You're not going to irritate me at all? You're not going to try to manipulate me into—"

Dirk snapped. "I just want to look at the damned casket, if you don't friggen mind!" he shouted, his face dark red.

Eileen said nothing, just turned abruptly and walked away. But she left the door open behind her, and Savannah and Dirk took that as a yes.

They scurried inside before she could change her mind.

"Smooth," Savannah whispered to him. "Quite the silken-tongued laddie you are."

"Oh, back off me, woman. I'm not in the mood."

She laughed at him. "If I had to wait until you were in the mood, I'd never get to harass you, and life would hardly be worth living."

He ignored her and looked around the enormous room for his evidence. Eileen had returned to her lab bench in the back. Her assistants were helping her or sitting at computers.

A couple of the techs shot Dirk wary looks, but none offered to help him.

Fortunately, an item as large as a coffin wasn't difficult to find. In the rear of the room near where Eileen was working was a large, long cardboard box that was sealed across the top with evidence tape.

"That's gotta be it," he said as he walked over to the box and knelt beside it.

Savannah did the same and read the evidence label taped to the top. One of the techs had written on the label, describing the contents as "stage prop coffin-victim found inside."

Dirk looked over at Eileen, who was peering into a microscope. He opened his mouth to say something to her, but without taking her eye from the scope, she said, "Go on. Open it. Just be sure to sign the chain of possession label."

Dirk grumbled something that sounded re-
motely like, "Thanks," then did as she said. On the
top of the box, a large piece of paper had been
taped. It bore the same description as the evidence
label but also had a number of blank lines below the
description where those handling the evidence
could write their signatures.

Dirk scribbled "Det. Coulter," the date, and time.
Then he and Savannah both put on rubber gloves,
and he used his pocketknife to slit the tape that
sealed the top of the box.

Savannah helped him open the flaps, and they
found themselves staring down into the black coffin
where Andrew Dante had been found.

It was a cheap, plywood box made in the shape of
an old-fashioned, toe-pincher style coffin—wide about
one-third of the way down, and narrow at the head
and feet. The edges were rough and unsanded, and a
quick coat of black paint had been slapped on.

For all of its spooky effect in the semidarkness
with blood-red lighting, it looked pretty tacky in the
bright light of the laboratory.

But even under high-tech illumination, the black
background made any blood difficult to see.

"Here. You'll need these." They looked up to see
Eileen holding out two pairs of orange wraparound
plastic goggles and a portable light source, which
looked like a small black box with a handle, and a
lens similar to a flashlight on the front.

"Thanks," Dirk said, taking the scope from her
and one pair of the glasses. He actually sounded grateful this time.

Handing the second pair to Savannah, she called
out, "Mike, dim the lights back here."

A few seconds later, the ceiling lights in the room
went down to the level of a romantic restaurant in
the evening.

"I assume you're checking for blood spatter," Eileen said, putting on a pair of goggles.

"Among other things," Dirk said.

"Like?"

"The bullet that killed our victim."

Even behind the goggles, Savannah saw Eileen's eyes widen. "Get outta here! No way!"

"Yep," Savannah told her. "We were just at Dr. Liu's. He was shot through the heart. The old-fashioned way—with a gun."

"But the wooden stake?"

"Apparently, it was inserted postmortem." Dirk switched on the light source and directed the beam onto the casket. "Holy crap! Look at that!"

"Wow, talk about lit up! It's Times Square on New Year's Eve in there," Savannah said as all three stared at the eerie glow inside the coffin.

Tiny fine dots glistened on nearly every square inch of the black wood. But the densest area of illumination was about three-quarters of the way down from the top of the coffin. And it had a strange, almost triangular shape to it, with the apex of the triangle toward the top of the coffin and broadening toward the bottom.

"That's weird," Eileen said.

"Not really," Dirk replied. "Dante was shot in the back, exit wound in the front. And Dr. Liu thinks he may have been sitting when he got it."

Savannah looked down at the triangle and realized that if, in fact, Andrew Dante had been sitting in the coffin, his legs partly spread, and someone shot him from behind . . . that would account for the triangle of dense blood deposited on the bottom of the coffin. Very simply, the exit wound spray of blood and tissue would have gone between his thighs and legs and onto the casket bottom, leaving this very shape. She noticed that the cleanest area was just above the triangle, where his buttocks would have been.

"That's pretty nasty," she murmured.

"No kidding." Even Eileen seemed impressed.

Savannah was only dimly aware that the other lab techs were standing around them, also wearing goggles, staring at the evidence of Andrew Dante's gruesome demise.

Dirk leaned closer, examining the spatter along the inside edges of the coffin. "This confirms the shooting," he said. "This is definitely high velocity spatter. You don't get this fine mist from a stabbing or bludgeoning."

Savannah leaned even closer and peered at the bottom of the coffin. Amid the thickest part of the glowing biological gore, she thought she saw a glint. "Can somebody hand me a cotton swab?" she asked.

A moment later, a small, long white box was pressed into her gloved hands. She opened the end of it and shook out the long cotton swab that was inside.

Bending over the coffin, she carefully swabbed away a tiny bit of the blood covering the area where she thought she had seen something.

And there it was.

"A slug," Savannah said. "That's gotta be our bullet."

"And hopefully," Eileen added, "it won't be too badly deformed. Human tissue and wood are fairly yielding as materials go."

Dirk took the swab from Savannah, reached down, and cleared away more of the debris. "I think I can get this out for you," he said.

"No pocketknives!" Eileen barked. "You know how I hate it when you cops do that!"

"Hey, I only did it once! You chewed me out for it royal, and I never did it again!"

"I just don't want you using anything hard to dig it

out with. It can leave marks and make it harder for us to match—"

"I know, I know." He held the bullet up between his thumb and finger. "There you go. No pocket-knife, no tweezers! Are fingers soft enough for you?"

Eileen held out a small manila envelope. "Just put it in here, and I'll look at it right away for you."

"What a gal!"

"Unless you piss me off again."

"What?" He shrugged and looked at Savannah. "What did I say? Man, working with all these chemicals in a room with no windows sure seems to make people cranky."

"Sh-h-h," Savannah told him. "Don't you know how to quit when you're ahead?"

But Eileen didn't hear the exchange. She was already examining the bullet under a microscope.

"It's a .45. There's some damage," she called out to them, "but the rifling is pretty clear, the lands and grooves pronounced enough that if you find a weapon, we'll probably be able to get a comparison."

"Excellent." Savannah got up off her knees and tried not to groan at the twinges the movement gave her. No groaning in front of younger people who would then consider you an old fart.

"Okay," Dirk said, standing. Less vain, he went ahead and groaned. "I guess we need to send a team back out to the Dante estate and have them look for a .45-caliber weapon."

"You think the shooter was stupid enough to leave it there?" Savannah asked.

He shrugged. "Hey, you can always hope."

"So, how are the alibis checking out?" Savannah asked as she and Dirk headed over to the Dante mansion.

"Robyn Dante was where she said she was," he replied as he unzipped his bomber jacket and tried to pull it off over his shoulders.

Savannah reached over, peeled it off him, and dumped it on the backseat. "She was at the spa the whole time she said she was?"

"Yep. I dropped by there this morning before I even went to Dr. Liu's. The gal at the desk remembered seeing her. I talked to the guy who massaged her and the chicks who did her face, her nails, and even her toenails. She was getting pampered for hours."

Savannah sighed and closed her eyes. "Ah-h-h-h . . . can you even imagine the bliss?"

He snorted. "The day I have to actually pay people to touch me is the day I get a girlfriend who'll do it for free."

"Always the economist. You know, occasionally, you have to feed a girlfriend and buy her presents."

"If I were going to buy food for somebody, I'd just get myself a dog."

She shot him a death ray look. "I can't believe you just said that."

"I can't believe you didn't know I was teasing. I said it just to get a rise out of you." He leaned over and put his hand on her knee. "Don't you know that if I'm gonna buy any presents for anybody, it would be for you?"

"But you don't buy me presents, except at Christmas, when you *really* have to."

He nodded once and smiled. "See what I mean? So you shouldn't take it at all personally."

"What?"

Fortunately, for his sake, they had arrived back at the Dantes'.

Although there were plenty of paparazzi parked in front of the mansion, the throng had thinned a bit. And they only had to threaten a few reporters with torture to get through the crowd.

"When are you going to let them take all of this crap out of here?" Savannah asked as they, once again, made their way through the nightmare display.

"I was going to release the scene today," he said, stepping around a werewolf who was chewing on an alien's green foot. "But now that we're going to be looking for a stashed weapon, I'm going to have to hold it a bit longer."

"Are you telling me we have to search through all this crap? I can't. I'm just sick to death of looking at it."

"*We* aren't going to. I've risen to the highly respected level of sergeant, and you are a lowly civilian. We'll pawn it off on the standard-issue beat cops."

"They'll be thrilled," she said dryly.

"Actually, they will. I just talked to the chief. Considering the high profile status of the case, he's authorized some overtime. They'll be all over it."

"When are they getting here?"

He glanced at his watch. "In less than an hour, so we'd better get on these interviews. I'll take the maid."

"The one in the French hotty costume? I'll bet you will. And what am I supposed to do with myself?"

"Give me plenty of privacy? Oww!"

The moment they reached the front door, it flew open, and an angry middle-aged woman charged out.

Tiffany came running out after her dressed in a bright red, highly spangled belly dancer's costume.

"You had better not touch one thing here!" Tiffy was screaming at her. "I mean it! I hired you, not my stepmother. You'd better do as I say!"

The woman whirled around and stuck her finger in Tiffany's face. "You're nuts! You know that? You are just crazy! Your father was killed here less than twenty-four hours ago, and you're going through with a party? That's just . . . sick!"

"My father would have wanted me to go ahead! He would! He loved me, and he always wanted the best for me. The party is going on, no matter what that bitch in there says!"

"No, there isn't. I'm having nothing to do with a fiasco like that. Your mother—"

"Stepmother. She's my wicked *step*mother!"

"Whoa!" Dirk said, holding up one hand. "I'm sorry to tell you ladies that neither one of you is going to get what you want." He turned to the older woman. "You can't take your things out of here yet. They're still part of my crime scene. We're going to be searching every single piece of this junk before it goes anywhere."

"Yes!" Tiffany said. "Excellent!"

"And you . . ." Dirk said, turning to her, ". . . are as crazy as this woman thinks you are if you think you're going to have a party the day after your father is murdered here. Nobody is coming inside this house. I was being kind to you and your stepmom, even allowing *you* to stay here last night."

"Kind? You think you've been *kind* to me?"

"Yes, more than reasonable. And if you mess with me, you'll be packing your bag and moving into a local hotel. Got it?"

"Are you telling me that I'm not going to be able to have my big Halloween party tonight? Is that what you're saying to me? With food arriving any minute and entertainers and . . ."

"Nobody's arriving. Nobody." He took out his cell phone and called the station house. "Coulter here," he said. "I'm going to need at least half a dozen radio cars at the Dante place right away. And could you get that team over here for the search, too?" He hung up.

"What do you mean, search? What search?" Tiffany demanded. "You people were crawling all over this place last night. I thought we were done with you."

"You aren't done with us until we're done with you, Tiff-fy," he said in his most condescending tone, the one that made Savannah feel the desperate need to box his ears.

Apparently, Tiffany felt the same urge. She even went so far as to raise her hand, then seemed to see something in his eyes that made her drop it.

"And now," he said, "if you and your red, sparkly costume would get out of my way, I have work to do."

They left a furious Tiffany in the middle of the sidewalk and walked on into the house.

In the foyer, they found Robyn having a conversation with the maid, who was dressed as the Bride of Frankenstein. Her fine figure was covered, neck to toe, with a shapeless white sheet. Her wig stuck straight up at least a foot, black hair with the traditional jagged white stripe on each side.

Dirk looked desperately disappointed.

Savannah chuckled to herself.

"Yes," Robyn was telling the maid, "you most certainly *may* change out of that stupid costume and back into your . . . wait . . . no, from now on just feel free to wear a simple blouse and slacks of a neutral color. Something that looks nice but is comfortable and easy to move in." She reached over and patted the maid on the shoulder. "I'm sorry that you ever had to wear that disgraceful outfit. Things are going to be different around here now."

The maid nodded, setting the enormous wig bobbing wildly, and hurried away.

"Hello, Savannah, Detective Coulter," she said as

she walked over to them and shook their hands. "How can I help you today? Is there anything new about Daisy . . . or Andrew?"

"Uh, nothing about Daisy," Dirk said.

Savannah could tell he was debating how much to tell her. It was never easy, deciding how brutally honest to be with the family.

But she knew Dirk. He would eventually tell it all.

"And about Andrew?" Robyn said. "What is it? Have they finished with the . . . uh . . . autopsy?"

"Yes. It's done." Dirk cleared his throat. "I don't know if this is going to make you feel better or worse, but as it turns out, Andrew was actually shot to death."

"Shot?" She stared at him, her mouth open, for a long time. Then she seemed to come back to consciousness. "Shot?" she repeated. "With a gun?"

"Yes," Dirk said. "In fact, we're going to have to go over the premises again thoroughly to see if we can find the weapon. I'm sorry that we have to disturb you again, but . . ."

"No, don't apologize," she said. "You have to do your duty, and we'll cooperate any way we can."

Savannah nodded toward the doorway. "We ran into Tiffany out there and some lady. I guess she's the party planner or . . . ?"

"She's the woman who brought in all these ghastly props. I think she works with the movie people, supplying this sort of stuff. I told her to get it all out of here, and Tiffany seems to have this ridiculous idea that she's having a party here in a few hours."

"Don't worry," Dirk told her. "It isn't going to happen. I'm seeing to that." He glanced down the hallway where the maid had disappeared. "Do you mind," he said, "if I talk to your housekeeper now? I just want to ask her a few questions."

"I'll go get her," she offered. "And then, if you don't mind, I'm going to go back upstairs to my room. I have some very important phone calls to make."

"Phone calls?" Savannah asked. "Like to inform friends and relatives?"

The friendly smile fell off her face, and her big blue eyes blazed with a deep hatred that was a bit startling. "No," she said, "I've already made those calls. I'm going to see if I can find an attorney who can keep that rotten kid from totally screwing me out of everything."

"Good luck," Savannah said, meaning it.

"Yeah, really," Dirk added.

"Thank you."

As they watched her disappear around the corner, Savannah leaned over and whispered in Dirk's ear, "I don't know who killed Andrew. But if Tiffany ends up dead, I'll know who did that one."

"No kidding."

It was quite a while before the maid returned, and by then, Dirk was outside, giving orders to the search team, who had arrived.

So Savannah decided to do the honors herself.

She took the young woman into the living room where they sat on a sofa to talk.

The maid had changed out of her Halloween attire and was wearing a simple white blouse with black slacks. Her long dark hair was pulled back and held with a large barrette.

Savannah approved of the change. She looked elegant but dignified. A far cry from the overtly sexy costume she'd been wearing when they'd first met her.

Dirk wouldn't agree, but his judgment couldn't be trusted when it came to a great pair of legs.

"My name is Savannah Reid," she told her. "What's yours?"

"Libby Jefferson."

"How long have you worked here?"

"Six months, maybe seven," Libby replied. She glanced around as though looking for eavesdroppers and added, "I guess it just seems like a long time."

"Dog years, huh?"

Her eyes sparkled with mischief, and she giggled. "Yes, no kidding. With all the fighting and having that . . . that Tiffany . . . boss me around all the time. You wouldn't believe what I have to put up with around here."

"I can only imagine." Savannah shook her head. "Actually, I don't even want to go there mentally. She must be impossible to work for."

"Oh, she is! And now that Mr. Dante is gone . . ." Tears filled her dark eyes. She blinked, and they ran down her cheeks. "He was really nice to me. I'm going to miss him."

"I'm sorry for your loss," Savannah said, offering her a tissue from her purse.

"Thank you. Do the cops know who killed him yet?"

"They're working on it," Savannah replied. "But I was wondering . . . You were here yesterday when Detective Coulter and I took Tiffany away for questioning, right?"

She grinned broadly, for the moment, her mourning suspended. "I sure was. That was great!"

"Yes, it was rather fun," Savannah whispered. "Can you tell me what happened then?"

"Oh, all hell broke loose. One of the workers ran in and told Mr. Dante that you'd taken her, and he threw a fit. He called his lawyer, and then he ordered everybody to leave."

"Everybody?"

"Yes. There were all those people here setting up for the party. And he yelled at everybody and told them to get out of here. So they did."

"And how about any others?"

"Others?"

"People other than the workers. Like the Skeleton Key girls, Bunny, Kiki . . . their mothers . . . anyone else who might have been here?"

Libby thought for a long time before answering. "I think they were here earlier. Bunny and her mom dropped by, but I think I heard Tiffany asking them to run some errands for her. And I know she sent Kiki off to the seamstress to see if her costume was ready . . . that red belly dancing thing she's got on today."

"And where did you go, what did you do when Mr. Dante ordered everyone to leave?"

"Well, I live here in the servants' quarters, an apartment over the garage. So when he screamed at us all and told us to go, I went to my apartment."

"How long were you there?"

"I stayed up there until last night when I saw all the lights and weird things going on around the pool area. That's when I came down and realized that Mr. Dante was dead." She started to cry again. "My God, I'll never forget how he looked in that coffin. It was just horrible. I dreamed about it last night and woke up screaming!"

The thought occurred to Savannah, not for the first time, how wide the ripples from a murder spread, how many victims there were from such a grave crime.

"It'll get better," she told her from experience. "But not for some time."

Savannah allowed Libby to cry for a while, but as soon as she had composed herself a bit, she decided to press on. "Can you tell me, please, where are the guns kept in this house?"

"The guns? Sure. There's a pair of old dueling pistols in Mr. Dante's workout room and a hunting rifle in the top of the closet in the master bedroom, and Mr. Dante's father's gun is in the desk in the library in the bottom drawer."

"Can you show me that one?"

"Of course."

They left the living room and ran into Dirk again in the foyer.

Savannah pulled him aside long enough to tell him, "Check for a rifle in the top of the master bedroom closet and dueling pistols in the exercise room."

He nodded but looked mildly perturbed to see she had taken over the maid. "I'm going to check Miss Twerp's room again, too," he said. "I saw her drive away a minute ago. It seems like the good time. The team is going to start out in the yard."

"Sounds like a plan."

They split up, and Savannah followed Libby into the library.

The maid went straight to the desk and opened the top drawer. Reaching beneath the drawer, she pulled off a small key that was taped there.

"Mr. Dante was careful about how he stored his guns," she said. "He knew that with kids coming in and out of here, you have to be responsible."

She used the key to open the bottom right drawer and looked inside. "It's right . . . oh . . ."

"Oh?" Savannah asked with a sinking feeling.

"It isn't here."

Now, how did I just know it wasn't going to be? Savannah asked herself.

"What kind of gun is it?"

"I don't know much about guns, but it's one like you hold in your hand."

"A pistol, not a long one, like a rifle."

"Yes, a pistol. That's what he called it. He called it something like his horse or maybe his pony."

"His horse? His pony?" A lightbulb came on in her head. "Did he maybe refer to it as his Colt?"

"That's it, his Colt! That's what he called it, his dad's old Colt from his army days."

Colt, as in a Colt .45? Savannah thought, her heart starting to pound.

"Is there any other place it might be?" she asked Libby. "Any other place he kept it sometimes?"

"No. Mr. Dante was big on knowing exactly where his guns were at all times. None of us were allowed to touch them, and he always kept them in the same places."

Savannah sighed and said, "Well, I'm afraid somebody broke the rules. Somebody touched one. Probably this one."

She reached over and patted Libby on the arm. "Thank you," she said. "Thanks a bunch." She gave her one of her business cards. "If you think of anything else, anybody you might have seen yesterday afternoon, before or after the incident with Tiffany, please give me a call."

"Sure, I will. Good luck."

"Thanks."

Savannah went upstairs and soon located Dirk in Tiffany's bedroom. He jumped when she opened the door and caught him with his hands in one of her dresser drawers.

"You scared me," he admitted with a weak chuckle as she closed the door behind her.

"You thought I was Tiffany. Big, bad you is scared of that little brat."

"Am not."

"Are, too."

"Okay, I am. Not exactly afraid, but sick of her. One more round and I might do something to her that really would get me sued and fired."

"I hear you."

"I see you already questioned that maid," he said, closing the drawer and opening the one beneath it.

"Yes, and I think I know what gun we're looking for. There's a Colt .45 missing from Dante's library desk."

Dirk froze in midsearch. "No way!"

"You heard me. The maid—Libby's her name— took me in there to show it to me. It was supposed to be in a locked drawer. She unlocked the drawer, and it was gone. She says he always, always kept it there."

"Wow! Good work, Van."

"Thank you."

She looked around the hot pink room, at the canopied bed with its pink organza bed curtains spilling down onto a frilly pink bedspread covered with frilly pink pillows. A fainting couch in the corner was pink, as was the fur throw that was laid across it. The folding privacy screen was pink and had an enormous pink feather boa thrown over it.

Savannah was a girlie girl in many ways and liked pink as much as any other female, but this room made her want to gag.

She walked over to the bed and slipped her hands beneath and among the mountain of pillows. Then she moved a giant pink teddy bear out of the corner and looked behind him.

Dirk was finishing with the dresser, so she dropped down onto her knees beside the bed, lifted the pink satin dust ruffle, and looked underneath.

"Dirk," she said.

"Yeah?"

"Come here."

He hurried over to her and knelt beside her. "What is it?"

"Give me your penlight."

He handed her the tiny flashlight. She pointed it at the dark object in the corner near the bed's carved claw-foot.

"Get me a pen," she said.

He grabbed one off the nightstand and gave it to her.

She reached far under the bed and a moment later, came out with the big pistol dangling from the pen by its trigger guard.

"Whoa! Van, you scored! Good goin', girl!"

She held the gun close to her nose and gave it a sniff. "Oh yeah," she said, a huge grin on her face. "What's better than finding a Colt .45 in bratty Tiffany's bedroom? Finding one that's been recently fired."

He laughed out loud. "Makes my day," he said. "Bigtime!"

Chapter 17

Tammy sat at Savannah's kitchen table, staring at the computer screen in front of her, while the entire Moonlight Magnolia Detective Agency, plus Gran, sat around the table, waiting and watching with great expectation.

"Drats," she said, shaking her head. "Nothing."

"No! Do not tell us that!" Savannah said, sinking low in her chair.

"Are you telling me . . ."—Dirk leaned over and tried to see the screen as she typed—". . . that I went to all that rigmarole to get that search warrant and seize her computer for nothing?"

Tammy threw up her hands in frustration. "What can I say? Tiffy doesn't compute much. Apparently, she's too busy."

"We're all too busy," Ryan said from one end of the table. "But we still find at least some time to waste on the computer every day. Don't we?"

Savannah shook her head. "I don't."

"Me either," Gran added. "I'm still complaining about how much the telephone interferes with my day. Don't need anything else, like a computer, to make it even harder to get my chores done."

"Maybe she uses a BlackBerry or some other sort of handheld mobile device to receive e-mails," John suggested.

"I thought of that," Dirk said, "and I had them include that kind of thing in the search warrant. But she wasn't home when I went there to seize the stuff, so I'll have to wait on that."

"Oh, hey, hold on," Tammy said. "I think I found something here. She's stored a few e-mails here. I just found them."

"That's more like it!" Savannah said. "But are they recent?"

"Last week." Tammy typed away and squinted at the screen. "They're from somebody whose screen name is SwizMiz62."

"SwizMiz62," Savannah mused. "Tiffany's mother lived in Switzerland. I suppose it could stand for Swiss Miss? But I doubt she's 62."

Ryan added, "It could be her birth year. That would be about right."

"You're right," Tammy said. "It *is* her mother. There's some really nasty stuff here about Robyn. Her mom's real name is Crystal. And boy, they both really hate Robyn's guts."

"Can't really expect it'd be otherwise," Gran said softly. "Most women don't take kindly to the gal who took their man away. And you can't really blame that Tiffany girl either. It's hard for a young'un to deal with grown-ups' nonsense. They've got enough trouble just being a kid."

"But it's been a couple of years since all that went down," Dirk told her. "You'd think they'd be over it by now."

Gran shook her head. "No. Some hurts go too deep for a body to ever get over."

Dirk considered that for a while. "You suppose she's nursing a grudge still deep enough to kill the guy over?"

"Might be," Savannah said. "At any rate, we've got to add her to the list of people to check, make sure she's still in Argentina with her polo player."

Dirk said, "That list of ours seems to be getting longer rather than shorter. And us with a missing kid still on our hands."

A cell phone lying on the table began to play a merry tune. Dirk reached for it and looked at the caller ID. "It's Daisy's cell," he said. "And it's her boyfriend calling again. He keeps leaving messages every couple of hours and has been since we talked to him. He's getting more and more frantic."

"You haven't told him that we have her phone?" Tammy asked.

"No." Dirk continued to let it ring without picking up. "I wanted to hear what he was saying to her. But so far, he just sounds like a boyfriend who's worried sick."

"Her mom is a mess," Savannah said. "She went on the news at noon and begged for whoever has Daisy to let her go. It broke my heart."

"Well, hopefully, it'll break somebody else's heart," Gran added. "Maybe somebody who knows something will come forward, and then maybe you guys can get a lead on what's happened to her."

"I've been trying to get hold of Kiki," Savannah said. "I swear, if I could get her alone one more time, maybe I could pry something out of her. But she's obviously avoiding me. I've called a dozen times."

Dirk rubbed his eyes wearily. "I'll try to get hold of her again. It's just that with this Dante thing on top of it all, I don't know if I'm coming or going."

"That's why we're here," Ryan said. "Really, let us take part of this for you. What can we do?"

"We've been known to pry a few things out of unwilling parties from time to time ourselves back when we were with the Bureau," John replied, a twinkle in his eyes.

"I thought it was a kinder, gentler FBI now," Savannah said.

"That's the IRS," Ryan replied with a laugh. "The FBI is still as mean as ever."

"All right," Dirk said, admitting defeat . . . or something close to it. "If you two really do want to help, I'll give you the address of a certain travel agency, the one Dante always used. I'll call the gal there who's expecting me to drop by and tell her that you'll be interviewing her for me. I need to know a couple of things."

Ryan grabbed a legal pad from the middle of the table and reached into his pocket for his signature fountain pen. "Okay, shoot."

"It's on the corner of Charles Avenue and Eve's Place. The gal's name is Marilee. I need you to get every bit of info you can on any traveling Dante's paid for these past six months. I'm particularly interested in a trip to Amsterdam that he took four months ago in the middle of June. I want to know if he went alone, and if not, who he went with."

Ryan scribbled away on the pad. "Got it. And . . . ?"

"Also, I want to know if he's booked anything recently. Supposedly, there was a note saying he was going to London at the time he was killed. See if he bought a ticket."

"Anything else?"

Dirk thought for a moment, then said, "I think that's it."

Ryan tore the sheet off the pad and said, "No problem. We'll take care of that this afternoon and give you a call when we're done."

"Thanks, buddy. I appreciate it," Dirk said with uncustomary warmth.

Savannah couldn't help being surprised and pleased.

"Anything to help you find a missing youngster," John said. "We all carry a soft spot for those adolescents who can get themselves into such serious trouble so quickly."

"Well, this travel agency thing is more related to the Dante murder than the missing kid," Dirk said.

As Ryan folded the paper and stuck it into his shirt pocket, he said, "Don't you really think that one has to do with the other?"

Reluctantly, Dirk admitted, "Yes. I'd like to hope that Daisy's disappearance has nothing to do with a cold-blooded, gruesome murder. I'd hate to think she's on the bad side of somebody who would drive a stake into their victim's chest just for fun."

"No kidding," Savannah said under her breath.

Another cell phone began to play a tune. This time, it was Oingo Boingo's "Dead Man's Party."

"It's Dr. Liu," Savannah told the group as Dirk answered his phone.

"Coulter," Dirk said. He listened for a moment, then said, "Oh, yeah? What?" Grinning a little, he said, "No, you neglected to mention that detail. Did you swab it for DNA? Okay. What shade?" He chuckled. "Thanks a lot, Dr. Jen."

"Well, are you going to share with the rest of us?" Savannah said when he'd hung up.

He glanced over at Gran and cleared his throat. "Um, it seems the good doctor noticed something else during her autopsy after we left."

Savannah nudged him under the table with her foot. "And . . . ?"

"It seems our Mr. Dante had, um, enjoyed a form of sexual activity the day he died."

"You asked, 'what shade,' " Savannah said. "What? Did she find lipstick on his collar, as the old song says?"

Again, Dirk shot Gran a quick look. "Mm-m-m-m, not exactly on his collar."

There was a long, heavy silence in the room before Savannah finally said, "Ah, okay, gotcha."

Everyone nodded knowingly, including Gran.

Another long, uncomfortable silence reigned until once again, Savannah broke it. "Well, what shade was it?"

"Dark red, very dark. Almost black." Dirk pushed back from the table and stood. "I guess I need to go back out to the Dante place and ask Mrs. Dante if she and her husband got friendly that day and see if she has a tube of dark, dark red lipstick in her makeup drawer."

Gran stood, too, and walked over to the refrigerator. She reached inside and pulled out a pitcher of iced tea. "Well, if she does have a tube that color in her stuff, then you know she wasn't the one who kilt him."

They all mulled that one over for a minute, then Savannah asked, "How do you figure, Gran?"

She grinned as she poured herself a tall glass of the tea. " 'Cause there ain't no wife alive who'd get *that* friendly if she was figurin' on killin' her man the same day. That'd be a pure waste o' time and energy."

"That was nice of Ryan and John to volunteer to help us out, huh?" Savannah said as she and Dirk drove through Spirit Hills to the Dante place.

"Yeah, they're stand-up guys, those two," Dirk admitted.

She reached into a bag on the floorboard and pulled out a Snickers bar and a can of Pepsi. "You didn't like them when you first met them."

"Well, it's not for the reason you think."

She popped the top of the can and handed it to him. "What do you mean by that?"

"I mean that I didn't like them when I met them, but you thought it was because they're gay." He took a long drink of the Pepsi, then turned and grinned at her. "That *is* what you thought, huh?"

"Well . . . yeah. I guess so."

He tucked the soda between his thighs and took the candy bar she had unwrapped for him. "It's not true. That wasn't the reason."

"Okay." She got another chocolate bar and soda from the bag for herself. "I'll bite. Why didn't you like them?"

" 'Cause I thought they were stuffy and uppity."

Savannah knew exactly what he meant. Anybody who wore an ironed shirt and creased trousers was "uppity" to Dirk. And anybody who enjoyed classical music or knew the names of more than three artists was "stuffy."

"And now?" she asked.

"I know them now. And I mean, I don't have that much in common with them. I like baseball and football, and they like tennis and golf. I drink coffee and beer, and they drink tea and wine. I eat burgers, and they eat frogs' legs. Stuff like that. But they're good guys."

"And when did you decide this?"

"Oh, I've been making up my mind for a long time now. It was, like . . . an evolutionary process."

"Whoa!"

"What?"

"Watch out there, buddy, or you'll sound uppity and stuffy."

"Naw, never gonna happen. Not me."

A few minutes later, they pulled up in front of the mansion, their refreshments finished, their energy temporarily recharged.

They were met at the door by Libby.

She was thrilled to see Savannah and gave her a hug and a kiss on the cheek. Then she disappeared to summon the lady of the house.

"Hey, what was that?" Dirk wanted to know. "Since when are you two bosom buddies?"

"We bonded," Savannah said with a shrug. "We had our own little Hate Tiffy chat session, and now we're sisters. Why? Jealous?"

"A little, yeah. I mean, I don't want to be her *brother*, but . . ."

A couple of minutes later, Libby returned and said, "Mrs. Dante is on the telephone. But she asked me to show you outside to the patio and get you something to drink. She'll be down in a minute."

"If I have anything else to drink, I'll float away," Savannah said as they followed her out to the patio.

Savannah was astonished to see how ordinary the place looked. Dirk had finally released the scene, and apparently, the woman who had furnished the props had wasted no time in clearing everything away.

The only evidence of the violence that had happened here were the CSI techs' markings on the patio, specifically, where the coffin had been.

Dirk sat down in the chair that Libby offered, but Savannah walked around to the opposite side of the pool instead. She knelt near the markings and looked closely at the tiles that had been directly beneath the coffin.

After a while, she came back to Dirk and sat down on the chair next to his. "You can see where a little bit of the black paint rubbed off on the tiles over there," she said.

"Yeah? So?"

"I was just checking to see if the murderer dragged it. I was looking at the paint on the coffin there in the lab, and it looked fresh. I was looking to see if maybe the thing had been dragged here on the tile."

"O-o-okay. And this matters because?"

"Because we were talking about whether he was shot here or . . . I don't know, Dirk. Maybe I'm tired, too. We're kinda going in circles here. Nothing to really hang our hat on."

Dirk chuckled. "If what Dr. Liu told me is true, somebody could have hung their hat on Andrew's— hey, look who's here!"

Robyn Dante had just exited the house and was walking over toward them. She had a triumphant smile on her face.

"Good news," she said.

"Oh? Do share," Savannah told her. "We could use some good news."

"Just that I have an attorney who thinks I can get at least half of Andrew's estate."

"Tiffy's gonna be thrilled," Dirk said dryly.

"And of course, that's one of the sweetest parts." She sat down on the end of a chaise in front of them. "I know that isn't a very nice thing to say, but I'd enjoy getting some sort of satisfaction where that kid's concerned."

"I understand," Savannah said.

"Did Libby offer you something to drink?" Robyn wanted to know.

"Yes. But we really don't have time," Dirk told her. "We've got a lot on our plates here, between your husband's case and Daisy's."

Robyn's expression turned concerned and sad. "Oh yes, poor girl. Is there anything new about her?"

"Not yet," Dirk said.

"So, how can I help you?"

Dirk cleared his throat. "Actually, I need to ask you a couple of rather personal questions."

"Okay. Ask away."

"Did you, um, did you and your husband happen to have any sort of sexual contact the day he was murdered?"

"Did we what? Did we make love?" Robyn seemed shocked by the question. But as soon as she recovered, she said, "No. We didn't."

"No sexual contact of *any* kind?"

"No, none at all. Why?"

"We're just checking all sorts of things at this point, Mrs. Dante. We're just leaving no stone unturned. That sort of thing."

"Obviously." Robyn looked moderately perturbed.

Savannah decided to dive into the cold water with Dirk. "And something else. Would you mind terribly if I just quickly glanced through your . . . your makeup?"

"My *makeup*?"

"Uh, yes. Your makeup kit or drawer or . . . whatever."

Now Robyn definitely looked irritated.

"I don't see why you would want to do that," she said. "You've had free run of my home. I've allowed you to look absolutely everywhere and search everything you wanted. And now you want to—"

"Yes, you have," Savannah interjected. "You've been just wonderful, fully cooperative in every way. And if you could just allow us this one last liberty, I'd be so grateful. Then we can be out of your hair for good."

Robyn sat there for what seemed like a year, staring at her with those big blue eyes that suddenly, didn't look all that friendly. But finally, she said, "Okay. I keep my makeup in the master bedroom's bath—in the cabinet by the mirror, top drawer on the left. Help yourself."

Savannah jumped up, eager to get going before Robyn changed her mind. "Thank you, Robyn," she said, "so much."

Ten minutes later, Savannah was back.

Dirk was where she had left him, sitting in the chair. But Robyn was pacing back and forth on the other side of the pool, talking on her cell phone.

"Another call from her attorney," he told Savannah as she sat down next to him. "Find anything?"

"Nope. She's totally a pastel and natural tones sorta gal. Not a red, let alone dark red, in sight." She glanced around to see if anyone was within earshot, then added, "I also took a look in Tiffany's stuff."

Dirk gave her a disgusted look and shuddered.

"I know," she said. "Major ick factor. But when you've been in this business as long as we have . . . you learn to expect the worst from people."

"And you're seldom disappointed."

His cell phone rang. He answered it and said to Savannah, "It's Ryan." He continued his short conversation and when he hung up, told her, "They interviewed that gal at the travel agency, Marilee. She said Andrew didn't buy any ticket to London. And that trip to Amsterdam four months ago, he had a companion."

"Oh yeah? Who?"

He nodded toward Robyn. "Her."

"No way. But she said he went alone."

"Apparently, he didn't. Two tickets. One for Andrew Dante and the other for Robyn Dante."

"Well, that's a jackass of a different color."

Robyn had finished her phone call and was walking back to their side of the pool.

"I guess we'll just have to ask her about that one," Dirk said.

"Yes, you do that. She's probably still mad at me for going through her makeup. You have no idea what an invasion of privacy that is to a woman. Look through my knickers drawer, but keep your hands off my mascara."

"Did you find what you were looking for?" Robyn asked Savannah with a hint of sarcasm in her voice.

"No, I didn't," Savannah told her. "And that's a good thing."

"But I have a question for you," Dirk said. "About that trip to Amsterdam in June that Andrew took."

"Yes?"

"With you."

"No, I didn't go that time. I stayed home."

"Not according to your travel agent."

"What?"

Dirk gave her a long, hard look. "You're Robyn Dante, aren't you? There were two tickets bought for that trip. One for Andrew and one for Robyn."

Robyn sat down abruptly on the chaise, as though her legs had suddenly given out beneath her. She looked over at Savannah, tears welling in her eyes. "I told you," she said, her voice shaking. "I told you that's when it started."

"The affair?"

"Yes. He did what we used to do. He booked her ticket under his wife's name. Hell, he probably got her a fake passport, too."

"Fake passport?" Dirk perked up.

"Too?" Savannah asked.

"Yeah. Andrew knew this guy in Hollywood who

makes fake passports and sells them out of the back room of his tattoo parlor."

"What's the guy's name?" Dirk asked, already digging out his notebook and pen.

"Tank."

"Tank?"

"Yes, that's what Andrew called him. I'm not likely to forget a name like that."

"What's the name of the tattoo parlor?"

"Can't forget that one, either. Inky Dinky Do Tattoo. It's on Sunset Boulevard a few blocks north of Whisky a Go Go."

This time, it was Savannah's phone that rang. She was annoyed by the interruption until she saw on the caller ID that it was Pam O'Neil.

"It's Daisy's mom," she told them.

The moment she said, "Hello," she could hear the woman crying hysterically on the other end. She braced herself for the worst news possible.

"Savannah!"

"Yes?"

"She's alive!"

"Daisy's alive?" Savannah jumped up from her chair. "Oh, Pam! That's wonderful! Did she call you? Is she home?"

"No, Daisy didn't call, but someone did. Someone called me just a couple of minutes ago and told me that they've talked to her."

"Someone you know? A family member? A friend?"

"No, a stranger. She wouldn't leave her name, but she told me that she saw me on TV. She said she felt so sorry for me that she had to call me and tell me that my little girl is okay. Isn't that fantastic?"

Savannah felt her mood plummet as fast as it had soared. But she tried not to sound too disappointed when she said, "Tell me what she said, Pam, every word. Try to remember it exactly, okay?"

Pam calmed down a bit as she recited the conversation. "This woman called, and the caller ID said 'unavailable,' but it showed the number. Anyway, she asked if I was Pam O'Neil. And when I said I was, she said, 'You don't know me. But I saw you on TV earlier today, and I just felt so sorry for you. I know that your daughter is okay.' When I asked her how she knew that, she told me she wasn't at liberty to say but that she has heard from Daisy and will be seeing her sometime soon. She said she's a mother herself and knows how I must be hurting. She promised to talk to Daisy when she sees her and convince her to give me a call."

"Wow," Savannah said, her head reeling.

Dirk was on his feet, too, his face against the other side of her phone, listening.

"Get the number," he told Savannah. "Tell her to give you the phone number that was on the caller ID."

Savannah did as he said and wrote it down when Pam read it off to her.

"This is good news, isn't it?" Pam said. "This is what I've been praying for, right?"

"It sounds promising, Pam. It does," Savannah told her, walking that fine line between breaking her heart and offering too much false hope. Lunatics called victims' families all the time, some with horrible intentions and some well-intentioned but hurtful, all the same.

"Do you think Daisy will call me? Do you think this woman is really in touch with her?"

"We're not going to wait for her to call, Pam," Savannah said. "We're going to go ahead and follow up on it, starting with this phone number. We'll find out who made the call and talk to them if we can. I'll keep you posted."

They said their good-byes as Savannah reminded her, once again, to call anytime with anything.

Dirk was already on the phone, calling the station, to give them the number. He waited on hold, tapping his foot impatiently, as they processed the number.

"What do you think?" Savannah whispered to him.

"I think I've been on hold here for way too long."

"I mean, about this call."

"Could be legit. Could be a crackpot. Should know pretty soon." He held up one hand. "Wait. They're back. Yeah. You got it? Great. Oh, a phone booth. Where? Okay, thanks."

He hung up and said to Savannah, "It's a phone booth at Main and Blanche Streets."

"I know that corner. The phone is in front of a convenience store, and the owner's a buddy of mine."

Dirk nodded to Robyn. "Gotta go. Thanks a lot."

"Good luck," Robyn said. "I do hope you find her."

But Savannah and Dirk were already on their way.

Chapter 18

"Hey, Red! What's shakin', sugar?" Savannah asked the convenience store owner as she and Dirk walked up to the counter.

He set aside the box of frankfurters he was putting on the rotisserie and hurried around the counter to give her a big hug. "Savannah! Hey, girl! What have you been up to?" Seeing that she was with Dirk, he added less enthusiastically, "Ah . . . hanging out with What's His Face here."

Red McMurtry wasn't a redhead anymore. Far from it, in fact. His thick fox mane was now a lot thinner and all white. But Savannah remembered when he had been young and feisty enough to chase her around the store.

Games of Keep Away were as long gone as his red hair, but the sparkle in his eyes told her he remembered as well as she did.

Savannah didn't like it when her favorite people got older. It reminded her that none of them were going to last forever.

Today, in honor of the holiday, Red was dressed

like a clown with striped, baggy pants, a lime green shirt, and a round red nose.

"I need your help," she told him.

"An ice cream bar? Help yourself. It's on the house."

"No, thanks. Another time maybe. I have to ask you an important question," she said. Trying to be serious while questioning a clown wasn't the easiest thing to do.

"Okay. What is it?" he asked, pulling a white paper rose from one of his pants pockets and presenting it to her.

"Do you remember seeing somebody use that phone there in front of your store today? Maybe about a half hour or forty-five minutes ago?"

He glanced through the window at the pay phone that was less than ten feet from his store's front door.

"Well, yeah," he said. "As a matter of fact, I did notice somebody using it. Somebody who comes in here all the time, but she's never used it before. I thought it was a little weird since I know she carries a cell phone with her. She's a regular customer, and it's always ringing when she's in here."

"Great! Do you know her name?"

He shook his head. "No. I never heard her name. But she comes in here every afternoon to get a yogurt and a piece of fruit. Says it's her afternoon snack."

"Do you know if she lives around here?"

"I don't think she does. But she works right across the street."

Savannah's pulse rate jumped. "Really? Are you sure?" She hurried to the front of the store and looked out the window at the large brick building across the street.

"Sure, I'm sure," he said. "I've watched her walk

out of there many times on her way here. And I see
her go back. She works there at the clinic."

Savannah knew the clinic all too well. More than
once as a cop, she and others had been called to the
property because of protestors picketing outside.

The clinic specialized in women's health issues:
birth control, gynecological conditions, and obstet-
rics. But they also performed abortions at the clinic,
and that drew the occasional crowd of demonstra-
tors.

She turned and looked at Dirk. The expression
on his face told her that he was thinking the same
thing she was. If Daisy had contacted a woman working in that clinic—maybe even scheduled an abortion—the woman would not have been able, legally,
to tell Daisy's mother that.

There appeared to be hope, after all, that the
caller was something other than a crackpot.

"What does this lady look like?" Savannah asked
Red.

"Kind of average. On the short side, voluptuous."

"Like me?" she asked with a grin.

"No, more voluptuous than you, mostly around her
hips. Maybe fifty-five or sixty. Short gray hair. She's
wearing a bright orange dress today. You know, in
honor of the day. Sorta looks like a pumpkin, but I
wouldn't want her to know I said that."

"Thank you, Red," she said as she walked back to
him and gave him a kiss on the cheek. "You're the
best, and I love you!"

"I love you, too, pretty lady," Red returned, beaming. He bent over and planted a kiss on her cheek,
leaving some of his grease paint behind.

"I don't love you," Dirk told him, "but thanks."

"Yeah, you're welcome. I guess."

When Savannah and Dirk were back in the Buick,

she said, "It makes sense, considering the pregnancy test box I found. Daisy certainly wouldn't be the first girl to run away from home after finding out she was pregnant."

Dirk grunted. "I don't even know how I feel about this. I mean, I'm happy if that's all it is, if she's okay. But if I get the chance, I'm going to give her a piece of my mind about putting us all out like this. Especially her mom."

She turned his rearview mirror around and checked her reflection. "Of course, we don't know for sure that's what's going on. It could be something else," she said, dabbing at a bit of red and white makeup that her clown friend had deposited on her cheek.

"Want to go across the street and talk to the 'voluptuous' lady?" Dirk asked.

"I reckon we have to. Don't know how much good it'll do. She's not going to be able to tell us anything about what's up with Daisy medically."

"She may not be able to say it in words. But she wanted to reach out, to communicate something to somebody, or she wouldn't have made that phone call."

"True. Let's go."

The moment they walked through the clinic door, they saw the bright orange dress and the lady in it. She was the receptionist seated at a desk behind a large partition that looked like bulletproof plastic. She did indeed appear to be in her late fifties, early sixties, and she had short salt and pepper hair— more salt than pepper.

She had to be their caller.

Fortunately, there was no one else in the waiting room, so Savannah walked up to the window, introduced herself and Dirk, and immediately told the woman the reason for their visit.

"I believe you are the person who called Pam O'Neil today," she told her. When the woman looked shocked and alarmed, Savannah quickly added, "Don't worry. It's okay. In fact, I think that was a very compassionate thing to do. And I realize it wasn't easy for you, under the circumstances."

The woman glanced around frantically and whispered, "Please! You're going to make me lose my job. My daughter's in the hospital, and I'm taking care of my grandchildren. I can't get fired! I just can't!"

"I understand," Savannah said. "And if anybody comes in, we're just here to pick up some birth control, okay?"

Dirk chuckled behind her, but the woman nodded and seemed to relax a little.

"I know there are certain things that you can't tell me," Savannah said, "but can you at least verify that you've been in contact with Daisy O'Neil, our missing girl?"

The woman bit her lower lip, then said, "I really can't discuss any particular patient. That would be unethical."

Savannah nodded. "I see. So, if . . . say . . . somebody, anybody at all, were to want an abortion, they could just call in and schedule one?"

The receptionist looked behind her and down a hallway, checking to make sure it was empty.

"If," she said, "somebody, anybody wanted an abortion, they would have to come in for a consultation first, be evaluated by one of our staff psychologists. Then, if that went okay, they'd be scheduled for the procedure."

"I see. And when they came in for their consultation, that would probably be the first time you actually saw them in person. Before that, it might just be phone contact."

The woman leaned forward in her chair, locked eyes with Savannah, and said, "Yes. If someone wanted an abortion, they might have called, say, several weeks ago and set up the consultation appointment for maybe this afternoon or this evening."

"I understand. And is there any particular time you would recommend . . . this afternoon or this evening?"

A door in the hallway opened, and a man in a white smock walked into the office area near the receptionist's desk. He glanced Savannah's way and said, "Hello. May we help you?"

Savannah stuck her hand into a fish bowl on the counter and scooped up a handful of individually packaged condoms. "Just came in for our weekly supply," she said brightly. "Thanks a lot."

Taking a grinning Dirk by the arm, she marched him toward the door. "Thanks again," she said over her shoulder as they exited the building.

"How many of those do you have there?" Dirk asked as they returned to the car.

She glanced down at her hand, which was brimming with prophylactics. "Oh, I'd say a dozen at least."

"A week's supply, huh?" he said, laughing.

"Hey, boy, I thought I'd make you look good. That guy in there may be a successful physician, but right now, he's wishing he was you!"

"Hell," Dirk said, opening the car door for her, "right now, *I* wish I was me!"

Having called Ryan and John and asked them to surveil the clinic for the afternoon, Savannah and Dirk took off for Hollywood and the famous—or perhaps, infamous—Sunset Boulevard.

Once a Native American trail, the 26-mile-long

boulevard stretched from the Pacific Ocean to downtown Los Angeles. And if visitors to sunny Southern California traveled the entire distance, they would pass through such illustrious areas as the Pacific Palisades, Brentwood, Westwood, Bel Air, Beverly Hills, Echo Park, and Chinatown.

But Savannah and Dirk weren't interested in doing the tourist thing. They took the Pacific Coast Highway south from San Carmelita and turned inland on Sunset. And they only went as far as West Hollywood and Tank's Inky Dinky Do Tattoo Parlor.

For some reason, Savannah had pictured Tank as a white guy, seriously tattooed himself, wearing a tank top with some sort of rock band's logo on it, maybe an undershave haircut, and lots of studs bristling from his body.

He didn't disappoint.

What she hadn't anticipated, because she kept forgetting it was Halloween, were the enormous and amazingly real-looking fangs that showed quite clearly when he spoke.

It all seemed a bit adolescent for a guy who had to be forty-five, if he was a day.

"Whaddyawant?" he mumbled when they walked in.

"Tank, right?" Dirk asked.

He hesitated before 'fessing up to his own identity. Finally, he said, "Uh, yeah. I guess. Why?"

"We gotta talk." Dirk flipped his badge out and motioned with a nod of his head toward the back room. "Now."

With even greater reluctance, Tank led them into the back room where the tattooing was done.

Savannah had been in quite a few tattoo parlors during the course of her career, and many of them were as spotless and professional as a doctor's office.

Tank's wasn't one of those.

Of course, the walls were littered with the obligatory tattoo art designs, but Tank seemed to specialize in the grotesque and sexual. She saw a lot more reptilian monsters entwining themselves around buxom maidens in skimpy chain mail bikinis than butterflies, hearts, or unicorns.

The chairs where patrons would sit to receive their particular staining looked like they would benefit from a good cleaning. And the myriad bottles lining shelf after shelf were dusty and disorganized.

Something told her that Tank didn't do a lot of tattooing in his parlor.

Dirk got right down to his interview without preamble or foreplay. "I hear you sell bogus passports in here, dude."

"I do not! Who told you that—"

"Oh, shut up. I don't have the time to mess with you, so don't even start that shit. You've made up a couple of passports for a guy named Andrew Dante and—"

"Hey, man, I saw on TV that the dude was murdered. I didn't have nothin' to do with that! I'm a good guy. Just white-collar type crime. I don't kill nobody."

Dirk leaned far into Tank's personal space and said, "I never said you did. Although, that's certainly something I'll have to check into if you don't tell me what I need to know right now."

Tank mulled that over for a minute. "Um, well . . . what do you wanna know?"

"The passport you did for him, around last June sometime . . ."

"Yeah? I mean, I'm not saying I did, but if I did . . . ?"

"You put the name Robyn Dante on it."

Tank gave a half nod.

"And somebody's picture. Somebody's besides Robyn Dante's, that is."

"Hey, I don't know who it was. Dude brought the gal in, we took the shot, and I did . . . well . . . what he paid me to do. That was it."

"You know it wasn't Robyn Dante he brought in here. Who was it?"

"I'm telling you, I don't know! She was just this chick. She was all over him, so I guess it was his girl-friend."

"Describe her."

"I don't know, man. Average. She was just, like, av-erage. Brown hair, I think. Not cute, not ugly. Kinda young."

Savannah's breath caught in her throat. "Young?" she asked. "How young?"

Tank shrugged. "Maybe around twenty."

"A heavy girl? Or skinny?" Dirk wanted to know.

"I don't know. I don't really remember. Just sorta average, I guess."

"You're not helping me nearly enough here, Tank, my man." Dirk put a firm hand on the guy's tattooed shoulder, right over a demon whose tongue was lolling out to the end of his chin. "If I'm gonna walk out of this joint and forget I know you, you're going to have to do a lot better than 'average' and 'I can't remember.'"

Tank looked like he was about to start crying. It occurred to Savannah that if he did, it would just be too weird. She'd never seen a vampire cry before.

"Seriously, man," he was saying, "don't you think I'd help you if I could? You think I want to get busted? I'm a two-timer, man. One more, and I'm sent away for good. You gotta believe me."

Savannah groaned to herself. She hated it when they were telling her the truth . . . and it wasn't what she wanted and needed to hear.

The Tank was dry, flat on empty.

Dirk knew it, too. He took one of his cards and

stuck it into the top of Tank's tank top. "If you think of anything, anything at all—like what Dante might have called this disgustingly average girl—you give me a call. Day or night. You got it?"

"Sure, man. No problem. I will, really."

"Yeah, right."

Dirk turned and took Savannah's arm. "Let's get back home. Tank here knows the lay of the land, and he's our best buddy now. He'll be calling us soon."

He said it with all of the conviction of a thirteen-year-old professing a belief in the tooth fairy.

Once they were back in the car, watching a parade of incredible Hollyweirds march down the street in their outlandish Halloween garb, Savannah said, "You going to do anything about that back there?"

"Do anything? Of course I'm going to do something." He reached for a cinnamon stick, took a long drag on it, held it, and exhaled with as much relish as if it was a fine Cuban cigar. "I'm going to give the Tank Snake twenty-four hours to call me with something worthwhile. And then I'm gonna drop a dime to Homeland Security."

"Homeland Security?"

"Hell, yeah. We don't want him selling those BS passports to no damned terrorists, right?"

Savannah thought that one over. "He's not going to give you anything. Why don't you just go ahead and make that call on the way home? I'll dial for you."

Chapter 19

Savannah and Dirk had driven most of the long way home from Hollywood to San Carmelita when Savannah got a call from an excited Tammy.

"You're never going to guess where we are," she said.

Savannah knew this game. With Tammy, it could go back and forth for half an hour before the kid gave, and she wasn't in the mood. "Where?"

"Guess."

"No. Where are you, and who's we?"

"I'm at the library with your granny."

"That's nice. It's sweet of you to take her for an outing. I'm just sorry that I've been too busy to do it myself."

"We're not on an outing. We're *sleuthing!*"

Ah, Savannah thought, *if only Miss Nancy Drew knew how nerdy that sounds.*

But then, Tammy probably wouldn't care, she decided. Tammy was one of those rare people who was totally accepting of others and of herself—a quality that made her a lovely friend. And truly impossible to embarrass.

"You're sleuthing?" Savannah repeated for Dirk's benefit. He glanced her way and rolled his eyes. "And at the library?"

"Yes, and we have some really cool stuff here. You've got to come see it."

"Um, we're actually a little busy here, darlin'. We're on our way back to the clinic to relieve John and Ryan. They've been sitting there all afternoon and—"

"No, really, Savannah. This is some interesting stuff here. You have to come and see. Gran's really excited about it . . . says she's got a 'feelin'.' "

"Okay. We'll be there in ten."

Savannah hung up and told Dirk. "We have to make a pit stop at the library before we go to the clinic."

"You have to go to the bathroom again? I told you not to drink that soda. I'll just pull into a station."

"No. It has to be the library. Tammy's hot on a trail, she says."

"Yeah, but it's *Tammy*. She's cute, and she means well, but she's a ding-a-ling."

"But Gran's with her, and Gran has a feelin' about it."

Again with the eye roll. "Hey, if the bimbo's excited and Granny Reid has a *feelin'*, who am I to argue with that?"

When they entered the library ten minutes later, Savannah and Dirk found Tammy busy at one of the library's computers, which had a large pumpkin sitting on top of the monitor. Gran was beside her, perched on the edge of a chair, peering over her shoulder.

A group of children sat in the far corner of the

room, wearing fairy princess, ghost, and pirate costumes, listening to a Cinderella read them a story.

It really is Halloween, Savannah reminded herself.

This wasn't the first time she and Dirk had "lost" a
holiday to a frenzied investigation, and she was sure
it wouldn't be the last.

The instant Tammy saw them, she jumped up and
motioned them over.

"Look! Look at this! You gotta see this!"

Tammy pushed Savannah down onto the chair
she had been sitting on and pointed to the computer
screen.

Savannah stared at it a while and then said, "Okay.
What is it?"

"It's a picture, well, actually . . . it's a zoom in of a
satellite map of the Dante estate," Tammy told her.

Granny was practically hopping up and down in
her seat, too. She shoved some papers into Savannah's hand and said to Tammy, "First, you gotta tell
her how we came to be here, what we figured out,
and all that."

"Oh, right!" Tammy grabbed another chair and
pulled it over next to Savannah's and snatched the
papers out of her hand. "It was your granny here. I
was telling her how much fun I've had going through
people's computers, trying to get stuff on them or
figure out what's going on in their lives. But we
couldn't do that with Daisy because her mom said
that her computer's been on the fritz for weeks."

Gran broke in with, "And that's when I told Tammy
that in McGill, not everybody and their dog's uncle's
cousin can afford a computer. And most folks who
want to go online and look stuff up or get e-mails,
they go down to the library and do it there for free."

"And that," Tammy said, "is when I thought
maybe Daisy's been doing that! So I called her

mom—hope you don't mind—and asked her, and Pam said, 'Yes, Daisy's told me several times that she was going to the library to use the computer,' so. . . ."

"So, we came down here, and that nice lady over there . . ."—Gran pointed to the reference clerk, who was dressed as a green-faced, wart-enhanced witch—". . . told us that Daisy had been here. And not only that, but she let us look at the log they keep that shows who went on at what time and on which computer."

"Then I checked the cookies!" Tammy said.

"And those aren't the kind you eat, either. She just taught me all about computer cookies," Gran announced proudly. "They're little pieces of information in your computer that show what you've been looking up and when you did it. And boy, it's a good thing your sister Vidalia doesn't know about cookies, or your brother-in-law would be in the doghouse worse than he already is . . . him and his girlie pictures that he's always looking up and—"

"Gran, I'm sorry to hear that Butch and Vi are still fighting over that stuff, but what do you have here?"

"Yeah," Dirk said. He had been waiting patiently behind them, but was nearing the end of his leash. "We've gotta get crackin' here or—"

"Okay, okay." Tammy pointed to the papers in her hand. "I compared the times in the librarian's log to the cookies to see what Daisy was looking at. It took forever, but she was checking out Web sites that have to do with those horrible, sickening things called canned hunts."

Savannah's stomach contracted. As an ardent animal lover, she had been sick the first time she had heard of the atrocities. And she still felt the same— that hunters who were that cruel and unsportsman-like deserved to trade places with their so-called prey. Maybe if *they* were chased around inside a fenced-in area by a pack of hounds and drunken fools with guns for half an hour, they'd lose their taste for such activity.

"I didn't know what they were," Tammy was saying, "but Gran told me, and I about died."

"I guess I'm the only one here, then, who doesn't know what it is. Anybody want to tell me?" Dirk said.

Granny shuddered. "Some folks have too much money and not enough kindness in their souls. And instead of going out and hunting their game the old-fashioned way—the way my own daddy did in order to put meat on our table—they do it the lazy, cruel way."

"That's right," Tammy said. "They put the animal—a bear or a ram or a leopard or even a lion—in this big, enclosed area where they don't have a chance of getting away, and then they shoot them so that they can have a trophy head or whatever to hang on the wall."

"Enclosed area?" Dirk asked. "Isn't that like shooting fish in a barrel? Where's the sport in that?"

"And the sad thing is . . ."—Gran shook her head—". . . the animal is usually raised for these hunts and fed by people, so they aren't even afraid of human beings. They walk right up and get shot. But the worst part is, since the so-called hunters don't want to mess up the trophy, they shoot them in the hindquarters, and they die a slow, painful death. I'm telling you, it oughta be illegal."

"It isn't?" Dirk asked.

"Not in most states," Tammy told him. "And a lot of highly respected zoos that everybody goes to, they sell their surplus animals to these places."

Savannah shook her head. "It just makes me sick to even think about it. And Daisy was researching all this?"

"Yes, she was. We saw the Humane Society's Web

site there and Wildlife Protection. She was checking them all out."

"She loves big cats," Savannah said. "Has pictures of them all over her room. It must have been very disturbing to her. But what is this?" she asked, pointing to the screen.

"This," Tammy said, "is something else she was looking at the day she went missing. You know how you can look up maps on the Internet?"

"Uh, I hear you can," Savannah admitted. "I don't personally, but . . ."

"Well, you can. And not only that, but you can get actual aerial views of towns taken by satellites. They're so detailed you can see every tree and bush. That view right there, it's the Dante estate."

"Where's the house?" Dirk asked, leaning over Savannah's shoulder.

"This is way back behind the house. They own a lot of acreage there—I checked that, too, while I was here," Tammy said. "And those three square things there"—she put her finger on the screen—"those are cage enclosures . . . for canned hunts."

Savannah and Dirk both leaned closer, squinting at the screen.

When she looked closely, she could see that among the trails, trees, and bushes, there were several square shapes that appeared to be man-made structures.

"Okay, I see them," she said, "but how do you know that's what they are? They could be sheds or—"

"No. I did an Internet search and found a couple of articles about how they used to have those hunts up there. It was a long time ago, before Andrew Dante even bought the property. Some guy from back East owned it and had a house up there. It got torn down when Dante bought the land."

"I remember the place," Dirk said. "It was nice but old, and it didn't compare to Dante's mansion. I don't remember anybody living there."

"Why do you suppose Daisy was researching this stuff?" Savannah said.

"I was wondering that, too," Tammy replied. "So I called her mom again and asked her if she knew anything about it. She told me that Daisy had been hiking some of the trails there on the Dante's property a week or so ago, and she mentioned finding some old cage things. She'd told her mom she was going to ask Tiffany about them."

"Does Pam know if she did ask Tiffany or not?" Savannah said.

"No. That's all Daisy told her."

Savannah sat, staring at the screen, thinking. She didn't like the thoughts that were crossing her mind.

Glancing over her shoulder at Dirk, she could tell from his expression that he was thinking along the same lines.

"You don't suppose . . ." she said.

He gave her a slight nod.

"But Daisy's supposed to be showing up there at the clinic anytime now," she argued, more to herself than anyone present.

"Yes," Dirk said. "She could be fine."

But something told Savannah that even though Ryan and John were in place, watching, waiting to see a healthy, whole Daisy arrive at the clinic, something wasn't right.

Daisy's a good kid, Savannah thought. *She and her mother are close. Even if she was pregnant, she wouldn't just vanish into thin air and torture her mom this way.*

Savannah didn't know how to even word her next question. And when she found the words, she could hardly speak them. "Are you thinking . . . imprisonment . . . or disposal?"

Thoughts of Maggie flooded her mind. The old citrus packing shed.

They had been too late.

Dirk put his hands on her shoulders and squeezed. "I'm thinking," he said, "that we need to go up there and check those damned cages."

Savannah jumped up from her chair and said, "Yes, right now. Let's get Gran home, and then the three of us have some serious hiking to do."

Savannah didn't mind the idea of walking a narrow path in the middle of nowhere after sunset. Darkness didn't frighten her. The cries of coyotes in the not so far distance didn't spook her. And she liked to think that all the rattlesnakes were curled snugly in their dens with their little ones, watching TV or eating popcorn and playing Snake Trivial Pursuit, even though she had heard facts to the contrary.

The October night air was cool with a full moon overhead, so the hike didn't even cause her, Dirk, or Tammy to break a sweat.

The coastal foothills of San Carmelita had a romance all their own. Several varieties of sage that grew from one to ten feet high scented the air with a perfume that became even more pronounced after the sun went down and the evening dew settled.

And although the semidesert might have seemed uninhabited at first glance, the thick brush teemed with life. As they walked along, they heard the rustling of rabbits, rodents, squirrels, and birds.

Occasionally, Savannah saw a lizard slither off the path to avoid them. At least, she told herself they were lizards.

Lizards didn't watch television or play games at night.

And under better circumstances, the moonlight bathing everything in a wash of a thousand shades of silver might have soothed her soul.

But not tonight.

Savannah was afraid of what they'd find on the other end of the hike, and she knew her companions were just as afraid because for the past five minutes, no one had said a word.

"This isn't like Maggie," Dirk had whispered in her ear when they had begun the trek. "This time, it's going to be different."

After studying the Internet map thoroughly, they had driven to the Dante estate and taken a path that led from behind the tennis courts, up the hill, and into the undeveloped foothills.

Dirk led the way with a powerful flashlight, Savannah right behind him, carrying her own torch, and Tammy in the rear.

Once in a while, he stopped to consult the series of close up maps they had printed at the library.

"Those two trees over there," Savannah said as they neared the area where they believed the cages were, "they're right here on the map. Isn't that them?"

Tammy and Dirk leaned over her shoulders as Savannah directed the beam of her light onto the map. They both studied the paper, then Dirk flashed his torch up and down the trees she was pointing to.

"Yeah," he said. "Those are the only big trees we've seen so far. I think we're about there."

Savannah's heart was beginning to pound, and it wasn't from the hike. "The first cage should be up there, around that bend on the left."

"This is so exciting!" Tammy said. "I'm so glad you let me come! Thank you!"

"Don't thank me yet," Savannah said softly.

She had been regretting her decision to allow Tammy to tag along almost from the moment they got into the car to come here. But since the lead had been one-hundred percent Tammy's, it was hard to tell her no.

Savannah just hoped with all her heart that Daisy wouldn't turn out to be Tammy's Maggie. And if things turned terrible, Savannah knew she would never forgive herself. Tammy wasn't as thick-skinned as she and Dirk.

And even they hadn't gotten over Maggie.

They continued on up the path, which was getting steeper by the moment. And just as the trail was turning left, they came to a fence.

There wasn't much left of it, only a couple of rusted barbed wires that were lying on the ground, along with some rotted posts. They were able to step right over it.

"I guess this was the enclosure the Web sites talked about, to keep the animals in," Savannah said.

"Yeah, you gals watch yourselves," Dirk said in his best protective, manly voice. "Don't scratch yourselves on those wires."

"Why, Dirko," Tammy said. "I didn't know you cared."

"I don't." He put his hands on her waist and lifted her lightly over the fallen wires. "But you've both got great legs. Why risk scars?"

To Savannah, he only offered a helping hand. She took it and as she hopped over, said, "Thank you, Sir Galahad. You're too kind."

"People say that all the time."

"Yeah, right."

Dirk's jacket began to buzz. He reached into his pocket and pulled out his cell phone. Looking at the caller ID, he said, "Hey, it's Ryan."

Savannah glanced at her watch. It was 8:05. The clinic would be closing at nine. The last appointment would probably be arriving about now, so maybe . . .

She mentally crossed her fingers. What would be better than finding empty cages up here and a healthy, if pregnant, Daisy in town?

"Yeah," Dirk said into the phone. "What's up? Oh?" He looked puzzled. "You're kidding. Hm-m-m. That's not what we were expecting. Okay. Thanks, buddy."

"Well?" Savannah asked when he hung up.

"What is it?" Tammy wanted to know, tugging on his arm. "What's the stuff we weren't expecting?"

"Two of our gals showed up over there," he told them.

"Which two?"

"Tiffany and Bunny."

"Tiffy and Bunny?" Savannah worked at getting her mind around that one. "Tiffy and Bunny? What the hell would they be doing there?"

"Picking up a handful of condoms?" Dirk said with half a chuckle. "Which one of them do you suppose is pregnant?"

"Maybe one of them is just going for a gynecological exam," Tammy said. "The clinic deals with all sorts of women's health issues."

"I don't know," Savannah said, "and at the moment, I don't care. We have to get to those cages."

She headed on up the path with them close behind. In the moonlight, she could see something ahead, something too shiny to be natural. It was a structure made of wood and corrugated tin.

As she drew closer, she could see the front of the building . . . and metal bars. Further down the path were two more similar structures.

In her mind's eye, Savannah saw another old, dilapidated building, deserted, dirty, rusty, and falling down. An abandoned citrus processing plant. And inside, a teenager who had barely even begun her life, dead. Still warm when Savannah had gathered her into her arms, but gone forever.

"Not like Maggie," she whispered as she raced forward, her flashlight illuminating only a few square feet at a time.

She reached the first cage and swept the light back and forth inside, trying to figure out what her eyes were seeing. Strange shapes. A large metal tub. Chains and leather harnesses hanging from the walls. Piles of moldering, mostly rotted hay on the floor.

She was only vaguely aware of Tammy and Dirk on either side of her until Dirk shone his brighter light into the space and lit up the dreary interior.

"How awful," Tammy said. "Can you imagine putting an innocent animal in here?"

Savannah didn't reply. She hurried on to the next cage, which was filled with similarly dismal trappings.

When Dirk joined her and flashed his light into that enclosure, a pile of straw on the left rustled, and Tammy screamed.

An enormous rat scurried out of the mound and ran through the bars, past them, and into some nearby brush.

"Are you all right, kiddo?" Dirk asked her.

"Yes," was the meek, shaky reply.

Savannah was already on her way to the third cage. And a feeling that she recognized as a deep-seated premonition told her this one would be different.

"Daisy?" she began to call out even before she reached it. "Daisy! Honey, are you in there?"

She saw something inside, to the right, over in the corner. She shone her light on it, and what she saw made her knees nearly buckle beneath her.

"She's here!" she cried out. But Dirk was already beside her.

His light showed what they had been hoping they would find . . . and fearing they would.

Daisy was lying on some sort of wooden bench on her side, her face away from them. She was motionless.

"Daisy! Daisy!" they all three shouted. But there was no response.

Savannah was jerking at the door, trying to open it. But it was held closed by a chain and a padlock. She grabbed the padlock and yanked at it, trying to somehow rip it off the chains.

In some detached, far less emotional part of her mind, Savannah recorded the fact that the padlock was new, shiny in sharp contrast to the rusted metal of the bars. That part of her mind also told her that no matter how hard she tried, she wasn't going to get this door open with her bare hands.

Later, she would look at her bruised and cut hands and realize how foolish and futile her actions had been.

She would also remember that she had been sobbing while she was doing it.

"It's locked, Savannah," Tammy was saying. "You can't open it that way. Dirk, shoot the lock with your gun and open it!"

"That's only in cowboy movies, kiddo," Dirk told her, a grim, sad tone to his voice.

He reached over and grabbed Savannah's hands, pulling them off the lock. "Wait a minute, honey," he told her. "Find me something to pry it off with."

As she had been forced to do many times before, Savannah willed a stronger, calmer self to surface. She looked around, casting her flashlight beam over the ground in front of and beside the cage. Near the back, she found something—a short metal bar maybe six inches long.

She grabbed it and ran back to Dirk. "This won't give you much leverage, but—"

"It'll do," he said. "That's not much of a lock."

He was right. In less than five seconds, he had inserted the rod into the lock and twisted it off. Three seconds later, he had the door open.

Savannah pushed ahead of him to get inside, to get to Daisy.

She ran to the bench and grabbed the girl's body, turning it over.

Don't touch the body without gloves, a quiet, professional voice whispered inside her head. *This is a crime scene. Don't disturb the evidence.*

"Daisy!" she said. "Daisy!"

Dirk lifted his flashlight and shone it down on the girl's face.

Savannah expected to see open, vacant dead eyes staring up at her. But Daisy's eyes were closed.

"She's warm," Savannah said. *Not that it matters.*

Savannah pressed her fingertips to the girl's jugular vein and felt a pulse. It was weak but regular, and she could see the gentle rise and fall of her chest.

"She's alive," Dirk said. "She's alive, Van."

A wash of relief poured over Savannah from her head to her feet. And when it hit her knees, she went down. The next thing she knew, she was sitting on the dirty floor, holding Daisy's limp hand against her cheek, rocking back and forth and sobbing.

As though from far away, she could hear Dirk on the phone saying, "Yeah, we're going to need a medevac for an unconscious female. No visible signs of injury, but possible dehydration or . . ."

She rose to her knees and leaned over Daisy. Lifting one of the girl's eyelids gently with her finger, she shone the flashlight into her eye and watched as the iris contracted. The teenager stirred ever so faintly.

"You're okay, honey," she told her. "You're going to be all right. We've got you now. We've got you."

Daisy groaned just a little, but it was one of the sweetest sounds Savannah had ever heard.

"You're all right, Maggie," she whispered. "This time was different. This time we found you . . . before . . ."

Behind her, she could hear Tammy ask Dirk, "Is Savannah okay? I just heard her call Daisy 'Maggie.' Is she all right?"

"She's okay," was Dirk's soft reply. "Don't worry about her, kiddo. Right now, Savannah is very, *very* okay."

Chapter 20

"You were largely responsible for this, so I wanted you to see it," Savannah told Gran as she led her down the hallways of San Carmelita Community General Hospital.

They rounded a corner and saw the large double doors of the Intensive Care Unit. Through the pane of safety glass in each door, they could see the flurry of activity, the medical personnel in their pale blue scrubs rushing around, attending to the most severely sick and wounded of San Carmelita. The ICU was maybe two notches less harried than the Emergency Room. But since this was the only major hospital in the county, there was no area of San Carmelita Community General that could be considered laid back.

The semichaos worked to Savannah's advantage. In spite of their "only two visitors at a time" rule, she had come and gone from Daisy's ICU cubicle several times in the past two hours without anyone questioning her.

So she had sent Tammy to get Gran.

Gran needed this life-affirming moment.

They entered the large central room with its desks and counters in the middle, and around the hub were the individual glassed-in cubicles with the critically and seriously ill patients.

"Over here," Savannah said, leading her grandmother to their left. "She's the one there, with all the pretty red hair. And that's her mother."

They stood at the opening to the cubicle and said nothing as they watched Pam O'Neil leaning over her daughter, stroking her hair, and speaking lovingly to her.

Just before they had found Daisy, Pam had told Savannah that she thought she had finally run out of tears to cry for her lost daughter.

Apparently, she had found more. But at least these were happy, healing tears running down her face.

Daisy was conscious, the IV supplying much needed fluids for her badly dehydrated body. She was gripping her mother's hand and telling her not to cry, that everything would be all right.

Savannah glanced at Gran and saw tears welling up in her eyes, too. "That's a precious sight," Gran whispered. "It is, indeed."

Pam noticed them standing there and hurried over to greet Granny. She grabbed the older woman in a warm embrace and held her for a long time before finally releasing her. "Thank you," she said. "Savannah told me that if it weren't for you thinking of going to the library and checking the computers there, we never would have found my Daisy."

Granny shrugged and looked embarrassed. "Well, I don't know about that. I'm just honored that the good Lord gave me that word of wisdom there. And if He hadn't given it to me, I'm sure He would have given it to somebody else. Obviously, He wanted you to have your little girl back."

Gran walked over to Daisy's bedside. "Now, let's

see this young'un who's been causing all this ruckus." She took Daisy's hand between both of hers. "Hi, sugar pie," she said. "What a pretty thing you are! Your momma has been beside herself for the past few days, worried sick about you. You're gonna have to be a perfect kid for the next thirty years to make it up to her."

Daisy smiled a weak, but lovely, smile. "I will," she said.

"What I want to know," Gran said, "is how you got yourself in that pickle in the first place? What in blazes were you doing up there in that cage to begin with?"

Savannah started to reach for Gran, to gently pull her back from the bed and stop the conversation before it began. She and Dirk had discussed that while he was still up on the hill examining the cage where Daisy had been imprisoned and finding all he could there, she would question Daisy at the hospital.

And now, it seemed Gran was starting the interrogation herself.

The detective and former cop in Savannah insisted that she do the job herself. After all, who could get information out of a teenager better than a trained professional?

A grandmother who raised several children of her own and nine grandchildren besides, that's who, she thought. *Go, Granny, go.*

"I went up there because I wanted to show the girls the cages I'd found, the ones used for the hunts," Daisy told Granny.

"Which girls?"

"Tiffy and Bunny. They told me to drive up there into one of those canyons, and they'd meet me there. We got sort of lost, but eventually, we found each other, and then I took them up there to show them."

"Well, how did you get locked inside like that?"

Daisy started to sob, but no tears formed. The IV hadn't fully done its job yet. "We were all inside that one cage looking around. Then they slipped out, and before I knew it, they'd locked me in," she said.

"Why would they do a fool thing like that?"

"Tiffy told me it was an 'intervention.' That it was for my own good."

Pam reached over and grabbed Savannah's arm, her fingertips digging into Savannah's flesh. "It's okay," Savannah whispered to her. "We have to know what happened. Let them talk."

"What do you mean, 'an intervention'?" Gran asked.

"They said I'm fat and I need to lose weight. They said they were tired of being embarrassed whenever they went anywhere with me because I'm a fat pig."

Pam's nails dug deeper into Savannah's arm, and Savannah could feel her own rage rising.

Gran reached up and laid her palm against Daisy's cheek. "I'm sorry they said those hateful things to you, darlin'," she told her. "You're a beautiful child of God, and nobody on this earth has a right to hurt you with words like that."

Daisy sobbed quietly, but she turned her face into Gran's hand and closed her eyes for a moment, savoring the contact.

"So, they locked you inside that awful cage," Gran said. "And said those terrible things. Then what happened?"

"They gave me two bottles of water and a handful of vitamins. And then Tiffany told me she'd be back every day to bring me more water and vitamins and my daily allotment of calories—a salad. She said that one way or the other, I was going to lose weight."

"That bitch," Pam whispered to Savannah. "I'm

going to kill her. You just wait until I get my hands on her, I—"

"Sh-h-h. I know how you feel, but later. Later, Pam."

"And did she do that?" Granny asked. "Did she bring you water and food every day that you were up there?"

"No. She did the first day, but after that, she didn't come back. And I ran out of water. It was so hot in that metal cage." Daisy shuddered. "In the daytime, it was like an oven in there. I could hardly even breathe. And then at night, it was so cold. They didn't even give me a blanket or a coat. All I had was that hard bench. And there were rats and. . . . It was so awful."

"I'm sorry, sugar," Gran said. "I really, really am. But it's all over and done now. The worst has already happened."

Gran looked over at Savannah and Pam, and Savannah couldn't ever remember seeing her grandmother look so angry.

Savannah stepped up to the bed and said, "Gran, would you take care of Pam while I just ask Daisy a couple more questions?"

"Sure." Gran bent over, smoothed the hair away from Daisy's face, and kissed her forehead. "You just rest now, sugar. Rest and get well. You've been through a real trial, but it's going to make you a strong, strong woman. You just wait and see. Someday, you'll find a way to use all this bad for good. I just know it."

"Thank you. I will," Daisy replied with a glimmer of strength and determination in her eyes that confirmed Granny's prediction.

Gran walked over to Pam and said, "While Savannah does what she has to do here, why don't we go get us a cup of coffee and a donut? I always think better with some strong coffee in me."

Pam hesitated, but finally, she submitted and left with Granny. Gran looked over her shoulder at Savannah and said. "We'll see you later. Do your detective thing there, Savannah girl."

"Thanks, Gran."

"She's your grandmother?" Daisy asked weakly.

"Yes, she is," Savannah replied.

"You're lucky."

Savannah laughed. "You have no idea how fortunate. And you're blessed, too. Your mother loves you so much, and she has enormous respect for you."

"She told me so many times not to hang around with those stupid girls. She told me they'd get me in trouble. But I didn't listen, and they nearly killed me."

Savannah couldn't argue with her about that. The emergency room physician had told her and Dirk that if Daisy hadn't been found in the next twelve hours, she would have died from dehydration. She had very nearly been murdered.

"Why do you think they really did it?" Savannah asked. "We know it had nothing to do with weight or any stupid intervention. That was the excuse. What was the reason?"

Daisy thought about it for a while. "I think it's a couple of reasons. I think Tiffy was super jealous of me getting that part on the TV show. She hated me for having something she wanted and couldn't buy for herself."

"Yes, I'm sure she was."

"And Bunny . . . Bunny told me something, and I think she decided later that she shouldn't have told me. I think Tiffy was just going to keep me up there for a little while because she was mad, but I think Bunny was really hoping I'd die."

Savannah was pretty sure she knew the answer, but she asked the question anyway. "What did she tell you?"

"That she's pregnant. She asked me to buy a pregnancy test for her; she was afraid her mother might find out if she bought it. And she took it, and it was positive. Then she asked me to call the clinic here in town and make an appointment for her to have an abortion, all under my name."

"And you gave your permission for her to do that?"

Daisy shrugged. "I was stupid. I did anything any of them asked just to be part of them."

"It's okay. You've learned. That's all any of us can do. Live and learn."

"That was a pretty hard way to learn."

"It sure was, but like Gran said, it's over now. Daisy, do you know who the father of Bunny's baby is?"

Daisy nodded. "Andrew Dante, Tiffy's dad. They've had a thing going since last spring. She was on the pill, but she went off it deliberately so that she'd get pregnant. She wanted to have his baby more than anything in the world."

"But you said she scheduled an abortion."

"That was only after he told her to. She had this big idea that if she got pregnant, he would dump Robyn and marry her. Then she'd have him, that big mansion, everything. She wanted to be the lady of the manor, even above Tiffany."

"That's mighty ambitious."

"Yes, and dumb. Andrew told her, 'No way. Just forget about it.' So she asked me to schedule an abortion for her. But then she got to thinking about it and threw a big fit. She threatened to tell Robyn. That's when he offered her a luxury trip to Europe to have the abortion there."

"How did she feel about that?"

"She hated him for that. I mean, *really* hated him. I'm even afraid she might kill him over it. She's said a bunch of times that if he won't marry her, she might."

Savannah hesitated, then decided to go ahead and tell her the truth. "Daisy, Andrew Dante *is* dead. Someone did kill him."

Daisy's eyes widened. "No! No! Really?"

"Yes. We've been working on trying to solve his murder."

"Oh my God! That's awful. I mean, he wasn't the greatest guy ever. He shouldn't have been fooling around on his wife, and not with a young kid like Bunny. But still . . . that's terrible."

"It is. So if you can help us in any way, we'd really appreciate it."

"Sure. I'll tell you anything I know. It's not like I need to have any loyalty toward them, considering what they did to me."

"Do you know anything about a false passport?"

Daisy nodded. "Yeah. Andrew got one for Bunny so that she could go to Amsterdam with him last spring. They went to Hollywood to some tattoo parlor and got it."

"Do you have any idea where it is?"

"Yes. She keeps it and other stuff she doesn't want her mother to know about in a secret place under the floor of her bedroom closet. Her diary's there, too, and she writes everything in there. If that helps you any."

It was all Savannah could do not to scoop Daisy up off the bed and squish her with hugs. "Oh, yes, that will help."

"If Bunny killed Mr. Dante," Daisy said, "she should pay for it."

"She will. And she and Tiffany will pay for what

they did to you. False imprisonment is a very serious crime. They're going to prison for a long time for what they did."

"Really?"

"Absolutely."

"Good."

Daisy gave her a smile that Savannah recognized all too well. It was the smile of a victim who believed they might get some justice, the ultimate validation of their suffering.

"Daisy," Savannah said, "how much does Tiffany know about Bunny and her dad?"

"She knows it all. Everything except that Bunny threatened to kill him. Bunny never said anything like that in front of her, just to me and Kiki."

"She didn't care that her dad and Bunny were having an affair?"

"Oh, she cared some because she's jealous of anybody who gets any kind of attention from her dad. But she hates Robyn, so she didn't care that he was fooling around on his wife."

"And how did she feel about the pregnancy?"

"Oh, she was furious about that. She loves being her father's only kid. She was all for the abortion, just not the big European trip. She was pressuring Bunny to have one here in town."

"Does Bunny's mom know any of this?"

"No, nothing. She thinks her little honey Bunny is perfect in every way."

"And Kiki?"

"Kiki knows all about Bunny and Andrew, too. But she wasn't there when they put me in the cage. I can't believe she would know about that and not tell someone where to find me. She's always been a better friend to me than the other two."

Savannah didn't have the heart to tell her that she was pretty sure Kiki knew, too. Daisy had suffered enough in the past few days. And she was looking tired, so Savannah decided it was time to end the interview.

Besides, Pam was returning with Gran, and she wanted to give the mother and daughter the healing time they needed together.

"You get well, sweetie," she said, leaning over and giving her a kiss on the cheek. "When you get out of here and are feeling better, I want you and your mom to come over to my house. I'll cook you a dinner that will knock your flip-flops off!"

Savannah waited as Gran said her brief good-byes, and Pam thanked them both profusely one more time. Then the two of them left the ICU.

Once they were in the hallway, Savannah grabbed her cell phone out of her purse and called Dirk.

"Where are you?" she asked him.

"I just came down off the hill. You're not going to believe how bad that place was. The straw in there was full of rats, and they'd given her this one little pot to—"

"I know," she said. "I just left the ICU. Daisy's doing a lot better now, and Gran and I got to talk to her. It was Tiffany and Bunny who shut her in there. And it's Bunny who's pregnant . . . with Andrew Dante's kid."

"Whoa!"

"Yeah."

"What do you want to do next?"

"Why don't you nab Tiffany and Bunny and take them to the station for questioning? I'll meet you there." She glanced down at her watch and smiled. It was ten minutes until eleven. "If you hurry, maybe we can get them in there and squeeze a confession out of them before midnight. That would make this the best Halloween ever!"

Chapter 21

Savannah wasted no time dropping Gran off at home and then hightailing it over to the police station.

Normally, she didn't like hanging around the station. Some years back, she and the San Carmelita Police Department had parted ways with a less than amicable divorce. And even though she was close friends with many of the cops, she still loathed the bosses who had unfairly dismissed her. And she avoided running into them whenever possible.

Fortunately, none of them worked the night shift.

So when she walked through the front door, she was greeted like a long lost family member.

"Savannah!" Officer Marianna Weil shouted from the front desk. "We heard you guys found the O'Neil girl! Good goin'!"

"Thank you," she said. "Is Dirk here?"

Marianna's bright expression dimmed ever so slightly. "No, but I heard he's on his way. They're bringing that Tiffy Dante gal in with some friend of hers. He called and asked for two radio cars with cages to transport them."

Savannah laughed. "How appropriate."

"Hey, what's that?" Marianna stood up, and she and Savannah hurried over to the window. A crowd had appeared out of nowhere—cars, vans pulling up in front of the station and people spilling out of the vehicles, carrying cameras and microphones.

"Looks like we've got a departmental leak," Marianna said.

For a moment, Savannah flashed back on the moment she had dropped Gran at her house. Had she remembered to warn her not to call her girlfriend Martha Phelps in Georgia? She was pretty sure she'd forgotten to. Oh, well.

"This stuff gets out," she told Marianna. "You just can't keep a lid on it."

Within less than two minutes, there wasn't an empty parking space on either side of the street for as far down as they could see. And the yard in front of the station house was filling up, as well.

Officer Weil walked back to her desk and picked up the phone. "Yeah, uh . . . you may want to send somebody out there for crowd control. Coulter's going to be bringing those bimbos in any minute now, and all hell's gonna break loose."

No sooner had she hung up than they heard sirens and saw the lights of the squad cars coming down the road.

"Dirk's not stupid," Savannah said. "And he doesn't give a hoot about headlines or getting his picture in the paper. He'll bring them in the back way."

And he did. She saw the two cars take a sharp and abrupt turn left down a side street. And like lemmings following each other, the crowd shifted and moved in unison, going after them.

Savannah hurried through the station, racing to the back door, and arrived there just as Dirk and three uniformed cops escorted Tiffany, Bunny, and her mother inside.

All three ladies had looked better. Apparently, they had been plucked from their beds and hustled into the radio cars because they were all wearing pajamas and no makeup and their normally perfect hairdos were askew.

"Come on, come on, come on," Dirk was telling them. "We have to get you inside and safe. You don't want those media nuts to get their hands on you. Move along now!"

Savannah knew the reason for Dirk's haste, and it had nothing to do with the paparazzi crowd out front. He was keeping their minds on other things for as long as possible to forestall the moment when he would hear those most unwelcome words, "I wanna talk to my lawyer!"

Fortunately, all three females looked too stunned to be thinking straight yet.

"Here," he was telling them, "just go in there, Tiffany, and you, Bunny, into that room there, and Mrs. Greenaway, if you could just wait for me in—"

"No!" Bunny wailed. "I want my mother! I want my mom to come in here with me!"

"Sure, sure, no problem. I'd be happy to do that for you," Dirk said, all sunshine and cooperation . . . for the moment. "Just go in there, and I'll be right with you."

"Are we in any kind of trouble?" Mrs. Greenaway said, trying to smooth her tousled hair.

"You? Naw, not at all," Dirk said. "There's just been some new developments in Daisy's and Mr. Dante's cases, and you ladies would want to know all about that, right?"

Bunny glanced around her, uneasy. "Uh, yeah, I guess."

Then she and her mother went into their ap-
pointed room.

Dirk motioned for Savannah to follow him, and
they hurried into the interrogation room where he
had stashed Tiffany.

She was pacing the tiny room, and the moment
they entered, she yelled, "You can't question me! My
attorney said that I didn't have to say another word
to you *ever again* if I don't want to. And I don't want
to, so *there!*"

"I'm not here to question you, Ms. Dante," Dirk
said far too calmly, far too politely. "I don't need to
hear another word from you ever again. I know all I
need to know about you. I'm placing you under arrest for the false imprisonment of Daisy O'Neil. And
after a few more conversations with the prosecutor, I
may even be able to add kidnapping and attempted
murder to the list of charges. So *there!*"

Tiffany gasped, and the sound was like air escap-
ing an overinflated balloon. She staggered back and
sat abruptly down on a folding chair. "False imprisonment? What is that?"

Savannah stepped forward and leaned over her.
"It's putting a human being into a hot metal cage
and then leaving her there with no food and no
water and—"

"Oh, that!" She looked instantly relieved. "That
wasn't imprisonment. That was an intervention.
Daisy is so-o-o fat! Have you seen her lately? She has
totally blimped out. We just did that for her own
good. I explained that to her. She didn't need food.
She could just live off her fat for, like, a year at least.
And then she'd look a lot better!"

Savannah fought the urge to slap her off the chair
and onto the floor. "When we found that poor girl a
few hours ago, she was nearly dead from dehydration.
She's in the hospital now in intensive care."

"Oh, ple-e-ease. We left her some water. And I couldn't go back. My dad had been murdered! I was busy."

Dirk stepped forward, and for a moment, Savannah was afraid he really would hit her. "I don't have time to mess with you right now," he told her. "But you are under arrest. You have the right to remain silent . . ."

Savannah turned and walked out of the room, her stomach tightening into a hard, bitter ball in her belly. Still, after all these years, she couldn't get over the way human beings could rationalize the most vicious acts.

It simply boggled her mind.

Dirk came out a few moments later and asked a female uniformed cop in the hallway to keep an eye on Tiffany. "Don't let her out of your sight," he said. "She's under arrest."

"Really?" the cop asked.

"Yeah."

"Cool!"

Dirk turned to Savannah. "You know," he said, "we don't have enough to actually nail this Bunny kid for killing Dante. I know she did, and you do, too, but we've got squat. The fake passport, some lipstick, and maybe some DNA when it eventually comes back from the lab—that's not enough."

"She threatened to kill him several times in front of Daisy and Kiki."

"Still not enough."

"There's a diary stashed in her room that may have some good stuff in it."

"But for right now, we've got nothing."

Savannah raised one eyebrow and grinned. "Yeah, but she doesn't know how nothing the nothing is that we've got."

"What?"

"Exactly. Watch this."

* * *

"Let me tell you what we already know, Bunny," Savannah said as she leaned across the table that separated her and Dirk from Bunny and the girl's mother. "Not the stuff we *think* or the stuff we're just *guessing* about . . . but the stuff that we absolutely, positively *know.*"

"Okay," Bunny said, flipping her hair back over her shoulder in a very Tiffanyesque move. "Go right ahead. You tell me what you know about me, lady detective."

"No," Mrs. Greenaway interrupted. "I think we should have a lawyer here before anybody says anything."

Savannah felt Dirk tense beside her. The L word during an interrogation was the last thing any cop wanted to hear.

"Sure, Mrs. Greenaway," he said. "If you think your daughter has done something illegal, you probably should get an attorney. Although, of course, as soon as you start calling around, it's out of our hands. We won't be able to keep a lid on this. Thanks to your daughter's notoriety, the whole town, the world will know about it in fifteen minutes."

"I don't need an attorney, Mom," Bunny said with a classic sixteen-year-old eye roll. "They have nothing on me because I didn't do anything wrong."

"Oh, yes, you did." Savannah fixed her with her best blue laser stare. "You absolutely did. And we have all the proof we need to convict you."

"Oh yeah? Of what?"

"Of the false imprisonment of Daisy O'Neil, for starters. That's a biggy, a felony, Miss Bunny. And you and Tiffany are both going to do some serious prison time for that."

"I'm a minor!"

"Yes, but that's a *major* crime, and the prosecutor is sure that he can try you as an adult. You're known around the world for how very adult your behavior is. I'm sure it wouldn't be hard for a jury to see you as all grown-up."

That seemed to take at least one puff of wind out of Bunny's sails. She sank slightly lower in her folding metal chair.

"And," Savannah continued, "then there's the matter of the murder of Andrew Dante."

"She doesn't know anything about that!" her mother said.

"She knows everything about that," Dirk told her. "Your daughter killed Andrew Dante in cold blood."

Bunny sniffed and shook her head. "That's just so dumb. I did not, and you can't prove it."

"I think we need a lawyer," Mrs. Greenaway said. "I'm going to call one right now, and—"

"No, Mom, that's just stupid!" Bunny shouted in her mother's face. "I don't need a lawyer. *Criminals* need lawyers. I'm not a criminal. I didn't do anything that anybody else wouldn't have done in the same situation."

"And what situation is that?" Mrs. Greenaway asked.

When Bunny didn't respond, Savannah said softly. "She's pregnant, ma'am. I'm sorry to be the one to tell you, but your daughter is pregnant with Andrew Dante's baby."

"She is not! Are you?" She turned to her daughter. *"Are you?"*

"No. They're lying."

Savannah shook her head. "No, we aren't lying. Bunny, you were at the clinic this evening having a consultation about an abortion. Tiffany Dante took you there. She's pressuring you to go through with it, isn't she? She doesn't want to share her father's fortune with any other siblings. Aren't you smart enough to know that's why she's 'helping' you?"

Bunny's round little face flushed with anger. "I am too smart! I'm smarter than Tiffany will ever be. I don't want Andrew's stupid baby. He turned out to be a total creep."

"Bunny! No!" Her mother began to cry. "You are pregnant? Really?"

"Oh, Mother, catch up, will you? Jeez, you can be so irritating sometimes."

"Andrew was a creep?" Savannah prompted. "He didn't treat you right? He wasn't willing to divorce Robyn and marry you? That's what you were hoping for. That's why you got pregnant in the first place."

Mrs. Greenaway gasped, but Bunny just crossed her arms over her chest and said, "Maybe."

"Oh, no 'maybe' about it," Savannah continued. "He told you no way on the marriage. And when you realized that you weren't going to be the new Mrs. Andrew Dante, the mistress of his big mansion with a fat bank account for everything you ever wanted, you killed him."

"Did not."

"We know that you did," Dirk told her. "We know a lot about you, young lady."

"Like what?"

Savannah glanced at Mrs. Greenaway and then said, "We know that you had sex with Andrew the day he died. We collected DNA from his . . . body . . . and compared it to yours. It's a match."

Lie number one, Savannah thought. Not that it particularly troubled her soul, but she did like to keep track of such things.

Bunny snickered. "Yeah, right. I watch a lot of those forensic shows on TV. I know all about that stuff. You don't have my DNA on file. I didn't give you any samples."

"We took it off a soda can that you drank from there at the Dantes'. You threw it away, and we dug it out of the garbage. It had your fingerprints and your DNA all over it."

Lie number two.

Bunny looked a bit less cocky. "You did not."

"Did too. And we compared the lipstick you left on his genitalia to a tube of yours. It was a match."

Lie number three.

"Lipstick?" Mrs. Greenaway looked like she might faint at any minute. "On his . . . oh . . . no!"

"And," Savannah continued, on a roll, "we know that it was you who left the note on the refrigerator that was supposedly from Andrew, saying he was on a plane to London. And after Robyn saw the note and threw it away, you dug it out of the garbage before we could find it and disposed of it another way."

"Nope. I didn't."

"Oh, yes," Savannah said. "And then there's the clincher. The gun."

"What about the gun?" Bunny wanted to know.

The girl was far less calm now. In fact, she was breathing so hard and fast that Savannah thought she might hyperventilate at any moment.

"The gun that you stashed under Tiffany's bed. Nice touch, that. But it had your epithelials on it."

Lie number four.

"What are those?" Mrs. Greenaway asked cautiously, as though she was afraid to hear the answer.

"Oh, Mother, just shut up." Bunny looked absolutely miserable, which was fine with Savannah. Better than fine, in fact. Her Halloween was just getting better by the minute. "I know what epithelials are. They're like cells that come off of your hands when you touch something. They can get DNA out of them."

"Gee, you could be a CSI tech when you grow up," Savannah said. "Oh, wait . . . I forgot . . . *You're* going to be in *jail.*"

"I don't see why I should go to jail," Bunny said. "I really don't. If people knew how he treated me, they wouldn't blame me for anything I did to him. He was so rude! I did everything he wanted . . . even that morning, and then he called me very nasty names and told me he didn't want me or our baby."

"So you got the gun and made him go sit in one of the coffins on the patio," Savannah said. "Was he scared?"

Bunny shrugged. "Yeah, a little. But he kept saying I shouldn't be stupid, acting like a dumb kid, waving the gun around like that. He sat down in the coffin like I told him to, but he didn't think I'd really do it. Boy, I'll bet he was surprised."

The nasty smile that crossed her young face sent a chill through Savannah. She had seen some pretty evil people in her day, but this girl was so young. It usually took a lot longer for a soul to become embittered to that degree.

"Why the wooden stake?" Dirk asked.

"Because *he* drove a stake through *my* heart!" she said. "Do you know how it feels to love somebody so much, to do everything they want you to do and then be told to just go away, just get lost?"

Mrs. Greenaway clapped her hands over her face and shook her head back and forth as though she simply couldn't believe what she was hearing. She kept whispering, "No, no, no, no."

"Yes, Mother," Bunny said to her. "I did it, and I'm not ashamed either. If you've ever felt like I did, you'll know exactly why I killed him. That's why no jury will convict me of murder. If there's even one woman on there who's been through what I have, she'll understand and vote not guilty. And that's all it will take for me to get away with it."

Savannah sighed. "Oh, Bunny. We've *all* been through what you went through. We've all loved and lost. The difference is we didn't murder our former lovers. We might have felt like it, but we didn't pull a gun on him, make him sit in a coffin, put a bullet through his heart, and then drive a stake through it for good measure. You blew it, kiddo, bigtime."

"Well, he deserved it. And I'm not sorry, and I'm not ashamed."

"That's too bad," Savannah said softly. " 'Cause you really oughta be . . . for your own sake, if for no one else's. You really ought to be ashamed."

Chapter 22

Savannah looked around her backyard at her guests who were having a good time, eating her food, soaking in a bit of Southern hospitality, Southern California style.

Daisy and her mother were hanging out by the barbecue grill, getting to know Ryan and John. Tammy and Gran were sitting on a swinging bench seat that Dirk had suspended from a tree branch in honor of Gran's visit. She always missed her porch swing when she came to visit.

And Dirk was lying on the grass, his Dodgers cap over his face, hands folded on his belly.

He looked a little like Andrew Dante had in his coffin, but Savannah decided not to mention that to him. The case was finally closed, and it hadn't been a particularly pleasant experience. Everyone present was all too happy it was over.

Two days ago, the prosecutor had announced that he would, indeed, be trying both Tiffy and Bunny as adults, and the media was going wild. It was the lead story on every television and radio news broadcast and on the front page of every newspaper and tabloid in the country.

But here in Savannah's backyard, among her various flower gardens, with barbecue smoke and lively, friendly conversation floating on the breeze, all was well, calm, serene.

She walked over to Gran and Tammy and sat down on a chair beside their swing. "What are you two hens clucking about over here?" Savannah asked them.

They looked at each other, guilty grins on their faces. "Uh, well," Gran said. "I was just telling Tammy that I talked to Martha on the phone this morning, and it seems she's come into a bit of a . . . um . . . inheritance of sorts."

Savannah raised one eyebrow. Gran's best friend, Martha, was Gran's age—in her eighties. "Oh? Did her grandmother finally pass away unexpectedly and leave her a chunk of money?"

"Something like that," Gran replied coyly. "I think she's going to replace that old blunderbuss of a car of hers and get herself a brand new Cadillac!"

"Ah, how nice for her. And how about you, Granny Reid?" Savannah said. "Are you going to be coming into any unexplained money in the near future?"

"I can't really say," was the sly answer. "But I wouldn't be the least bit surprised if the next time you come visit me, I have some new windows in my little house. Those old ones get stuck all the time, and I dang near suffocate in the summertime."

"Well, won't that be nice for you and Martha." Savannah laughed and shook her head. "Are you two hungry yet?" she asked.

"Starving," Gran replied. "It's been so long since breakfast that my stomach thinks my throat's been cut."

"Well, the steaks will be done in a few minutes. You eat one of those, a few ears of corn, some big scoops of potato salad and finish it off with a whomping bowl of that homemade peach ice cream . . . and that should take the edge off that hunger."

"It'll make a serious dent, to be sure."

Savannah smiled, reached over, and took her grandmother's hand. "You and I have some catching up to do in the visiting department. Where do you want to go? Disneyland?"

"Always. It's been too long since I've had a Mickey and Minnie sighting."

"We'll take care of that next week."

"Actually," Dirk said, sitting up and brushing the grass off his arms, "if you could get to Disneyland this week, I have a suggestion as to what you girls might do next week."

"Oh?" Savannah couldn't help being intrigued. Since when did Dirk act as social director for anyone? Anyone at all? "And what would you recommend?"

He grinned, walked over to the chair where he had tossed his jacket, and fished around inside one of the inner pockets.

He walked back to them, a shiny golden envelope in his hand. Laying it in Savannah's hand, he bent over and kissed the top of her head. "There," he said. "That's for you."

"For me?" She looked down at the envelope. "Why?"

"Because you mentioned to me . . . quite recently . . . that I never buy you presents unless I have to. And I realized that's true. So I figured it was time I changed that. I bought you a present."

She was dumbfounded. *"You?"*

"Don't be a smart aleck, or I'll take it back. Open it up."

As she pulled the fancy silver seal off the back, he said, "You helped me a lot with that case. You all did. So that's actually for all three of you. All of my girls."

Savannah reached inside and pulled out three gift certificates.

"Oh, oh, oh . . . Dirk! These are for . . . oh . . . I don't believe it! Gran, Tam, he's bought us all a full day of beauty at Euro-Spa in Twin Oaks! Facials, manicures, pedicures, massages! Can you believe it?"

"Full days of beauty!" Tammy leaped off the bench and threw her arms around his neck. "No way! Dirk!"

A moment later, he had Gran and Savannah hugging him, too.

"How could you afford that?" Savannah asked, while kissing his cheeks. "What did you do, sell your house trailer?"

"Naw, I couldn't have gotten that much for it."

"Did you finally have a winner in the lotto?" Tammy asked.

"Hey, I make good money, you know," he said. "And you may have noticed that I never, ever spend any of it."

Gran nodded. "Uh, yes, we did notice you squeeze a nickel pretty tight before lettin' it go."

"Well, I decided you deserved it. All of you. So, go get rubbed the right way for a change . . . on me."

Gran and Tammy finally let him go and hurried across the yard to show their gift certificates to Ryan and John. But Savannah remained behind, still hugging him close, her arms tight around his waist.

"Thank you, buddy," she said. "This means a lot. You're the best."

Dirk looked down at her, his eyes warm with affection and more importantly, respect. "No, babe, you are," he said. He nodded toward Daisy, who was standing next to her mother, her beautiful red hair shining in the afternoon sun, her pretty face lit with the pure joy of living.

"This time, we did it," he said. "We got to her in time. We saved this one."

She leaned her head on his shoulder and nodded, too emotional to talk. When she could finally trust herself to speak, she said, "We sure did. We can't always save them all. But once in a while, we can pull one back from the edge . . . and that makes it all worthwhile."

"It does." He kissed the top of her head. "It really, really does."